# Wondermonger

# Wondermonger

## MICHAEL ROTHSCHILD

VIKING

VIKING

Published by the Penguin Group

guin, a division of Penguin Books USA Inc.,

d Street, New York, New York 10010, U.S.A.

Ltd, 27 Wrights Lane, London W8 5TZ, England

oks Australia Ltd, Ringwood, Victoria, Australia

uin Books Canada Ltd, 2801 John Street,
Markham, Ontario, Canada L3R 1B4

n Books (N.Z.) Ltd, 182–190 Wairau Road,
Auckland 10, New Zealand

Penguin Books Ltd, Registered Offices:
Harmondsworth, Middlesex, England

irst published in 1990 by Viking Penguin,
a division of Penguin Books USA Inc.

1 3 5 7 9 10 8 6 4 2

The following selections were previously
published, some in different form: "Wondermonger,"
"Dog in the Manger," and "A Land Without Fossils" in
*Antaeus*; "The Price of Pine" in *Works in Progress* and
in its present version in *Maine* magazine; and "The Austringer"
in *The Paris Review*. "The Price of Pine" and "The
Austringer" also appeared in Mr. Rothschild's
*Rhapsody of a Hermit and Other Tales*,
published by The Viking Press. Copyright ©
Michael Rothschild, 1973.

LIBRARY OF CONGRESS CATALOGING IN PUBLICATION DATA
Rothschild, Michael, 1947–
Wondermonger / Michael Rothschild.
p.  cm.
ISBN 0-670-83326-6
I. Title.
PS3568.O867W66   1990
813'.54—dc20        89-40660

Printed in the United States of America
Set in Garamond No. 3

*to my mother*
*Violet Capellaro Rothschild*
*and to Norman Rothschild*
*my father and first son*

# Contents

# *Wondermonger*

Long ago, when Sunbury Town was a particle of sugar on the rim of black and plotless wilderness, there lived a woodsman named Mordecai Rime who was, until his fortieth year, the most ascetic and profligate man in the north country.

Late in the fall of every year a coldness formed inside Mordecai Rime and before snowfall he left Sunbury Town and journeyed for days to reach some opening in the forest where a camp and low hovel stood, and roads were swamped from stands of pine to the landings along riverbanks and upon the frozen lakes. There, he bedded the winter long with fifteen or twenty woodsmen—other choppers, swampers, barkers, the ox teamster, and a boss—and with them, in monkish silence, ate beans, salt pork and drank the pitch-black tea. Before each sunrise he tramped over crust to his chance and, from December until the mud or rotten ice of March, felled the old pines and bull saplings, with scarfs smooth as the cheeks of women he tried not to think on before the freshet came.

Then the sun hesitated longer at the top of the sky, moist winds blew, the river rose, and when the drive started every man knew that death, which only now and again visited winter camp, lived on the river. Crushed while breaking a landing or jam, drowned, dead men were wrapped in bark and buried without fanfare. While water mounted no drive could hold back, so there was little time for the soul which, according to the oldest loggers, hastily transmigrated into meat-birds, gray jays, moose-birds, or whatever else the brash thieves chanced to be called. Besides, as Mordecai Rime once remarked carving a late friend's initials in a tree below the man's hanging calked boots, the toes slit so rainwater could drain out, "Death don't have much character."

And after a winter's work in grimmest seclusion no amount of fatigue or fear was enough to sweat out a winter's accumulation of lust. The spring of his fortieth year, when the meltwater rose high and the rollways were broken at last, Mordecai Rime felt as blister-hot as his red flannel shirt. Steel-calked boots on his feet, cant dog in his fists, a whopping desire and a bit of money in his poke, he was riding the thaw on the big logs to the brothels of Sunbury Town.

All the people of Sunbury Town gathered at the riverfront when they heard the distant grind and grumble of log upon log chafing downriver to the mills of the town; for the townspeople, too, had endured a dull, cold time of winter. And so they gathered: merchants with raucous racks of suits, jewelers, barbers with scented fingers, smiling saloonkeepers and ministers, widows, farmers, husbands closeby their curious wives, whores and especially schoolchildren were all variously eager to rejoice in the brawling prodigality, the tales of death and skill and love; in sum, gathered to warm themselves by the hot squander about to burst upon Sunbury Town. And more than any other name, the name Rime was in the minds of wives standing on their toes and shading their eyes to see over the calliope of crowded heads. The bright lips of whores whispered and laughed, "Rime," and "Mordecai Rime" squealed from the shining tongues of children as they surged along the riverbank to catch sight of him first.

"Once I seen'm jig on a log."

"I saw Rime break a jam by himself."

"Liar!"

"So didn't I."

"I heard'm sing."

"Rime! Look out there! Rime! I see'm!"

"Which one?"

"I see'm too. Look!"

And indeed, there in the middle of the heaving corduroy river, a red-shirted, red-sashed man was prancing as if those careening froth-beating logs were flat and steady as a stage. Short of body, thick of neck, skin waffled by calk-booted foes, teeth of a size and number that only his own outsized mouth could hold, and eyes small and bright as a bird's, Mordecai Rime was in no wise a handsome man. Taken one piece at a time, there was not a lovely piece to be found in all of him; and yet, whatever held those pieces together was of a stuff so grand and innocent and rare that the children who beheld his capers atop the death he seemed to ignore were astonished to silence, and Rime, on spotting those bands of children, waved his cant dog, jabbed it into the log he was riding, and of all things, walked the length of that slick, battered log—on his hands!

Some children covered their eyes and dared peek only through fingerchinks, some started to bawl or howled with terror and wonderment, but every cheering one of them scurried back toward Sunbury Town to keep pace with that fantastical man on the water.

Hopping here and hopping there, a dozen bright figures were sighted far upriver, small as blood-filled fleas. A united whoop roared from the gathered townspeople. And above the groans of the clotted river the faint, answering whoop of a lone throat was heard; and each passing moment it grew louder and wilder, until the blue-faced whooper himself hurdled from a log, dug his spikes into the muddy bank and bellowed for all that merry but speechless assembly: "Pickin' time's come sure as I'm Mordecai Rime an' a man, the fruit's red, ripe an' near rotten. So let's get an' pick till it's gotten!"

No sooner had the mayor of Sunbury Town, in official greeting, tipped his beaver-felt top hat to the riverman than the hat was gone and like a king and fool in one, Mordecai Rime marched up the bank amidst a festive court of children, a painted queen on each arm and a glorious new top hat cocked upon his head.

The whole red-shirted brigade of bachelors followed suit, and before long, other crews landed, each with its distinctive brand in the scarf of its logs. Wooden sidewalks were quickly pocked by all their boots, black with tobacco spit and wet with rum. The dizzy screech of fiddling and jubilation commenced; mothers hunted for their children; hustlers their marks; husbands their wives; and but one thing was certain— Sunbury Town was topsy-turvy.

By nightfall, however, a different note, less playful and charming than before, intruded upon the screeking logs and strains of merrymaking. Most townspeople understood at once, disappeared from the streets and in their places, bolted themselves in. "Put the boots to 'im," a man yelled past midnight. The sharp, frantic note of hunger and zeal was unmistakable now, and all over town open-eyed husbands lay beside their wives in the dark and, not without pleasure, listened to the carnival break into menace.

The fierce night wore on, the revels wore down, and at dawn they ceased, as though first daylight had chased the wood demons back to the wilderness and restored a gloss of sweetness to Sunbury Town. Everyone knew this lull of early morning was a respite, that the satyr was catching his wind and so long as money held out, misrule was in town to stay. And so while broken glass was swept up, windows were replaced and the blood and urine mopped off the sidewalks below the snoring brothels where men and their ladies mended and charged themselves for the coming night, Sunbury Town readied for business proper.

Now, among those up and about at this hour was the young schoolmistress, Lucille Triller, and it was evident that neither her high-necked shoe-shining dun dress nor the hard bun she had rolled at the back of her neck could conceal the juice and bloom of her face. At the edge of the schoolyard Miss Triller spied a ring of excited children and drawing nearer to them she paused a pause which, however ordinary it may then have seemed, led to the transformation—if not the transmigration—of Mordecai Rime's soul.

She had hesitated because in ring-center one of her pupils had struck a heroic posture. A wooden staff held high in his tiny fist, he erupted all in one high-pitched, hurried exhalation, "Show me a hole'n I'll fill't, hole ain't there'n I'll drill't." As when the hawk bolts upon the chicken-yard and in dust and din hooks one self-concentrating bantam, so Lucille Triller broke that ring of children, got hold of one scalding ear and in a trice twisted a bawling apology from the youngster, and the name Rime.

That restless morning—counting the desks of truants, confiscating lewd doodles, ever demanding attention—the schoolmistress discovered that the disorder which visited Sunbury Town had, in particular, subverted its children. And once school was out she marched toward the river district, resolved, in behalf of her pupils, to search out and upbraid this Rime, the sound of whose name alone incited children to deplorable antics, and herself to such ferocious ill will.

"Where might I locate Rime, sir?" she inquired of a grandfatherly man pipe-smoking on a stoop. He shook his head, fondly puckered his eyes and lips to say, "Git'n line, honey, he's the king log," and spat by his boot.

A smile so vulgar and presumptive answered each query that she began to fancy an image of Rime, Lord of Boors, and stalked it with such intensity that the old woman who finally directed her to an establishment known as Pink Chimney thought certain she had been wronged by her man and was about to get even.

When the schoolmistress stood beneath Pink Chimney itself, and gazing upwards, saw that the mortar between the pink brick of its prodigious stack had been dyed vein-blue, she lost hold, and shuddering, tripped inside. Her eyes smarted from the gray and yellow bands of smoke. She inhaled the exhaust of tobacco-sweat-rum-perfume, choked, and as if blinded in a house afire, reeled in panic while the floor bounced to the jagged fiddle and rowdy, rhythmic clap of hands and stomp of feet. Bit by bit, colored shapes revealed themselves through the hot murk of the barroom; but though her eyes cleared, her muddle worsened. She knew it was daytime in the civilized town of Sunbury where she lived and taught school, and yet here was neither day nor civilization, but the sort of woolly land she had toured only when, unable to sleep, she read her Shakespeare and was afterward tossed in wicked dreams of cannibals and the Anthropophagi.

Tree-necked men and bare-backed women thronged to view one stocky man atop a table. In wads of smoke, this man's head was thrown back, motionless and soaking. His enormous mouth was locked in such an immense smile and his teeth were so big, he looked ready to bite a chunk from the hewn beam high above him. Both his arms were crooked rigid at his chest. Indeed, for half an hour not a muscle moved above his red-sashed waist. But no one was looking there. Every admiring eye watched his legs and feet going like crazy, on and on in time to the hoarse wail of a fiddle.

He leaped off that tiny stage and crossed his legs in the air; he twirled; he pigeon-winged and whirled; he pawed heel and toe; the fiddling speeded fast, and faster, and at its peak the fiddler's bow blurred, the Jigger jumped up, twice crossed his legs before landing and then, to each sharp, separate squeal of the finale, he stamped, hopped, stamped again, and his feet came to rest as the fiddle, which seemed to make those feet move, fell silent.

In the stillness a bare braceleted arm lifted up a ladle, the panting Jigger kissed the arm, drank down the rum, grinned, took in a deep breath and roared, "By the chimin' blue balls o' Jesus an' sure as my muscle be long, hard, an' not so straight as a steeple, I can jump higher—squat lower—hump longer—jig better—bite harder—drink deeper—piss further—sing sweeter—fart louder—an' talk quicker'n any man made in the slipp'ry knot o' love tied 'tween a woman an' the creature she's found fit to tie with—whether she trapped it in woods or pulled it from sky or grow'd it in 'er garden—an' if a body doubts me I'll swear to it by the sweetest blue milk I ever sucked from the flowin' teats o'my good mother to start growin' into who stands before you now, Mordecai Rime, an' a man." And with that he spread a large scarlet handkerchief over his head and jumped with three heel snaps to the floor of Pink Chimney, rocking in cheer and cockalarity.

Drenched from his jig, Rime was on his way to cool himself out of doors when his eyes snagged upon the sole partridge in that roomful of brash-colored parrots. Beside the entrance, her bun unrolled and dangling over her hands, the schoolmistress stood. Without a noise but with the entire confused might of her body, she was weeping.

Mordecai Rime stopped dead. He pulled the wet handkerchief off his stiff hair, wrung his sweat onto the sawdusted floor, and gently commenced to sponge her scarlet forehead. She opened her eyes to his great-toothed smile, started, let out a faint, surprised sound, went slack, and was waltzed into the fresh air and down to the riverbank by the partner of her choice.

"Where d'you hurt, Ma'am?" Rime soberly asked, and paused, and continued, "Ma'am, suff'rin' aches an' pains, are you?" adding nervously, "Now y'ain't dyin' now, are you?" to which she managed after a time to say, "I am the schoolmistress Lucille Triller, and I am lost," an answer that frightened Mordecai Rime into trying to cajole her to a sensible calm, and so he said, "Up in the woods we call twin-boled trees, those crotched ones with their legs stuck fast, well, Lucy, we call'm schoolmarms," and he made a chuckle before she made more tears, so many, in fact, they infected the good-hearted Rime who joined in with his own awful, big tears until, mysteriously, one of them laughed and, before long, there they were, sitting together in the mud of the riverbank hugging, kissing, and the both of them laughing mad.

Every man and woman was hushed, huddled outside of Pink Chimney. They saw the couple pass through the thick, black shadow of the chimney which slanted far up the road; and afterward they waited, watching the shadow be sucked down into the gray dirt road and be gone. All at once, jewelry jangled up the Madam's plump wrist. "Ain't no wake," she cracked, and jostling her way first inside, yelling "Free round!!" she ducked behind the pine bar.

2

Along a dead, flat stretch of river in a solitary intervale far to the northwest of Sunbury Town, a trapper and timber cruiser's stopover had lately grown into Tantrattle, a farming settlement so small it was said that when one of its women gave child, all the rest came to their milk. And upon a narrow rise of meadow not half a mile downriver from Tantrattle, the rantipole logger who had always made mock of the husbandmen's staid plight (who had branded "farmer" any woodsman slow of foot, hand, or tongue), himself planted pumpkins, corn, potatoes and peas on a burn, and built a low two-room house modeled on the hovels he had wintered in since becoming a man.

Although the husbandmen of Tantrattle were hospitable enough whenever Mordecai Rime entered the settlement for supplies or asked their advice on some practical matter, he returned to his homestead sadder than he set out. There was

an awful design to the way these farmers settled one spot
with one woman under one God and from a lifelong scrutiny
of soil and sky, lived guardedly and wasted nothing. They
answered Rime as if each word moved death one day closer.
The foolishness native to man had been burned out of them
through constant, necessary prudence. And so that summer
Mordecai Rime visited Tantrattle only when he had reason.
There were no diversions to be found in the village, and he
had much to do.

From late in May when he chose the site, he lived alone
except for a black hound puppy, and labored as long as there
was light to labor by. The first time in his life he washed
regularly, after dark in the river, and for the first time, however weary he was, he could not sleep. Half the nights he
strolled through the cherry and fireweed speckling the
charred meadow with the puppy tripping alongside him; or
he sat by the river and listened to the last songbirds sing like
wet fingers on glass. He lay in the damp sedge, hour after
hour following the dark concert of sounds until it appeared
that each song was mated to another and no note was left
unanswered. Above the river, love bellows of bullfrogs
fanned the heavy air and from behind his half-built cabin
began the incessant heave of whippoorwills. But when the
exultations of woodcocks fell breathless from the skytops,
when it seemed concord was come to earth, then miserable
Mordecai Rime thought up songs about his woman in Sunbury Town, and as he made them up he sang them out loud,
along with all the rest of the nightsongs, and felt better
for it . . .

*I dreamed up a woman*
*Skin red everywhere*
*I kissed her heart gentle*
*Afraid it'd tear.*
*Go away summer*
*Hurry up fall*

*Sleepin' alone*
*Ain't sleepin' a'tall,*
*'Cause I dreamed o' that woman*
*An' such was 'er fright*
*When flat on my bed*
*She turn'd frosty white*
*But I kiss'd her womb gentle*
*She open'd so wide*
*We held on for dear life*
*We took such a ride*
*She planted my seed*
*An' I took me a bride.*
*So go away summer*
*Hurry here fall*
*Sleepin' without her*
*Ain't sleepin' a'tall.*

If his lids closed, late night rains sometimes jarred him from half-sleep in the sedge, or he woke before dawn in a chill shroud of dew that the spidery swallows, glancing in and out of the fog on the river, appeared to have wound him in.

Relieved and busy with the start of day, Mordecai Rime toiled so for the completion of his task that no progress seemed to be made. He imagined he would never be done; he would never return to fetch her in Sunbury Town. Often he wondered if she existed at all.

The air had already turned clear and bright on the afternoon he realized in a daze how high the cob-laid chimney had grown above the bark roof. Two small windows were oil-papered, and around the farm cabin, stacks of wood bled and seasoned. Beans were busheled in the root cellar and cornsilks darkened above the weeds. With a start, Mordecai Rime stumbled into the jungle of garden to investigate the golden-orange blossoms which overnight had burst, bugle-like, along the pumpkin vines. He squatted over the first cluster he reached, bent his head, lifted one large, fuzzy blossom and intently cupped it to his nostrils.

How long a while he knelt there, Mordecai Rime never knew or, indeed, if he did kneel or hover, even, midair. For the hound began to yelp, a shadow fell over him and his shoulders were squeezed hard. More bear than man, he turned on his knees, clasped her skirt and bawling as a bear bawls slashing a honey-trunk apart, he tore at her skirt and there in the garden beneath the pumpkin blossoms that had powdered his nose dull orange, beneath the prancing paws and prying snout of the hound, Mordecai Rime held his wife Lucy Rime and she fast onto him.

Upon waking, he blushed as bright as the ruby burns she displayed on the insides of her thighs, and straightway shaved his cocklebur lips and chin and swore to keep them barbered ever after. Honeymoon continued the rest of August and on in festive earnest through September, October, and still it went on. Summertime, however, which had dallied like a snake upon a sun-hot rock before her arrival, now, as if startled at her coming, slickered by. Mordecai Rime began to pray that the air would never cease its hum nor the haze fall away. He prayed for Indian summer without end, so he might never return to the wifeless forests of winter. He loved Lucy Rime as if each of the women he ever had held during all the spring nights in Sunbury Town had been pressed into a single, vivid body; and more than that, he loved her as he loved himself, for her belly and her breasts showed traces of his child.

They swam at dawn, harvested the days and, at twilight, washed in the cool river. Lucy wove a rug for the rough, chill floor and stitched a crazy quilt for their bed. From the village they toted sacks of goosedown, stuffed a mattress plump, and promptly buried themselves in it. She often read aloud from books he could not fathom in a voice that nonetheless made sense of everything. Of the rapidly changing season, however, neither spoke. The earnings she had saved as a schoolmistress were nearly gone and both sickened to consider winter, separation, the birth of their child.

Lucy Rime tried and largely succeeded in keeping her terror concealed. Only once, on a picnic by a beaver pond where she went wading and afterward tweezed a tiny leech from between her toes and scraped it off on a stone, did she suddenly begin to cry.

Mordecai Rime was a different matter. The leaves had fallen by the start of November, and with a husband's eye he gazed upon the bleached rushes, coarsened to knives along the black river. Never before when winter began to lock the ground had fears of loss and schemes to protect against that loss so locked up his mind. But this November he dwelt within a different law and smiled bitterly to see stalks lose their bend and the brittle stems let go. When pods split and emptied, he tagged a morbid dream to every seed cast on the sharpening wind. And while he sat, his wide, scaly hands cupped on his knees, he figured what was the matter with him:

> *My eyes look'd in*
> *Beneath my skin*
> *To see what I could find.*

> *Old Sin, new Dread*
> *Was newly wed*
> *An' kiss'd inside my mind.*

The ground crackled as Lucy advanced down the path with a quiltful of laundry. "Why so grim, Farmer Rime?" she asked, but he remained stooped in gloom, and she settled beside him.

"True, a farmer, an' scar'd somethin' awful," Mordecai Rime abruptly said. "I love you so, Lucy. Why I seen five toes settin' by themselves like beans on the snow, an' I seen men froze stiff an' drownd'd, burn'd an' squash'd, but nothin' of't scar'd me till now I'm shakin' like ev'ry other fart-fill'd sheep-toppin' farmer in Tantrattle. What's to happen t'you and the child, wife? What're we t'do?"

Lucy Rime felt panic rise in her chest and she stopped it up. "I've lived alone before," she said giddily. "And see here," she added, tapping her belly with a smile, "I've stored plenty of fat to live on and feed a cub besides. I'll just hibernate until thaw when you come back to us." Wind lashed hair across her freckled, ruddy nose and Mordecai Rime watched her tongue flicker a glisten on her dry lips while her eyes wandered over the cold water.

"Know somethin', you're so pretty I'm pain'd and jealous." He had on a face she hadn't seen before. His mouth teetered between a smirk and a grimace and there was a mean, dull suspicion in his eyes. "I swear it, wife, you're pretty enough for killin'."

Afterward, when he had set out to arrange for the services of Midwife Cawkins in Tantrattle and Lucy was scrubbing the quilt clean in the river, she remembered the strange spite which had warped his face. With difficulty she tugged the quilt onto the bank to squeeze out the frigid water. "Pretty enough for killin'," she repeated, and abstractedly scanned upriver. On the last skirt of bank before the river curled behind woodlands toward the settlement, Lucy thought she glimpsed him standing out among the black cattails.

Mordecai Rime, meanwhile, crunched along a hardened mud path through the ice-scarred willows and poplar of the flood plain, and kept to the burnished dirt road that passed over the cribwork bridge and cleaved the village. At last a natty blue and red sparrow hawk sighted him, drawing too near its prospect atop a maple. Rime heard its scream and followed the skating flight down the field of dun stubble, above long rows of stumps and a small graveyard. Tilting crazily before the Cawkins farmhouse, it was gone.

Rime went striding down the bouldered field, pausing to scoop a fat yellow apple from the fresh chippings around an apple-tree butt. Perplexed, he bit into the apple and regarded the hundreds of other stumps that had recently been an orchard. The apple tasted so good he concentrated upon eating it until stopped short by a neat, marble row of headstones. Although he had helped bury a dozen corpses in the acid mold of the wilderness floor, Mordecai Rime was a stranger to such a civilized cemetery as this, with a winter vault on its river side. A marble lamb reposed there above a body's face, and there, the pearly index of a sculpted hand pointed straight up to the low-covered sky. Mechanically he tore off a mouthful of apple, glanced at the line of five same-sized slabs at his feet, and unable to chew or swallow, gaped.

| Vilda A. | Freedom A. | Arletta A. | Sampel A. | Letitia A. |
|----------|------------|------------|-----------|------------|
| Dau. of | Son of | Dau. of | Son of | Dau of |
| Freedom and | Freedom and | Freedom and | Freedom and | Freedom and |
| Solemna Air | Solemna Air | Solemna Air | Solemna Air | Solemna Air |
| Ae. 10m. 16d. | Ae. 2 yrs. 8m. 19d. | Ae. 1 yr. 7d. | Ae. 9m. 23d. | Ae. 1m. 2d. |
| Our Bud | Our Bud | Our Bud | Our Bud | Our Bud |
| is | is | is | is | is |
| blooming | blooming | blooming | blooming | blooming |
| on high | on high | on high | on high | on high |

"Must be one Christly bloom up there!"

"It is indeed," replied a creased, shawled woman.

"An' one witchery o' marriage down here, I'll wager, ma'am," twinkled Rime, the plug of apple in his cheek.

"T'was I delivered the little ones into this world and the Reverend Cawkins, he . . ."

"Life is hard, sir," pronounced a sturdy sunburned farmer with an authoritative snowdrift of hair piled on his head. "Your business?"

Mordecai Rime stared into the healthy red and white face of the old man in consternation. "I'm 'bout ready to pack off for winter an' Lucy's goin' to be needin' a midwife come Feb'yary. She's my wife, see, an' she's with child."

The Midwife Cawkins pinched a fold of throat and smiled. "Why then, you must be the woodsman settling downriver?"

"Mordecai Rime, missus."

"Keep to home," counseled the Reverend Cawkins. "Lumbering and farming don't mix. Build a stout fence about your garden and keep to home." The reverend fell silent when he noticed the woodsman's eyes drift to a stop alongside the meetinghouse where the apple orchard was stacked horizontal, and barrels of ash caught rainwater to leach their lye.

"Fine-tastin' apples," Rime remarked, beginning to chew again. "What ailed your trees?"

"No price for cider," the midwife said, and her husband added, "Serves the enemy. If there be a way to serve, man will find it. Do you pray, Rime?"

"Only that you an' your missus don't lay hold o' my wife an' child," he answered, and with a low bow to them, started up the rise. He hurdled every apple-butt along his way, skipping queerly up the knoll toward the bare maple, never once looking behind.

Later on that cold, still evening Lucy Rime was darning one of his wool mittens when a terrible thought visited Mordecai Rime, and he let it stay and nursed it while the fire played on her hair and buffed her brow orange. Before long the thought had lodged inside him as a certainty, and he winced at her as if he had freed something fierce that someday would kill him. "How many before, wife?"

"Many?" she asked drowsily.

"Men. Other men. Before me."

"There are *real* things to worry us. Don't be a fool."

"Real things? A fool?" Rime grinned nastily, ear to ear. " 'Cause you're so friggin' book'd up you look down your lyin' snout at me."

"What is it, say," she begged, setting the mitten in her lap. There were no more words, however, and Lucy Rime was awakened in the night by a dream she was to dream and wake from on many another night of the coming winter. She called and called for Mordecai to come help her, but the windows were shuttered and the door bolted against the snow-carving wind. She screamed for his help, she screamed for help, but she was alone, she knew, and this night she clasped Mordecai Rime's throat and soaked him with her sweat. Throttled from sleep, his daytime malice forgotten, he pressed his mouth into her scalding hair and hummed tunes, rocking her jumping eyelids together to the rhythmic groans of the quilt stiffening on the line outside their door.

The last cricket straggled in from shocks of weed to get warm, an ice-skin thickened at the river's edge and as green lights lashed the night sky, frost sank deeper in. First snow soon crusted the weeds, ice and metal-hard sod and then, their final night together passed by. He looked her hard in the face and before he turned said only, "You'd best be true, Lucy Rime, or you'll make a meat-bird o' me."

She watched him enter the tangle of cherry, birch and poplar on a once-burned hillside northeast of Tantrattle, and she waited there while the snow slowly blurred, dimpled and effaced his nearest boot track.

Mordecai Rime drove himself dumb for three days, through damp tracts of cedar where little snow gathered and half-frozen earth puckered around boulders, across boglands of spruce and naked tamarack, pushing for an exhaustion so great he might sleep some of the nights.

The fourth morning he was buffeted over the frozen surface of a long, thin lake. He recognized it from a decade before when he had lumbered its margin and seen the shafts of many thousands of pines crowded upon its ice to be girdled in a boom. Several old pines, those with hollow heart, had been left to topple of themselves; yet here and there, rising high above a glittering desolation of decaying slash, they remained, and more massive in their isolation than he had remembered them.

He paced the flat stretch of lake hour after hour, and before twilight climbed the steep, slick eastern shore and camped without sleep in the ruins of the hovel where he had lived that earlier winter.

Not two days from his destination, at dawn, he tunneled into the constant half-night of a spruce and fir wilderness and walked the frozen pathway of the Quick River. Small as a mite that burrows under the shag of some huge beast and works its methodical way down to the beast's tail, Mordecai Rime picked along the barren floor where he had lived to make himself Mordecai Rime and a man, and he sensed his death might be hidden behind any black needle of the trees above him, and he feared he was a woodsman no longer.

### 3

Amidst scattered hardwoods, hemlock, fir and spruce, the lumber camp and hovel had been built at the foot of a ridge where old white pine clustered around the expanse of Lower, or Little Mooselip Lake whose outlet, the Quick River, flowed beneath the softwood wilds and fed the Sunbury River sixty miles northwest of Sunbury Town. It was here before each December dawn that Mordecai Rime and the chopping crews meandered down blue crystal corridors of snow on the packed branch roads. Sled runners smoked and squealed beneath mammoth pine boles and Clarence Smiles cursed his three yoke of oxen to and from the landing until not enough day was left to see those hazards that might be seen. The crew straggled to the warm camp, ate and, under a communal spread of cotton batting, slept in a row on hemlock boughs.

Every man on that operation had heard the large tales and claims made for and by Mordecai Rime. Those who had worked other winters or blown into Sunbury Town with him were now particularly baffled to find such a man resigned, separate, stingy with melancholy. Rime's chopper and barker, old John Gorges, privately ascribed the transformation to some bodily disease like hollow heart, at work inside of Rime; one swamper speculated that he had burned himself out and suffered horrors from the fierce way his first forty years on earth had been lived; and asquat on the frozen manure of the hovel floor to rub bean grease on his oxen's puffed legs, Clarence Smiles confided to his beasts that, "On'y a woman coulda broke a back hard as Rime's."

Theories abounded, but no one asked Rime for reasons. Many avoided his murky black eyes, others swapped pitying or ironic glances. Nevertheless, the crew stayed respectfully aloof and tried to pretend he was still the same man; all, that is, but one young newcomer, a vain, well-muscled chopper by the name of Rudolph Sarsen.

From the very night Rime arrived and tucked himself in his own crazy quilt apart from the crew, Sarsen let it be known that he slaved for more than a winter's wage. "Seems our lice's too ugly for the gent," he announced while he sat on the deacon seat and brushed out his orange, shoulder-length hair. Rime offered no rejoinder; and cheated, Sarsen was put in a sullen rage. Presently, as became his custom each night, Sarsen heated a bucket, stripped down before the flabbergasted crew and, whistling a melody, poured the steaming water down his huge orange-haired body.

"Ain't no human bean," Mordecai Rime said sleepily. "Holy Jesus, I seen one o'them things in a picture book. 'Xact same size an' same red hair all over. I do believe we're hovel'd with a rang-tang."

"Get outta your friggin' quilt, Rime, an' I'll kick your asshole so hard your eyes'll bleed," screamed naked Sarsen, but the jeers and laughter drowned out his threat, and Rime rolled over.

From then on, Sarsen was known in camp as Rang-tang Sarsen; and from then on the camp understood that his business was not so much to fell pine as to absorb the skill and the courage accorded everywhere to the name Mordecai

Rime so that he, Rudolph Sarsen, might ride the swollen spring rivers and reach Sunbury Town, resplendent in Rime's place.

Boss Urban Burlock made certain that Sarsen and Rime worked chances that were far apart. He had seen the preservative framework of game and insult come apart, and the sole prevention he knew was work. The second week in January a cold snap hit, stayed on a week, another, and Burlock refused to let up. Warm breath turned beards bone-white and the laboring oxen drooled icicles. Men complained of how their brittle axe-heads broke or bounced weirdly off icy trunks, and frequently pine fell with unpredictable jumps and twists. Numb fingertips started to crack open the second week of prolonged cold, and they were sewed up like socks. Already, the pine closest to shore had been twitched onto the ice, and each day the crews ranged farther, to skin the exposed clumps of pine rolling and crackling higher up the ridge.

Early on the severest morning of the cold snap Mordecai Rime was circling an ancient ivory shaft of pine halfway up the ridge when there appeared a throng of gray jays, diving and squawking around Rime's toque and mackinaw. Instead of notching the pine, he clamped his axe under his arm, made fists inside his mittens and settled on a nearby butt. "Them meat-birds's tellin' us t'ain't safe," he told his chopping mate Gorges.

"A bitch," John Gorges mumbled and tamping his pipe, huddled beside Rime on the wide stump. Neither of them turned toward the scrape-scrape of snowshoes side-stepping down the ridge behind them until Boss Burlock asked, "What's holdin' up, Rime?"

"Too mean a mornin' to cut I should say, Urban."

"That so?" shrugged the boss, "Is't really so?" He glanced at his stiff bindings and briefly searched Rime's face which squinted after the sooty jays, hollering away in the dead, indigo air. "Never know'd a freeze an' a coupla birds to spook

Mordecai Rime," whispered Burlock, hesitating to let the ring of axes working elsewhere speak for him. "Do what you see fit," he said, and shuffled off to traverse the ridge and reach the next chance.

Rather than hazard a word, John Gorges sneaked a sideways look and decided, from Rime's passive attitude, to light his pipe when up Rime bolted, hastily paced a line parallel the skidroad and shouted, "Bed 'er here."

Gorges nodded and began to cut young spruce and fir along the designated pathway. Of the many axemen Gorges had observed, he considered Rime best and smartest. He had seen a thousand pines felled by the careful, redundant ease of Rime's musical stroke. No shock drove up Rime's arms and neck when his blade half-vanished into a tree and magically sprang back with a flat orange chip the size of a head. Long ago, mystified Gorges had asked Rime how he managed to throw his axe at the wood with no effort and yet such devastating result. " 'Tain't me," Rime had claimed, "I but squeeze the helve. 'Tis the thinkin' head o' my axe does the job."

But now, all the while he spread evergreen saplings to cushion the falling pine, Gorges fixed a disturbed eye upon Mordecai Rime and shuddered in his chest. In the clearing the monster pine grew seventy straight feet before a first horizontal limb stretched out beneath another shelf of limb, itself overhung by a higher tier, and still another that lidded the surrounding birch and spruce forest. Tapering upward, the pine tree rose to a single, fluent lead shoot one hundred and fifty feet above the spot where Mordecai Rime had got his footing and slashed his poleaxe into the gray-plated trunk as though he meant less to fell that tree than murder it.

"Quit't now, hey Rime, quit," yelled John Gorges once the sparking bit glanced off a frozen fiber and Rime skidded to one knee. But Rime would not stop. He grunted onto his feet and with blue vapor rolling over his pinched white lips, with fingers bleeding from his barked knuckles, hacked at the tree and could stop for nothing.

Near to an hour passed, marked by an incessant thump of cleaver on bone, the hard, dull, uneven, urgent pound of Rime's axe as it opened a cleft and drove home to the heart of the pine. Gorges was first to sight a tremor in the pine-top. He shouted warning and scrambled up a rise, out of reach, and looked on.

Rime pushed his pole against the trunk and heaved; from the topmost shaft a spasm reverberated, down to the spur roots; the ponderous bole nodded slightly as if to fall, then, despite its all but severed base, remained perfectly erect, motionless.

Rime contemptuously hurled aside the pole and shouldered the trunk. "Clear out!" Gorges screamed in alarm. Rime half-circled the yawning girth and leveled a mad flurry of axe-blows into the back-cut. Nothing remained now to keep the pine upright, but there it stood and did not budge.

Twice, Rime butted the tree. His boots kicked and fists smashed and tore on the bark. Smoldering from sweat and cold, he staggered backward, stretched out on the snowcrust, and John Gorges heard but could not believe a human throat able to make the laugh Mordecai Rime laughed then.

Gorges maintained afterward it was the laughter itself which gave the final prod—for no sooner had it commenced than slowly, the pine leaned and, clawing and wrenching loose everything within reach, tumbled with a horrendous crackling and with a quake and hollow boom, bounced precisely where Rime had indicated it would, atop the evergreen bedding.

Black twigs, bark and ice rained down in the wake of the pine and Gorges lost sight of Rime until the destruction in the air settled. Then, there he was, still flat on his back beneath a skim of debris.

Inspecting the hole ripped in the forest roof, Gorges rushed fast as he could down to Rime and reached out his hand. Rime pulled himself up, chattered the same ugly, braying laugh as before and as suddenly stopped and gave a hearty slap on the back of Gorges's mackinaw.

"Limb that stubbo'n mother," Rime said, "skin 'er extra snug." He set his jaw hard but his black pupils were so dilated and glossy that Gorges felt ashamed staring into them. "Meatbirds wanted to carry me off with'm somethin' wicked," Rime said quietly.

He fetched his poleaxe and returned, chuckling. "Didn't. Miss'd. Miss'd me." And with that he dragged himself through the marsh grass and manure strewn over the glassy skidboard to brake the ox sled, and staggered toward the lumber camp.

"Man's goddam good an' lucky," scowled John Gorges. He fidgeted for his cold-stemmed pipe and crouched beside the toppled pine to use it for windbreak. "Haywire," he said. "Haywire as hell."

4    .

On the day her husband departed for camp above Little Mooselip Lake, Lucy Rime had returned home in a warm fall of thick, gentle-dropping snow, despising the flakes which alighted on her cape as though curses fell from the sky. Wind now and again rattled canes and seeds in the hollowed pods that poked above snow level beside her path. She wrapped the cape snugly about her and watched the footprintless trail, not lifting her head before she heard the hound yelp. Tethered beside the threshold of her cabin, he was half-strangled in his eagerness to greet her, be fed, and stretch before the fire.

The milky afternoon air darkened and further dimmed the two rooms where she banked the fire, bolted shut the door, gazed at the musket, the hooded hemlock cradle, and knelt to stroke the hound's winter fur and quiet the scrabble of his dream. Mice chirping, the hiss and collapse of logs and the snap of walls contracting in the colder evening air: house-sounds, like spruce at the rim of a vacant snowfield, struck her now with remarkable and unpleasant sharpness. But the keenest and the strangest of the sounds she heard was the noise of herself, movements in an empty house, her terrible intimacy with the fetus burrowing, relentlessly scooping its way out of her.

Through a chink in the wall some snowflakes seeped and sifted over Lucy Rime crouched by the hearthstone, her eyes pinched and dry. Back and forth she rocked with one palm upon her flat breastbone. Her chest seemed ready to burst from the tread of tiny feet on her heart. Slowly, as if to rock away the anguish, she swayed before the fire and her mind journeyed back to the genial bustle of Sunbury Town, her schoolhouse, the uncanny ease with which her reasonable life had come unraveled that spring twilight on the bank of the Sunbury River. She remembered the strange, beguiling tales he told her of sullen and holy Indians, and a crew snow-cribbed in a burning hovel; of handling a bateau over treacherous falls, fingers clutching a log in a black eddy, a human skull on a gravelbar; the many dozens of cleat marks in his chest and belly and finally, the bashful revelation of the entire coded map of his skin which they deciphered, greedily hunting like children after a treasure they discovered anew each night.

Fire-red with sweat, Lucy Rime spied the hemlock cradle from the corner of her eye and a shrill desire seized her to cast it upon the fire and see it burn. Her head shook from side to side. She began to cry. For a long time she wailed out hatred for her husband and for his child who fed upon the marrow of her bones. Weariness at last dulled her heart and silenced her mind, and her first night alone in their cabin she slept beside the querulous hound who now and again rolled his tongue along her thin wrist.

Miserable, and bewildered to find herself at the edge of the hearthstone, she awakened, breathing gray vapor into the dark chill of the room. At once she scraped aside the ashes, blew and blew on the dull embers until the kindling ignited, and considering the prospect of a winterlong marriage to this fire, she crossed the gloomy cabin and let out the whimpering hound.

The flash of yellow sky and blue snow made her recoil. While the hound pecked mouthfuls of fresh flakes and like a needle threaded in and out of the soft drifts, Lucy Rime gradually adjusted to the abstract brilliance which left so little for the eye to grapple with and insinuated its glare upon the mind.

Winter fostered neighborliness among the denned-up settlers of Tantrattle. Just as deer, to survive the depth of snow and boreal winds, yard beneath a sheltering stand of cedar and paw after browse within the steep-walled confines of their maze, so the scattered families tunneled out from storm upon December storm to call upon friends or, with new fervor and frequency, congregated, Sunday morning and Wednesday evenings, at the Reverend Cawkins's meeting house.

And so it was that before December, the eighth month of her pregnancy, had gone by, Lucy Rime, despite her increasing fatigue, began to give weekday morning lessons to a small group of children, receiving in return a loaf of bread, pale green candles, half a jug of milk, and the grace of occupied morning hours. As the shrinking days deepened isolation and sharpened need, she was particularly grateful to hear the shrieks of children when they leapt from a sledge and skittered atop the snow to her door, to hear their laughter whenever the same crust caved beneath a parent's weight.

Once the children had gone, however, her mind would be filled with morbid confusion about the childbirth she knew so little about and which the several farmwives who did pay visits spoke of as they might of damnation, Indians and woodsmen, in whispers. Then one afternoon she heard sled bells and opened her door to see a shaggy horse in traces, and to be greeted by the Reverend Cawkins himself. Behind him stood Midwife Cawkins, a basket, filled with eggs and a bar of soap, crooked on her arm.

During this brief interview the Reverend Cawkins stood by the inglenook and kept his austere gaze directly upon Lucy while the midwife asked how the children got on with their schooling and proceeded to ramble on about old Culverwell's death, and the storage of his coffin in their winter vault. Ice had to be broken in the christening bowl and the Rabbow infant never once complained. As soon as the reverend walked to the door the midwife fell silent, patted the back of Lucy's hand saying "In due time," and they took their leave.

Left alone, Lucy Rime grew irked and puzzled at why, when she suffered grotesque fancies of childbirth, she had never interrupted the midwife's gossip with questions and proposals. Something in the reserve of the Reverend Cawkins had unnerved her. Even now his mute condescension lingered, to disquiet her mind. She dismissed him as the darkness settled in, but however much she worked to beat down her thoughts, they disobeyed.

A confirmation of her disquietude arrived later that evening when there was a soft knock on her bolted door. She opened it and drew back, frightened to see the Reverend Cawkins planted at her threshold like a monstrous snowman. That stern, censorious reverend who had visited earlier bore scant resemblance to this simpering gentleman who hesitantly presented her with a sack of precious salt, tottered between cavernous drifts and faded behind the scrim of continuous snowfall.

And two nights later, carrying a small block of butter, appeared the Reverend Cawkins. This time, a large red fist poised upon each knee, he remained long enough to speak of how winter seclusion compounded the dreadful loneliness brought on by the winter of a man's life. Indignant at his sad duplicity and humiliated by her acceptance of his offerings, Lucy Rime could not touch the butter.

The second week of January, on the eve of the cold snap, the Reverend Cawkins paid a final, and for Lucy Rime, most destructive visit. Standing, he spoke of his prospering estate: the grist- and sawmills he planned to build; tanning, potash, the land already purchased. He set an earthen crock of honey on the table and pacing the room, halted at the hooded cradle and started to whine—uttering now a hoarse confession of reverence for Lucy, now bellowing brutal abuse upon his long-barren wife.

"Get out!" ordered Lucy Rime, a trembling edge to her voice. Aghast, the Reverend Cawkins flinched as if she intended to strike him with the crock she shoved into his chest.

When not a single child arrived for lessons the next morning, she attributed it to the extraordinary cold. But then, no one came the following day. Nor the next. And at last, Lucy Rime comprehended what had happened and for days afterward, seated on the pallet bed pushed close to the hearth, she plotted and hoped for little else than Cawkins's death.

So long as half a dozen children had scribbled on their slates or, when the mornings were warm, clambered out of doors to roll great snowballs into figures and forts, Lucy had secured some respite from herself. Abruptly now, the brittle cohesion of busyness, distraction, was gone.

And now the meager extent of her intercourse with the settlement of Tantrattle was over, her life shrunk to the torrid perimeter of light shed by her fire. Pain, like a fierce night animal, stole out from her heart and chewed at her mind. These were the hours when her love and desire for Mordecai Rime summoned the image of his countenance and received vague and gruesome distortions: the peevish head of the Reverend Cawkins grafted upon her husband's bull neck and shoulders. Invariably, when she willed her perverse creations to be gone they came nearer, became more vivid, so that Cawkins might grimace and gravely exhibit to her the reach of his tongue. The moment she scoffed, aware of and disgusted with herself, her composite man vanished. Despite the numbing cold she often prowled her two small rooms as if entranced by the quick drum of her pulse. She employed one of a thousand devices to balk at the bridge to unreality, a plank across a brook, and keep sane. She might open a book and chatter its words aloud; once, when the neglected hound rolled onto his back, his legs crooked, she abstractedly dug her nails along his belly, causing him to squeal and skulk off. As the final month of pregnancy began, she crossed over that bridge more readily and took asylum in the bright ambitious time before her marriage. And if each passing day aggravated fiercer yearning for Mordecai Rime's return, the frozen nights inspired a parade of suitors, half-seen and unknown men who often amused her and tantalized her. Increasingly too, she looked upon this or that man's attentions favorably and thereby stimulated such burdensome self-despisal that she was overwhelmed with sorrow for herself and furiously despised the spectral marshal of every parade, the wondermonger who had entrapped and stranded her on this margin of nothing and nowhere. She began to fathom a profound justice in her creation of a man having the body of Mordecai Rime and the head of the Reverend Cawkins; the pathetic old farmer who sneakily reviled his childless wife, and the infantile woodsman able to do nothing but abandon her to an isolation so abysmal that it seemed she had fathered and carried and would surely deliver her child, alone. Indeed, were not the righteous farmer and the nomadic woodsman but different phases of the selfsame illness? She bitterly recollected Rime's parting threat—"You'd best be true, Lucy Rime, or you'll make a meat-bird o' me"—and wondered how she had held back from cursing, jeering, spitting in the face of his cruel egoism.

Week after week, these were the characteristic rounds of that night animal whenever it got loose from her heart and turned her mind in its sharp jaws.

5

> *Red Hot holes*
> *Hot as coals*
> *Step right up*
> *Mad Molly said.*
> *Sup an' sup*
> *'Fore you're dead,*
> *'Tain't no sin—*
> *Shove't in!*
> *Moll rides a cock to heaven.*

Whoooo-oo-eee, tongues clacked, fingers drummed the deacon seat and the wiry young swamper, flushed with his election, went another round:

> *Red hot holes*
> *Hot as coals*
> *Step right up*
> *Mad Molly said.*
> *My knee's spread*
> *My hole's as red*
> *As the day I wed*
> *Moll rides a cock to heaven.*

There ensued then a debate concerning the various merits, breadths and depths of vaginas to be met with in the natural world. Sheep, as ever, found a champion, as did women, goats, bears, deer and dogs. Continually teased about the length and frequency of his visits to the hovel, the teamster Clarence Smiles confessed a preference for the oxen's company to their own, as he considered the ox the more sensible beast.

Above catcalls and hoots, Smiles yelled, "You bullshit

ba'stads do all your screwin' here in camp an' all your lumb'rin in Sunb'ry Town," and bundling up, he plunged scowling into a chest-deep drift outside the entrance.

John Gorges folded his arms on his anxious chest and scanned the grimy fume-filled heads which cramped the room. In particular, he scrutinized Mordecai Rime who for days had kept to his corner berth carving a chunk of yellow wood. Since the crew had become snowbound Gorges regretted having talked of Rime's lunatic bout with the pine tree; and the more so the night Rang-tang Sarsen snapped his red galluses off his yoke-sized shoulders and jeered, "Whittlin' out a tree-beatin' club?" Sarsen drew the tin dipper to his humid, orange lips, his eyes narrowed upon Rime.

"Nope," answered Mordecai Rime without lifting his eyes, "a doll."

Uproarious Sarsen tried to stem the tea snorting out his nostrils. "Doll!" he gasped. "Feelin' need o' somethin' to sleep nights with? Myself, I'd hafta start off with a bigger slab so's the hole'd accommodate me."

Snickerings broke out in the close camp. They were not in sympathy with Mordecai Rime and so, with a derisive huff, Sarsen let be. Whipping back his bushy mane Sarsen began, "Know'd this Witch Woman"—staring up at the cupola as if the woman in question were hung there—"an' Christ a'mighty, did she have a way with wild things. Seen 'er walk straight up to a bull moose an' rub on his lip whiskers."

Sarsen waited to make certain the ears of the camp were his. "Happen'd I was trappin' late that fall an' doin' poorly, so's when I hear talk o' the Witch Woman I get this idea in my head. Witch Woman lived in the middle o' nowhere an' my ass was froze to get there but when I get there I seen grown wolves, cat'mounts, bears, wildcats, foxes, an' all manner o' coons an' weasels, and they was all circlin' her dooryard.

"Not a one o' 'em was quarrelin'. Too busy, what with their

moanin', howlin', pissin', pawin' an' scratchin', an' I warn't five minutes inside with the Witch Woman an' I know'd the reason why."

Sarsen's head tilted back, he tousled his shaggy red eyebrows and whistling appreciation and disbelief, he jumped up. Holding apart his hands nearly a foot he whispered, "Yay wide," nodding to confirm the distance.

"Like a chuck hole, an' so slipp'ry 'twas, so wet an' slipp'ry, the miracle of't was no toadstools grow'd along her walls. No problem soakin' both hands at a time clear to the elbows, an' I rubb'd her cracklin's on my lips an' nose 'cause they was chapped an' by next mornin', they was healed up.

"But the real gift o' the Witch Woman, what had them beasts moonin' an' wastin' themselves so, was the smell o' her. Trappin', I know somethin' about smells. I musta mixed every stink there is: eel oil, beeswax, alc'hol, them blue an' green an' yellow asshole sacs, junks o' meat—but there never was no rut-musk an' never no bait like that o' the Witch Woman.

" 'Twas a smell to craze.

"I'd only to slip outdoors, pick the handsomest beast, stun it, skin it, and flesh'm out. I tell ya, if that woman's juice'd been bottl'd, her man 'ould been richer'n any man in the north country."

"Where's this Witch Woman live anyways?" asked the pop-eyed swamper.

Sprawled on the field bed, another man crooned, "Big as a chuck hole," and fell silent.

"Slipp'ry wet too," said his bunkmate.

"Rang-tang, jus' why ain't you wed to that Witch Woman?" challenged the riled sled tender when Sarsen, beginning to undress, appeared done.

Cross-legged, listless at the far corner of the camp, Mordecai Rime felt mud slug through his veins. He marked Sarsen standing amidst the blue and yellow coils of smoke, how he stretched in full pride above the tiers of mute, blurry heads and, like a handkerchief, dropped the words: "She's dead," and how the squabbling crew cried: "How? Dead? When?" to try and pick up that handkerchief first.

The exasperating Rang-tang heated a bucket of water and tossed a pitch knot on the camboose. "Busted in 'er door," he revealed at last. "Gang'd 'er. Bull moose, bears, wolves, cats, weasels—the whole lot of 'em claw'd an' slash'd an' mobb'd her an' all the while she was able she pump'd back an' sung out songs, right up the time that Witch Woman was prong'd to death."

White and orange in the flare of the pitch knot, Sarsen snorted a period to the end of his tale and commenced his shower.

When Mordecai Rime perceived the awe on the crew's faces, he could not determine whether Sarsen had created those faces or they Sarsen. Together they made an inseparable unit. There was no question as to why this crew had fallen out with him. He had cheated on all of them: The master passion of his former life, of woods life—the passion among men—he had betrayed; its cardinal law—that women be the meeting place of men—he had broken.

These men in the thick steam and fumes appeared utterly contented. It was this contentment which disgusted and angered Mordecai Rime. Bereft of fight and language, he gazed upon the men and they were alien as the Reverend Cawkins had appeared alien to him. They watched Sarsen, entranced, while Sarsen stood wailing out an old ballad with a cruel, new edge:

*To the woods he will go*
*With his heart full up with woe*
*And he w-a-nders from tree to tree*
*Till six months are gone and past, he forgets it all at last.*

*It is time he should have another spree*
*It is time he should have another spree.*

*When old age does him alarm*
*He will settle on a farm*
*An' he'll find some young girl to be his wife;*
*But to his sad mistake, she* Mock *love to him will make.*


*And kind death will cut the tender threads of life*
*And kind death will cut the tender threads of life.*


Stroking himself daintily dry, Sarsen minced, "Sung that special for Deacon Rime."

"Wonder why 'tis dogs chew hardest on the dog that's hurtin'?" said John Gorges.

Sarsen bent his soaked chestnut body near to Gorges, clutched his woolen shirt, and easily hoisted him into the air. "Old man, hope you ain't callin' Rudolph Sarsen a dog?"

"Nope," Gorges promptly answered, adroitly mouthing the pipestem, "I was jus' wond'rin' why. You'd 'spose the sound 'o pain so scares 'em, they try an' eat the pain up."

Sarsen glared at the grizzled vacancy of Gorges's face and kept him harnessed. The crew watched, absorbed by how the strained buttons unraveled on the red shirt and squirted one by one between Sarsen's clenched, ruddy paws, and spun to the ground.

No one noticed that Rime quit his place in the remote corner of the camp and no one heard him stalk along the log wall. With the dry scrunch of a boot in frozen snow he ordered—"Set the man down!"—and every head swung around to see Mordecai Rime, his upper lip lifted on his wry, dark-yellow face, crouched twenty steps from Rang-tang Sarsen.

There was a stone-still moment: the crew gaped; Rime bunched in a ball; Gorges dangled; Sarsen smiled, fascinated, abstracted but for the plum-colored splotches exploding on his throat and brow. His gray eyes grew larger, shinier, rounder, and green veins inside his arms and on the sides of his neck and forehead swelled and twanged.

Then, all at once Sarsen giggled, hugged Gorges to his bare

chest and like a moody child, cross of a sudden with its doll, he hurled Gorges into the live coals and ash that buried the bean-hole.

Although Sarsen wheeled instantly about and planted his feet, he was not among the swift-eyed few to glimpse Mordecai Rime rear from a crouch and shoot headlong across the room. Rime's neck recoiled into his shoulders, his skull battered Sarsen's abdomen, and Sarsen, a benign sheen to his eyes, bellowed what sounded like a life's-breath, jackknifed backward through the air, straightened, half-somersaulted, and cracked his head on the packed earth where he came to a crumpled halt, his superb naked bulk unconscious and an expression of astonishment upon his face.

Mordecai Rime had forgotten what it was that had incited him. He was oblivious to the crew whose respect and devotion he had so vigorously reclaimed and which awaited now his victor's cock-a-doodling.

A pallor washed over Rime's sallow, impassive countenance. Transfixed, he hunched over the body as if it were a tree trunk, some thready cedar tree which, but a moment ago, had wind-toppled across his path.

Filmy eyes starting from their sockets, Adam's apple seething, Sarsen's rosy head was flung back, glistening in the unsteady fireglow. His long, brick-colored shock of hair spread, fanlike, upon the dirt.

It happened so swiftly, or else so appalled the already agitated crew—Rime's seizing of the heavy broadaxe off the wall and concentratedly wielding its curved helve, as if to hew a log, at Sarsen's upturned face—that no man stirred to grab hold of Rime before that fire-bright broadaxe had bitten off a sheaf of auburn hair and riven the earth not half an inch from Rang-tang Sarsen's deaf ear.

A relieved thunderous laughter broke the stillness and its roar kept up all the while Mordecai Rime lifted and heaved down the broadaxe to score an outline around Sarsen's tight-cropped head.

Rime cast the broadaxe aside. Fury continued to gather and crowd his chest and he could not yet be done with the flesh inert at his feet. He swayed above the body and searched it that it might disclose, and he inflict, that humiliation potent enough to expel the terror at large inside him.

The smug fashion in which Sarsen's languid tongue licked along the tufted edge of his mouth struck Rime as so hideous that he desired only to make a corpse of him.

Rime knelt beside Sarsen and frantically scooped the severed locks into one red wad. Underhanded, he chucked it onto the fire and slapped clean his palms while the burning wad came apart, snapped, writhed and stank.

That instant the flame bent, riffled, the door thudded open and down the snow dune slid Clarence Smiles. "Easin' up outside," he reported, "Warmin'," and he frisked patches of snow off his rump. The teamster perceived the bewildered stillness in the camp, and Mordecai Rime, and then the prostrate Sarsen, shorn and stomach-up, blinking in groggy disbelief at the splint roof. "Hey . . . what's," was all Smiles had stammered when pell-mell, Rime snatched Sarsen's wrist, jolted him to a sit and crooking an arm around his neck, gripped a thigh, jerked the dormant hulk across his shoulders, toted it to the door, and dumped it like a skinned carcass atop the snowdrift.

Rime latched the door. He crossed the room and sagged in his corner berth—wrists propped on his knees, head on the log wall, eyes slitted, steadfast upon the latch. In openmouthed silence the crew listened, and they too eagerly eyed the latch. After a most protracted moment the bar lifted from its strike. The halting shove which opened the door loosed such riot indoors as to blast with insult the abject and scalded man who reeled, doubled up, in the doorway. One hand clawing his shorn hair, the other cupping his genitals, he plunged into the noise.

Some few men guffawed and badgered him as he tripped toward the fire and his clothes, but the din had broken off.

Everything brazen appeared to have been smelted from Sarsen's aspect. He pulled a red toque on his head, rushed into all his four layers of scarlet underwear, his stockings, stagged trousers, and moccasin boots. Then, padded in a stout mackinaw, he hunched shivering above the fire. His lips pulsed, parted imperceptibly and released "Boss" in a whisper. He never looked at Urban Burlock when he asked for and was given his pay from the chamois pouch hung on Burlock's chest. And he never spoke or raised his eyes the while he packed his gear. He skulked to the entrance, reached for the latch, and stopped. Though his head kept depressed and did not turn, his throat raved as only an animal badly shot or at the peak of rut can rave: "YOU'RE GONNA DIE, RIME."

As the door cracked shut, Mordecai Rime had tried to rejoin, "Never thought diff'rent," but nothing had come out.

Some of the crew loitered, more crawled beneath the single cotton batting spread. "One helluva haircut!" exclaimed the swamper.

"Holy Shit'n Heaven!" agreed the sled tender.

"Serves the whorin' ape," said proud John Gorges, pondering his blistered fingertips and tapping empty his pipe bowl on the deacon seat.

Mortified, the crazy quilt drawn to his chin, Mordecai Rime watched and listened, and was watching and listening still many hours afterward, blood pumping so fast inside his head that the room jigged up and down with each heartbeat and the crew, wriggling and rolling in the mellow light, resembled one enormous centipede. He wished then to scream as Sarsen had—one steady, throat-cleaving noise to last the night long—but again, he found his throat horror-clogged. At last, sitting against the wall, he fell asleep and, deadly cold, directly awakened from a dream. There had been an infant in his dream, a bare girl infant, plump-jointed, his daughter. He tickled her along the arch of her rib cage and she grunted with glee and pedaled her arms and legs and displayed her tongue, gums, the patterned roof of her mouth. He spread his thick fingers apart and raised his arm. Of themselves those fingers made a fist, and he witnessed but could not halt the fist from driving her pliant belly right down, flush to her spine.

Mordecai Rime squeezed his ears to muffle the loud chatter of his teeth for he remembered finally how his baby's limbs had flapped and how she stopped, went limp and lay back whiter than paraffin, blank as the whitest snow.

## 6

Days of static dead cold were succeeded by a week of blizzard and wind, but when finally at the end of January a false thaw did come, Lucy Rime stayed sealed in, sleepily fingered her painful belly and mused upon the seductive lethargy which would let her mind burn down and go out. Then one afternoon on the verge of nightfall, there came a hollow thud outside the entrance. Had the noise not provoked a string of barks and growls from the hound, she would have considered it snow tumbling off the roof and ignored it altogether.

Immediately, hard poundings shook her bolted door and swept the vindictive face of the Reverend Cawkins across her mind. A voice shouted, the hound barked, and the hammering continued while Lucy Rime carefully inspected the muzzle-loader, ramrod, powder, balls, and vainly tried to recall how a charge was loaded. After a flustered moment, the question made no difference. Steeled by the queer calm which only the severest hostility can produce, and holding the unloaded weapon, she unbolted the door and stepped back, her thumb on the firelock.

From atop the crest of snow-wall that had drifted against the threshold, there peered and immediately vanished an unfamiliar bearded face. Concealed behind the edge of the bank he nervously asked, "This the Rime place?"

No reply came forth besides the wild barking of the hound.

"Crew'd with Mordecai Rime. You his missus?"

"What is it?" said Lucy anxiously, hearing the harsh quaver in her throat.

"Name's Sarsen, Missus Rime, Rudolph Sarsen. Would you set down that rifle? I come a long ways to get here an' I'm wet through." His head rose warily over the pitted ridge of snow and he glanced down into the room.

Every waking second of his tramp through the melting wilderness to Tantrattle, Rudolph Sarsen had been craving to play havoc with the place where Mordecai Rime lived. Humiliation had fabricated his scheme. Rage, indifferent to the leaden snow clinging to the webbing of his snowshoes, had lifted his screaming legs and staggered him onward. He lowered himself woodenly to the cabin floor.

Narrowing his attention to the hound, he scooped out tiny wads of snow caught inside his boot-tops and uttered the words: "I come straight down from camp on Mooselip to tell you Mordecai Rime's dead!"

A feeling of desolation, an unaccountable sadness overcame Sarsen once his hoax was accomplished. Suddenly he wanted to retract his words and like a child listening for his father's angry tread, be elsewhere.

"I mean you no harm," he said, and forced himself to look full into Lucy Rime's face. "I mean you no harm," repeated his dreadful voice. Opened unnaturally wide, her eyes gazed as the suspended eyes of a caught animal gaze dumbly about the advancing trapper.

Despite the anguish of soaked boots and trousers, Sarsen thought to run outside and keep running. She turned and moved away. While she hung the musket on the crotched brackets Sarsen noticed her fine, bony profile, her slender wrists, and for the first time, the frightful low-slung jutting between her hips. She sat on the pallet bed and nestled beneath a heap of woolen stuffs, blankets, and a goosedown coverlet, entirely out of sight.

Sarsen waited and stared and listened intently, but not a

noise or a movement could he detect in the mound on the pallet. Fearing she had crawled underneath the pile and died, he pulled off a sopping mitten and gently pressed his red fingers to the coverlet, feeling the faint rise and fall his eye had missed.

He took a deep breath and, shivering, collapsed into the chair at the foot of the bed by the hearth corner. As though burdocks were matted in his hair, Sarsen tenderly fingered his scalp. He would show her exactly what Rime had done to him. He would explain, apologize, and leave. Strangely, once Rudolph Sarsen determined to remain only until she awakened, the oppressive cabin and the horrible wrongness of his presence in it ceased to rack his mind. He followed the aimless play of shadows on the bark ceiling, touched the hound curled in a knot to one side of him, glimpsed the huddled woman concealed on his other side, and before long, suffused with an almost domestic well-being, slumped toward the blazing warmth and was fast asleep until dawn.

Still tired from the long journey and his uneasy dreams and hunger, he shifted in the rude chair and drowsily looked at the curled tongue of the yawning hound. The fire at his feet had burned low. Sarsen also yawned, stood, and stretched.

Then, he caught sight of Lucy Rime. Although she took no notice of him, that single look convinced him that her mind had broken overnight. Seated on her heels in the crumpled bedding at the edge of the pallet, she seemed to scan the cabin corner to corner, as from a great height. Her rigid eye flashed upon Sarsen and kept turning. Suddenly pain screwed up her remote and haggard face. She rolled onto her back with quivering legs akimbo and made soft rapid noises. After several moments the noises subsided.

"Fits!" Sarsen mumbled. Spellbound, he watched her strain up and perch motionless as a hawk on the rim of a nest.

Time and again paralyzed Rudolph Sarsen saw her throw back her disheveled head, arch her spine and shake her fists all about. Twice, unmindful of Sarsen's existence, she shuffled the length of the room, squatted over a clay bowl in the dark corner, urinated, and wavered to the pallet bed. For an hour, for two hours and longer Sarsen beheld elaborate and enigmatic sleepwalking procedures so alien to common humanness that he deemed her possessed.

And the whole time Sarsen stood planted in horror and did nothing but witness what he believed to be some potently unholy mechanism, Lucy Rime had felt her insides tugged downward, wave upon harsher wave, as if the moon had fallen out of the sky and buried itself under those very floorplanks. Not until the downward pull had become so great within her that all her muscles rolled in unison and fastened her to the hot stone hearth where she yanked her skirt and soaking layers of underskirt above her knees and groped between her thighs to ease herself—not until that moment did panicky Rudolph Sarsen comprehend the nature of the event taking place before his eyes. Hastily, he fetched a bucket of icy water, hung another to heat, and began to wipe sweat from her neck and brow.

Dazedly nodding, she clasped his stout wrist and guided it with uncanny strength between her shaking legs. The wet cloth dropped from his fingers, his hand shied and she let go gasping as a stronger wave crested with a pale spurt, and Sarsen saw the purple cone of head splay out her shining red flesh and be towed, the wave spent, back inside her. His trepidation sloughed off him. He fell to his knees and systematically wrung out rags, cleaned her vagina, swabbed down her thighs, his breathing quickening to coincide with hers.

Then the strongest wave of all mounted, pinned her fast, down, apart; her lips opened, jaw gaped at its widest, and grasping Sarsen's neck she hoisted herself into a squat just as there rode on the wave's brutal edge an astonishing and dented blue head.

Sarsen squealed a falsetto laugh which restrained him from hauling out the rest of the baby at once. He elbowed away the hound's snout and crouched, cupping together his trembling hands as if to catch the head which revolved to show him its impassive profile. The spot above Sarsen's stomach clenched hard as stone and allowed no breath until piecemeal, a shoulder, slippery chest, flailing blue fists and everything else had slithered into his grip, whereupon the impassive features of the infant girl inflamed and convulsed with an absolute purity of rage.

In the close cabin Sarsen gawked with awe and aversion at the sleek-ribbed infant he held clamped, ankles and nape. What with her wailing, sneezing, bending, and scraping her nails along her matted black temple; with her streaked coating, like frog eggs and curdled milk, and the thick smell of just-gutted animal rising up from her, the baby girl so dumbfounded Sarsen he nearly overlooked the cord spiraling down into Lucy Rime and walked off.

Between his curved knifeblade and thumb he severed the blue cord. Blood spilled over his fingers. Scrupulously, he washed the baby's head with warm water, and the chalky creases of her body. Lucy Rime never turned sideways when he arranged the baby in blanketing below her white arm. Eyelids slightly apart, Lucy twisted silently and left an enormous slab of bright meat draped over the inside of her thigh.

Once again Sarsen tried to bathe her and shift bedding as best he could. The whole room seemed to him one pudding of sweat, flesh, woodsmoke and blood, in which everyone bogged and swam about. Stupefied, he sloshed the heavy crosshatched afterbirth in a bucket of pink water and tottered out of doors, beneath icicles hanging, thick as legs, from the eaves of the cabin.

At each step toward the hooded river Sarsen sank, the hound plunging avidly at his heels. He quit halfway down the soft pitch, kicked a hole in the slush, emptied out the bucket and wearily buried its steaming contents. Once he had struggled a dozen steps back up the slope he felt dizzy and dropped onto his back for a rest. He was sucking a mouthful of snow and pressing another handful to his forehead, hoping to clear his brain, when he heard the whining. He sat up to see the hound shoveling away the snow he had packed into the hole. He scolded and hurled two snowballs, but the hound's forelegs dug on.

The faint, long-drawn yowl of the baby sounded through the gray air. Sarsen smiled and planted the back of his head in the rotting snow. Soon the hound, afterbirth adangle in his straining jaws, glided past Sarsen and secreted himself behind the cabin for a feast. Sarsen was unconcerned. Shallowly embedded in the snow, he abandoned himself to a most joyful, gratified, even triumphant smile. Rudolph Sarsen, with his two red hands, had delivered a baby girl!

And now, inside, Lucy Rime briefly surfaced, pulled back blanketing to discover the hapless enlarged sex of her child, and wanly tracing the clasping mouth with the yellow-crusted tip of her breast, she again submerged in a dream-swamp.

One drizzling day and night of sleet after the next Lucy Rime floundered in this swamp of reverie and fever with scarcely a word or gesture for Rudolph Sarsen. Fitfully, she rose from the heavy bedfolds and moved about, despite his scrutiny, like something in the damp privacy of a den.

Sarsen woke humiliated and regretful each day, determined anew to rescind his terrible lie—a resolve he shrank from each evening when her listless dejection gave way to chills and night sweat. Lodged thus, with a tormented somnambulant woman and her wretched infant, Sarsen worked to rid them of infection and the interminable nightmare he had precipitated. To this end he cooked and fed porridges, gruels, made tea, tended fire; he hunted partridge nearby, and snowshoe hare; and in the blunt, suspicious settlement of Tantrattle he exchanged his pay for eggs and clean cloths and goat's milk. Less and less frequently he thought to escape; and soon, all consideration of confessing his deceit had vanished.

It was singular, perhaps, that while he diligently nursed

Lucy Rime and attended her infant, nothing frightened him more than the very prospect of her recovery. Into the nights, seated on the floor beside the pallet bed, he sponged cold water over Lucy's white neck and lips while his knee rolled the hooded cradle. That Lucy Rime kept silent, insensible of his doings, captivated and encouraged Sarsen, and also relieved him of his characteristic bashfulness with females—a conceit so extreme and precarious that outside of brothels, he heard censure in a woman's laugh. When her fever had risen one evening, Sarsen was able to hazard an initial small tenderness: stroking back hair glued to her wet jaw he leaned down, tentatively, nuzzled a place over her ear, and drew back.

Fortified by the acquiescence of her delirium that night, Sarsen's confidence built until the extent of his audacity unnerved him. And after long restless hours, at the break of day, he first tasted the sweet leakage from her nipple and looked about, rattled by the calm stare of the hound. Sarsen turned then, to find himself the object of Lucy Rime's wide-awake and apprehensive watch. There seemed no blood in her head. She looked wasted and held up her head unsteadily, but the traces of fever and daze were gone. She wet her lips with pasty saliva, reached for Sarsen's hand and covered it.

"You've been awfully good . . . Mr. . . . ." and because she did not know the name she smiled gruesomely and dropped back, closing her eyes.

"Rudolph," and standing, he said "Rudolph Sarsen."

Lucy Rime wadded half the coverlet behind her shoulderblades and looked down her chin at one large, knotted breast sticking through her kersey dress. She winced and regarded the knife sheathed on Sarsen's hip. Then, without concealing the breast she glanced into the cradle. "You have kept us clean, I see," she said.

Over her bed he stood, baffled. More swiftly than any crisp silence or hair-and-heart-rending lamentation, the powerfully controlled frankness of Lucy Rime disabled him.

"How long ago did it happen?" she asked, shifting upon an elbow to examine Sarsen's bright thick-bearded face.

"The little baby, missus?"

"His death."

"I . . . lose track," he stammered, subdued. He edged into the chair.

"He warned it would happen."

Sarsen had broken into hectic sweat. " 'Twasn't you," he whispered, eyes averted. " 'Twas a birchtop. I seen't hit his neck. You ain't got nothin' t'do with the matter."

Unhappy Sarsen could not make her out. He resented her for having risen and thereby having summarily excluded him from the former intimacy of his office. Watching her now, he fell to pitying himself. "Rather I'd be off?"

The manner in which she lay back, smiled at the blackened bark ceiling and carefully pronounced "Ru-dolph" completed his relapse into timidity.

He went out and rambled over the slick, pocked crust, but try as he might, he could not bring himself to leave the vicinity of Tantrattle. By dark he had circled to a stop at the cabin door. He slept where he spent every night of the following weeks, uneasily crumpled on his mackinaw at the hot foot of her pallet bed.

The false thaw returned to winter without his noticing. The snow fell, shut them in, and kept falling. Sarsen noticed nothing besides Lucy Rime. He watched her sponge herself and suckle the snorting baby and gobble food and sleep badly and change her dress. What small distance might be kept in the cramped space before the hearth, Lucy Rime ignored.

Daily, the damage which Mordecai Rime had administered to Sarsen's physical vanity was delivered in subtle miniature by his nerveless wife. Close within his reach Lucy Rime held herself aloof, alert, secluded in herself. If she were a man, thought Sarsen, he would beat her outright. As it was, powerless to disengage himself, he bided in idleness and figured how to equalize things between them. Her health gained rapidly, together with this independence which Sarsen variously construed as hostility, fear, grief, desire, and whatever else, surely a deviant want of the decorum befitting of widow, mother, and woman.

And before long, she excited such a ferocious churn of energy inside him that he shoveled needless paths, split extra wood. Yet despite any number of brutal exertions, he throbbed and mulled away the nights. Warming his feet on the hearthstone one evening while the baby loudly grubbed out its supper, Rudolph Sarsen realized that he must be in love.

With a thick lip-smack the infant jerked sideways and distracted Sarsen by siphoning a powerful, fine strand of milk into the air. Lucy watched the spray a moment and capped it with the tip of her finger. "Lilah!" she burst out abruptly, "Lilah Rime. Do you like it?" She glanced across the pallet bed and caught Sarsen's eye. "Well?" she asked calmly.

Rapidly stroking whiskers along his upper lip Sarsen turned away in frustration and sulked with such conviction that Lucy Rime wondered what she had done to so offend him. She realized how unbearably exposed and abused he considered himself and it irritated her. "I'm certain you know my body better than I," she said.

Sarsen's brow and nose changed to the same bright orange as his beard and he glowered down at his heavy fists.

"What is it you want?" said Lucy Rime. "You want to sleep here, in my bed?"

Scarlet, he jumped to his feet, threw on his mackinaw, toque, and bolted into the soft blackness outside with so radiant and astonishing a display of outrage that Lucy Rime broke into a fit of silly laughter which he tried not to hear. He felt an intense sympathy for Mordecai Rime who had disgraced him, and who now was sure to try and kill him.

If Sarsen's terror and outlandish indignation had set off Lucy Rime's laughter, what kept it going was the sight of her daughter, smiling asleep in the hooded cradle; thoughts of men Miss Lilah Rime might some day meet. The hound groaned and cocked his head, as if the sound pained his ears. She laughed and she was empty. Her eyelids could no longer be held apart, and she could not prevent her emptiness from filling up with a landscape which even in dream she recognized from a day at the end of the past October. Once again, above the edge of the beaver pond where Mordecai Rime had led her for their picnic, the same chilly sun shone on the incandescent colors of decay when she unfurled the quilt beside a log tiered with fungus the shade of a red-winged blackbird's shoulder. Nothing had altered except that this time she sat by herself. The spank of a beaver's tail summoned her to a closer look, down among the crisp, rank grasses encircling the pond. Dozens of frogs spurted into the silt at her rustling footfalls while she strolled along and leaped troughs of bronze water. Clacking his red teeth, the beaver hooked up his hind legs, his paddle, and jabbed them into the water, diving with a surly whack. Happy for the company of the beaver's noisy surveillance, she smiled each time the beaver surfaced, farther from his wattled house, circling the dead cedars which stuck white and jagged above the water. The pondwater was warmer than the air and since she found herself naked, she entered the shallow, coppery water, waded, and settled down into the black leaves, in the thick sediment. Why the pond grew oppressive, suddenly darkening, she could not at first understand. Beneath the water her legs were spread and they seemed ugly to her, orange and stunted. Disturbed, she got to her feet and her long strides agitated the muck as she made her way toward the reedy shore. There, with a squeal of horror, she saw them— leeches, hundreds upon hundreds of tiny leeches hitched along the length of her legs, battening. Unable to move, her mouth rigid, she watched the one parent leech among the hideous gray swarm, a single black muscle cartwheeling, end over end across her knee-cap. Now and again it paused, waggled one of its tapered ends into the air as if to fix its course and slowly climbed on. Rigid mouth open, she screamed a plea for husband's help; screamed so hard that amidst the gnawed willows and alders she heard a miraculous crack of twigs and there beside her knelt Mordecai Rime, his small shiny eyes concentrated on his blunt thumb and forefinger which gently tweezed leech after tiny leech from her ankles and calves. An outsized tooth-chocked grin, a delighted chuckle and shake of his bristled head beguiled away her terror and he eased her down, his hands at work moving up her thighs until finally, the pudgy black leech was plucked from a red welt on her skin and her shock of wet pubic hair had engulfed half his hand. His whole weight rushed upon her then, and with stunning immediacy Lucy Rime was wrenched from dream and sleep, at once to feel milk soaking her from neck to belly beneath his smothering heat; against her forehead scratched a beard, and in the quivering firelight she glimpsed his red-haired shoulder, and with all the stark might of her fury she threw herself open to greet Rudolph Sarsen.

7

Nothing could be seen, and the squabble of crows scavenging the melting crust echoed in the grim air that closed upon Tantrattle at winter's end. Sunken, discolored drifts withdrew from tree trunks, the heat of dwellings, compost and piled excrement. First signs of spring were everywhere. Even the Rime hound, on sniffing the musky, wet air blowing from the settlement, had pranced into the fog and days later drooped back haggard, an ear torn. Nevertheless, Lucy Rime treated Rudolph Sarsen with the same sharp-eyed, even-handed disinterest which also informed her dealings with her daughter and hound.

The contradiction between this remote, ironical workaday

Lucy Rime and the amorous, anonymous woman of their nights confounded and entranced Sarsen before the beginnings of the thaw led him to the realization that winter camp on Little Mooselip had broken up; that if the majority of loggers stayed for the ice-out and drive into Sunbury Town, others had left already.

The transformation in him was apparent overnight. For hours he reclined indoors, torpid, and for impassioned hours he exhorted Lucy Rime to leave the intolerable north country and with him make a pitch somewhere to the benign west; recklessly he hobbled about the steaming thaw or lay wait above the path into Tantrattle; but most markedly, the change showed in the nights clasped alongside her praying down Mordecai Rime and wishing, as winter came apart, for cold and snow everlasting.

The dreamy thickness of the days was but a shade paler than the nights, and the air, concealing or misshaping the contour, depth and sound of the land, seemed not to move. With so little to help an eye gauge the passage of time, distorted time haunted Sarsen worst of all.

Upon tugging open the swollen door one morning, Sarsen stood peering into the lusterless space. And before the stagnant draft caused Lucy Rime to take notice of the open doorway Sarsen was already off, once again planting his boots in the packed surface of the path leading above the river to the settlement. Any day now the path would be impassable. Edgeless drifts, although some ten feet high in places, and the overall two- or three-foot cover, had rotted, and Sarsen heard snow puckering and oozing as cell by cell it dropped from canopies over the river below him and dissolved in the rising amber water. A shaft of sunlight penetrated the mist before him, illuminating a bush of willows and glancing off a towering slab of air. Then Sarsen heard a peculiar noise. Convinced that it was a human voice, he hid behind willows on the embankment. Chest to the snow, he watched the vertical band of light smear and dissolve until, unable to see, straining to catch a footstep, a voice, he heard several drops spatter from catkins of the willows overhead.

He had calmed enough to consider himself fooled by a nervous ear, when there resounded, as from the bottom of a well, the words: "I done the most haulin'."

"Shit, you did," said a second voice.

"So you do the talkin'."

"Nope."

"Well I ain't go'n'ta."

With a heartbeat so tumultuous it seemed a partridge was drumming on his neck, Sarsen hugged fast to the embankment. At the next moment, for an unbearable succession of moments, he expected men to halt beside the loudly drumming willows, and seize him. His uplifted eyes darted this way and that when the scraping, trudging, and laboring snorts appeared to shift directions in the vapor.

"Sona-abitch's boggin' down" was muttered, as if confidentially into Sarsen's ear, and then a silhouette cut through the fog, boots sank within range to kick his eyes, sled-runners churned, and then another, far larger silhouette plodded out of the mildew, passed, and nothing was left of the procession but murmurs and the faint splash of snow.

Rudolph Sarsen lay on his drenched stomach beneath the pussy willows, his whiskers lodged up to the lower lip in snow and his eyes locked straight ahead until his mind was made up to leave Tantrattle at once and forever. Cautiously, he quit his hiding place and crouched to examine the footprints and the soft, deep ruts left by the sled. He started to recall the fog-warped conversation and the fleeting outlines. To his positive astonishment, he realized that neither of the bickering voices and neither silhouette could have belonged to Mordecai Rime.

And when he remembered one of the travelers had said, "You do the talkin'," he whooped out a snicker at himself, cried, "Peddlers by Jesus!" and recklessly lunged in pursuit.

At the end of the track of parallel ruts Sarsen came upon the handsled, laden with a wet molasses cask, its runners wedged in the remnant drift in front of the cabin. He shouldered in the door and his eyes jumped from the black pipestem clamped in the miserable smirk of John Gorges to black-bearded Teamster Smiles, the hound snuffling the teamster's woolens, to settle upon the gracefully carved wooden doll held by Lucy Rime.

"They've brought the body," Lucy said in a flat, diminished voice.

Sarsen cast half a glance behind him, toward the black-staved cask, and went rigid as a pelt on a stretching board.

No one gestured and no one spoke until the bluff teamster winced at John Gorges and stammered, "Don't figure how she coulda know'da . . . the accident . . . 'cause how coulda Sarsen. . . ."

"Figures perfect," interrupted Gorges, ogling Lucy Rime's vexed, heat-burned features. "Figures perfect when you figure her an' him's in cahoots!"

Clarence Smiles fidgeted out of doors. The hound followed and commenced circling the cask, baying as if he had treed something. John Gorges lingered a moment beside Sarsen. "You was lyin', Rang-tang," he mumbled, "Witch Woman ain't been kill't," and he jammed shut the door.

"C'mon, lit's get," urged the spooked teamster.

"We ain't leavin'm," Gorges said, slapping a mitten on the caskhead. He wrestled the sled handles up and down, but the runners would not unstick.

"I want nothin' t'do with the ba'stads. C'mon."

"Take off," snarled Gorges. Landing a boot on the ribs of the hound, he resumed his struggle with the impacted runners. The burly teamster grabbed the sled handles, wrested loose the runners and vehemently sledged the difficult way back to Tantrattle, from where they were directed yonder, to a homestead where the entire party—the unnerving hound, teamster Smiles, Old John Gorges and the unwieldy cask—

stopped while Gorges beat and hammered until, risen from his early sleep, the Reverend Cawkins glared petulantly through the narrowly opened door.

"A barrel?" reproached Cawkins once Smiles had indicated the cask. "Savages do better by their dead."

"Weren't nothin' else," Gorges explained. "This man Rime was a . . . ," and at once, the reverend's door opened wide.

"Rime, you say? Mordecai Rime's in that barrel?"

"Curl'd up like a baby," declared Gorges.

Cawkins took measure of John Gorges: "A proper burying costs time and money. Gold money."

"Gold money," repeated Gorges.

"I'll be out," declared Cawkins, closing the door on them.

"Friggin' ol' Christer," growled the teamster.

Carrying a seething pitch pine torch, Cawkins emerged in a black greatcoat and waded stiffly around the cemetery. Torchlight shone on the tops of slate headstones. The hound bayed without stop. "What's into the creature?" shouted Cawkins, swishing the torch to scare the hound off. Reluctantly, Smiles helped John Gorges trundle the cask over the reverend's foot-holes, below the cemetery and down to the winter vault.

"Plague winter," uttered Cawkins as he knocked the cedar braces from the tomb's double door. Once the cask was set upright inside the vault, the woodsmen pulled back.

The long melt had begun to thaw corpses and neither would follow when Cawkins stooped deeper inside the putrid cavern. Cobwebs crisped like hair from the flame and the torch glowed upon frozen mud, caked spades, a stone boat and, stacked to the low ceiling, caskets of all sizes.

"Better than forty years," said Cawkins, nodding his torch at one short, slender casket, "the good midwife here shared my bed. And there, Rideout. Culverwell. Keen, Highstone, Gentle. These, the Rabbow children. Here, in my vault, one-third our settlement."

"Plague o' what?" queried John Gorges.

Reverend Cawkins had barely turned toward the entrance when the black hound sprang hallooing into the winter vault. Cawkins jabbed and lunged again, his torch clubbing the hound's back. One lunge singed the muzzle, driving the hound against the wall of coffins; another caught its glistening black nose—and the hound slipped under the sparking cudgel and rushed yelping into the outside darkness.

Winded almost to faintness Cawkins grabbed hold of the bank of coffins and wheezed, "No natural dog!" He tilted the spitting torch to light up the woodsmen, but they had fled, and he addressed himself to nothing besides the frigid glint of coins strewn atop the head of the molasses cask.

### 8

May, especially in the environs of Tantrattle, proved severely backward, a month of freezing nights which retarded the long thaw of April until the snow, full of trapped water, packed and broke into turquoise bits of ice. Seeping between snow and frozen ground, daytime rivulets of meltwater made shallow green ponds of every intervale depression and drained into the widening river. Indeed, such a multitude of jagged floes crammed the river by the end of May that a squeeze occurred in a narrow crook not far downriver from the Rime cabin, ice-boulders fused and before long amassed into one prodigious upheaval of ice. Catastrophe lacked only the rains which the first night of June delivered in abundance.

A sudden, tumultuous overflow of hillside ravines and gulleys and brooks and flooding streams descended upon Tantrattle that night with rush and roar enough to drive the Reverend Cawkins and a goodly proportion of the diminished settlement from their beds onto their knees. Loosing sheets of snow, ice and topsoil, the night torrent deafened the knock of stones and splintering wood and the bleats and bellows of the panicky stock. Incredulous farmers watched black rains tumble from eaves and drill moats in snowbanks outside their thresholds. Below their homesteads the shallow riverbanks were mauled and gave way. Swelling the floodplains, the boiling ice-freshet rose, to chase half-dressed farmers and their wives after herds of pallid, bawling children, cows, horses and tormented sheep—all groping through the splashing dark for higher ground.

The stone cribwork bridge in the midst of Tantrattle was filliped by the surging, thick current and swept downriver, toward the ice-dam. No one witnessed the thundering convergence of freshet and dam, but when rains ceased and at daybreak, winds began to blow, the outcome—a foaming troughlike reservoir flooding the intervale—was surveyed by the hapless survivors upon the hillsides.

Beneath a mud surface the frozen ground held the brown, scum-filled lake for days afterward. Families built shelters and salvaged what they could before the morning when the floodwaters began gradually to subside and an inventory of ruin was commenced.

Everything, everywhere had suffered the derangements of this freshet, and certainly not least was the Reverend Cawkins. That his entire meetinghouse had vanished, he had known days before this unhappy morning when he slumped in despair over the broken and missing headstones of the five infants, a marble hand in the silt of his ransacked cemetery. Not even the reverend's capacity for gloom however could withstand the surfeit of havoc awaiting him at the winter vault: cedar braces and one door ripped from the entrance; the remaining door buried awry in the dimpled mud; the center of the vault's earth roof fallen in.

While he viewed this harrowing debris, an explanation for it dimly lit Cawkins's mind. Scarcely a moment had passed when the explanation blazed forth with conviction. This man, deprived of a large portion of his wealth, his meetinghouse, his winter vault and his wife, began at once to trudge up the guttered knoll flinging about his arms and cursing. And all along his upland route to the settlement he grew ever more profane and embattled as he inspected the drowned landscape. He discovered a heifer, forked high in the alders of the floodplain; in the orange willows two chickens roosted, and a broken loom; and like an ark outside Tantrattle proper foundered the skeleton of his meetinghouse.

He soon met the forlorn group of nine settlers assembled upon the mound overlooking the former sites of the Airs' farm and bridge: neither the farm and the bridge nor Freedom and Solemna his wife had been accounted for.

"Terrible, Rev'rend."

"You seen the jam?"

"Was your place spared, Rev'rend?"

But Reverend Cawkins, squelching through the mud with long, patriarchal strides, marched on.

"Visionings," whispered one farmer.

"Wrath, you see the wrath and fever in those eyes!"

"Awful eyes," it was agreed. Smitten with wonder they followed him at a cautious distance. They no sooner had arrived at the wooded prospect outside the settlement than three of the party deserted. There, upon the washed-out slope, the Reverend Cawkins recoiled from an onrushing figure of a man, a large and fire-colored man galloping over the muck, tripping onto all fours, sliding, glancing behind and again scrambling his savage way in poor Cawkins's direction.

The creature swerved before laying hands on the swooning reverend, clambered uphill and lurched into the green poplars. Footprints near the scene of the ruffle were examined while Cawkins revived. It was clear that one of the man's feet had been bootless and that in all likelihood he had intended to escape rather than assault something.

Bedraggled and panting the Reverend Cawkins arose and proceeded to head the daunted group. When chimney smoke came into view, and the intact Rime cabin, Cawkins faltered. In the distance beyond the cabin the ice-dam moldered like a giant wall of butter and Cawkins's aplomb was so visibly enfeebled that two more farmers lagged behind.

Cawkins mustered himself, and perceiving the door ajar, made for the cabin entrance. The hearth was ablaze and on the floor of the musty room the baby Lilah, knees tucked to her chin, screamed as if poisoned. While Cawkins investigated the otherwise empty dwelling, one of his dwindled band noticed a moccasin boot lodged in the soft mud. Slurred tracks below the boot led them to such an appalling conclusion that when the Reverend Cawkins stormed from the cabin he spied those last four of his followers stampeding through the mud above the plain.

Crestfallen, he too saw footprints, only these had barely filled with cloudy brown water and they were, unmistakably, a woman's. Cawkins trailed them down the slippery rise, past the lone moccasin boot to the border of the receding floodwaters, whereupon the very mire reared up in the form of the black hound. The hound crouched, as terrified of the reverend as the reverend was cowed by the snapping hound and the wild woman cradling the blue head of the corpse. Cawkins's skin began to crawl. He staggered backward and fled Lucy Rime and the spoiled flesh doubled up in tattered crazy quilt.

Sentinels kept vigil that night on the perimeter of the encampment where all Tantrattle huddled around a single fire on the slope above their demolished settlement. However worn-out and beleaguered by the ice-freshet and its gruesome aftermath, none but children and livestock was able to sleep. At midnight, in the lavender smoke pouring up from the bubbling heap of wet twigs and branches, the Reverend Cawkins got to his feet, broke his silence and set them shivering in their greatcoats and blankets. The previous January, had he not apprised them of the cunning solicitations of the Rime whore? And did he not suffer the immediate loss of the Midwife Cawkins? The swirling glare of steam and fire aggravated the contortion of Cawkins's ivory-yellow face and lent dismal authority to his description of the black spy-dog he had beaten from the now decimated vault, the ice-jam behind the Rime place, and the dead woodsman Mordecai Rime run aground at the very threshold of his dwelling. "Winter plague . . . whoredom . . . hell dogs . . . flood . . . returning corpses . . . you behold Pestilence," exalted the hoarse, portentous voice of the Reverend Cawkins. "Pestilence infesting the north . . . spreading westward . . . Pestilence thriving, for thrive it shall until that golden . . ." and hesitating with an implacable scowl, he was interrupted by the ringing alarm of a sentinel.

Every smarting eye fixed upon the speck of orange flame pulsing beyond the poplars on the bluff downriver. Cawkins sat through the night hours hugging his knees and nodding at the spectacle of enlarging flame until the black smoke-column rising from the Rime cabin scored the dawn. And later that day, from an abundance of hieroglyphs made in the morass before the cabin (a groove running from the spot where the corpse had been stranded, up to the roofless and gutted dwelling), and the charred infant, preserved in a dug-out cradle beneath the bones and rubble of the pyre, the hellish fate of the entire Rime family was confirmed by several bold residents of Tantrattle.

All Tantrattle, however, had reason to consider the fireside prophecy of the Reverend Cawkins before that summer was out; for whether those direful forebodings had issued from a body ungratified to the verge of distemper or from a bona fide seer, there assuredly did come to pass hardships of such an inordinate nature that the succeeding months were to be remembered as the Ice Summer. Late frosts withered the buds of orchards throughout the northlands and early crops were blasted in the freak blizzard at the start of July. Birds' eggs hatched only to have nestlings frozen solid as the ice which formed an inch thick upon the streams. When the sleet of that weird season lashed down the first corn shoots and cold fever wasted entire households overnight, thousands of mystified, half-starved families surrendered, pulled stakes, and escaped before October snows had sealed the afflicted north country.

## 9

In the wake of the ice-freshet, the fire and calamitous summer, Tantrattle virtually disbanded. Settlers departing Tantrattle never talked about bad luck or happenstance as did emigrants from other stricken regions of the north. Hastening through Sunbury Town on their ways south and westward, those who had stayed in Tantrattle the longest, sowing and grimly sowing again, encountered woodsmen already heading north to set up winter quarters. These forthright husbandmen—possessed of little tolerance of ambiguity or fabrication—gave the superstitious woodsmen outlandish explanations for why the Ice Summer had befallen them. That fall, it was the talk of lumber camps.

While there was light on the shores of Upper, or Big Mooselip Lake, Boss Urban Burlock made certain that no one in his skeleton crew had leisure to brood and gossip and rail. Once the camp was established and the ox hovel built, Burlock tailored the operation to the run of the freezing water (which pinched through narrows and tumbled down a ravine, Quick Falls, into Little Mooselip), and its surrounding terrain. Burlock personally directed half the crew in damming the narrows and constructing a sluice for easing logs over Quick Falls; John Gorges supervised the clearance of windfalls, boulders and roots from the brookbeds and gulleys; skidpoles trestled ravines; rises were sheared; and as premature snows covered the frozen shores, a crisscross of branch roads was swamped in and out of every stand of pine, and each branch road connected with the main road alongside Big Mooselip Lake and ended at the landing upon the ice.

Each day woodsmen trickled into camp and then, with the

arrival of teamster Clarence Smiles and his oxen, hauling a long sled packed with goods and additional recruits, winter camp was sufficiently filled out to begin operations at dawn. None of the crew retired to the field bed after supper that night. They straddled the deacon seat, greased boots, and oilstoned axes, stared into the fire and listened to the sizzle of their brown spittle. A knot of three or four men hunched over a bedraggled deck of cards, and several others, while they stood watching the game, traded lies and plans for the faraway spring before the usual nightly fare of hunting and river-driving and rum-drinking stories was supplanted by accounts of the bizarre summer, Mordecai Rime, marriage tales and tales of death.

Straightway the teamster Clarence Smiles joined his cattle and John Gorges sucked a pipe and kept silent. Rumors were reviewed and savored until someone mentioned the all too recognizable man with the fluttering orange hair who had charged into the wilderness as if the King of Terrors were saddled on his back. Indeed, the destiny of this wild man had excited so many fabulous surmises that when the boy who toted nosebags into the swamp to feed the crew next day swore Rang-tang himself was arrived in camp, the poor youngster was scouted down by every man on that operation. Talk of a prank ceased after the crew ducked inside and milled around the swinging crane and bean-hole. Every amazed soul tried in vain to disregard Rudolph Sarsen as he combed out his auburn beard and then his hair with long insolent strokes. His tight-jawed leer singled out John Gorges and Clarence Smiles.

"Locks's grow'd back nicely, Rang-tang," said John Gorges. Sarsen nodded. Smoke, rising from the open fire to the log cupola, was blasted back upon them by winds shaving the cedar-splint roof. Coughing, spitting and rubbing red-rimmed eyes, the intimidated crew passed the dipper of tea and hastily couched for the night, fully dressed, upon the boughs of the field bed.

Chopping crews were scattered out at daybreak, felling pines along the marble floor. The binding ice of Big Mooselip Lake thunderclapped in the bitter air. Throughout a November of such cold it scorched nostrils and made brains dance, all the choppers but Rudolph Sarsen cut in pairs. He had no choice but to work alone. And after a day's labor, when crews trod the complicated night-blue shadows to camp, every man on the operation refused to eat so long as Rudolph Sarsen stood by the camboose wolfing down great heaps of beans and salt pork. Icy air clung to them while they clapped and stamped on the dirt floor to get their limbs working, and their bitterness grew by the day.

Had the unreasonable amounts of lumber felled and twitched from Sarsen's allotted areas not surpassed the output of any chopping team in camp, Boss Urban Burlock would never have permitted the dissension aroused by Sarsen's antics. The boy who carried grub into the woods told how the meat-birds always thronging about him chattering for food drove Sarsen to such states of frenzy that he held his head, took cover, or swung his axe as if to cleave the birds in midair. And Clarence Smiles, whose team snaked wood from Sarsen's chance to the landing, thought it strange that Sarsen was never once at work when he arrived, but leaning against a tree, grinning and watching.

The belief made its rounds that Sarsen napped or sat upon a stump while the day long his uncanny poleaxe chopped by itself. And since Sarsen conversed with nobody, showed no signs of needing to, and furthermore, slept, ate and worked apart from the crew, he was quickly considered something more and less than an ordinary man. Smiles said he was jinxed and treacherous. Another claimed he "didn't get all that skill for nothin'." He had signed away the gift of speech to cut such quantities of pine.

Level-headed John Gorges repeatedly took his stand on the phrase, "Fear's th' on'y devil can drive'n axe like that," and stood firm, until the night came when he no longer could believe his words, or, for that matter, his eyes.

It began, at first with relief that the wicked freeze of November showed signs of breaking. The gusts, which had filed Big Mooselip Lake and jiggled loose moss chinking the camp walls, slackened and died down when a low cloud blocked off the pure, cold sky. All night huge flakes of moist snow filtered under the log cupola and melted above the fire. Without wind the soggy snow mounted, and hours before dawn, when Clarence Smiles opened the door on his way to provender his oxen, snow had piled up groin-deep. By noon storm winds drove an icy snow sideways and the crew dozed, moodily bided time, and kept watch of Rudolph Sarsen who paced with an ugly expectant look in his eyes while the storm outside rose to a full blizzard.

Whenever Sarsen unlatched the entrance and held the door slightly ajar to check outside, he grimaced and kneed it shut upon the white snake of drift that squeezed in and along the earth floor. Again that night, and the following day, gray land was welded seamless to the gray sky, banking such energy indoors by the second evening that Boss Urban Burlock worried that his men would not stay pent another day.

A dozen grumbling woodsmen were sprawled in tedium on the field bed and a dozen more men ripped their shares of salt pork, sopped fat from the common kettle, and sat vacantly upon the deacon seat drinking tea—molasses-sweetened that night by Burlock's order—smoking, and glancing about, when Sarsen jerked open the door and stuck out his shaggy head. This time, to the alarm of everyone but Sarsen, the winds chanced to tumble past Sarsen's leg one ruffled and woozy gray jay.

Rudolph Sarsen practically jumped to the spot where, plumped against the opposite wall, black beak ajar, the stunned jay tilted its head.

Sarsen had dropped to his knees. As he greedily began to

inspect the bird someone jeered, "Some beans's left in the hole, Rang-tang."

"Never know who it mighta been."

"Shows good sense. Comin' in t' warm up."

"Let't be," pleaded John Gorges when Sarsen snatched up the gray jay. Fear shot through the room and drew the men into a subdued cluster. " 'Tis unlucky to harm a meat-bird, Sarsen. Toss't out or let't stay the night, but let the soul be!"

Wind made a dirge of roof shakes and joints while Sarsen, turning the bird before his nose, moved slowly to his corner and settled against the unpeeled spruce wall. And presently, for the first time that winter, Sarsen was heard to speak, his red whiskered lips inches from the gray jay's sharp beak: "Old man warns o' bad luck if Rudolph Sarsen don't treat you good," he whispered tenderly. "But the old fart's spoutin' out his asshole, 'cause this world don't have a grief that ain't been tried on Rudolph Sarsen." His red fist suddenly closed tighter around the jay's belly and he said, "You seen to't, ain't you mister, you're the one won't let *me* be." The jay squirmed, gagged out the single protest in the room, and leveled a formal series of pecks at Sarsen's thumb and bristly fingers. "Your comin' here's a bad mistake," he told the bobbing, straining head inside his knuckles. " 'Cause I guess'd you was comin', an' what with your pretty little eyes an' black hair an' cocky ways there's no mistakin' 'twas you chopped off my hair when you was a livin' man." Sarsen relaxed his grip so as to bare the jay's breast, and twisting his fingers, pinched out a mass of pale feathers. The bird wriggled without a squawk and pedaled its dark purple legs. "Dyin', you fool'd me good," admitted Sarsen while the passive crew, watching him pluck the last feathers around the slender pink throat, made faces as though each blood-filled quick of feather screamed as it was yanked out. When he had done with its breast, Sarsen flopped the shrunken jay in his palm, and exclaiming, "Some wicked, mean trick, sneakin' back through the mud when you was long dead," he commenced to strip the charcoal shoulders and back. " 'Twas so clever it spook'd me from the baby girl I pull'd outa the only woman I ever loved." Sarsen held the jay trembling up to his inflamed, gray eyes. " 'Fore your friggin' feather'd soul came 'round to cause me pains, you shoulda know'd there ain't a sufferin' left can pain me." With that, Sarsen got to his feet and pinning each wingtip, unfolded the alive and naked meat-bird like a paper doll he had finished cutting out. "There's nothin' now can overcome Rudolph Sarsen," he declared, and rushing to the door, he flung the gray jay into the riled snow.

The twenty-five woodsmen voiced no objection and made no gesture. They kept staring at the man who closed the door and took a breath as though he had just earned the largest fulfillment of his life. In no rush to let such satisfaction go, he unlaced his boots and peeled down his stagged trousers. Whistling a catch, unbuttoning his layers of red underwear, ruffing up his briary chest, letting the coverlet drop from his nakedness and stretching for the bucket of heated water on the swinging crane, he prepared for that shower and acknowledged no one. And the shower itself was the more pleasurable because he never responded to the gazes he knew were trained upon him and upon the water splashing down the contours of his orange skin to the cold floor. Ebulliently, he tousled his sopping hair.

But suddenly a queer whimper issued from that pillar of dispersing steam. Masses of hair were coming loose from Rudolph Sarsen's scalp. Hair clung to his arms and between his fingers.

He stood ankle-deep in hair rich and rusty as shed pine needles.

His fingers circled and scrambled over his utterly bald head. He touched and rubbed his beardless cheeks. He lifted his arms and saw his white armpits; peering down the gooseflesh of his pale chest at his white penis and hairless thighs, he started to tremble, weep and giggle.

Not a single strand of hair was left on his body. On his toes, the small of his back, in his nostrils and ears, his eye-lashes—nothing. He was stripped bare as the figure of a man made of snow.

There was an awful interlude of dumbness before confusion broke. Like an irate squirrel, one woodsman stuttered and gnashed his teeth; another coiled on the floor shielding his head while John Gorges leveled curse upon curse at Sarsen's whoredam and hellsire. Clarence Smiles barreled into the storm winds to the refuge of his oxen and hovel, and Urban Burlock managed but shakily to brace the head of the youngster who retched loud as the sobs and babblings that stirred those cramped quarters into bedlam.

And senseless as a man made of snow, Sarsen never cowered, indeed, never seemed to apprehend that the eyes closing upon him were crazy with terror and hatred. Slapdash, with neither his compliance nor his resistance, Sarsen's hairless legs were rammed into his trousers, his arms stuffed rudely into sleeves and mackinaw, an axe put in his hand and he was half-hauled, half-driven from winter camp into such whirligigs of snow that no trace of him was to be found the next morning when, notwithstanding the nightlong winds which had the entire ground scoured, doubting John Gorges concluded, "Devil don't leave no tracks."

## 10

From the beginning he had plowed through the black drifts with no destination save a place to hide his gruesome baldness and be done. He floundered in terror before he collapsed finally, lame and shivering in the orange break of day, upon a half-uprooted clump of white maple. Sweat had frozen the collar of his mackinaw and his woolen trousers were stiff with iced urine. Lacking the strength to lift his eyes and the courage to survey the brilliant landscape, he pried the axe-handle from his numb grip and hung his head.

Beneath the wall of snow and tangled maple roots, a glistening caught his eye. He tumbled down the wall, briefly held an ear to the frosted opening, sniffed, and hectically chipped ice and then plugs of grass and sod from the edge of the hole.

No sooner was the entrance enlarged to the breadth of his shoulders than he squeezed inside and shoving the axe ahead, crawled down the narrow tunnel toward the reeking, dark cavity. Shortly the axe touched softness, provoking a pother of grunts and sneezes. He squatted high as the verge of the cavity let him and held back the poleaxe in readiness. The moment his eyes adapted to the blackness, the instant he marked a snout paler than a brow, the axe-blade was driven into the bear's skull, the helve was wrenched from his fists and he was clubbed on the ear when the blind bear hollered and wheeled against the den-sides.

Many hours later, after tugging the fat bear up through the tunnel, he emerged. Underneath the leaning maples he rubbed the handsome, long fur, removing every bit of matt and burr and mud he found, while the dead bear, its turned-in legs flexed in the air, lay steaming in the new snow.

He stuck his knife between its hind legs, circled its vent and straddled the belly while he slit between hide and flesh, halving the white splotch on its chest and proceeding neatly up the heavily clotted neck to the tip of its lower jaw. Once he had opened each leg to the toes, he gently ripped web after silvery web of membrane, working loose skin from the hips, spine and sloping shoulders until the fine pelt was entirely free of its blue-white tendons, purple muscle and plates of buttery fat.

Despite the oncoming dusk he cleared no ground for fire, set up no wind-break and left the meat as it had rolled, unbled and undressed. The bearskin alone claimed his interest. Secure beneath the snow and frozen ground, at nightfall he smoothed the floor of the choking den, spread the bearskin, fur-down, and in darkness scraped flesh and gobs of fat off the skin with an edged stone. When he had finished, he removed his mackinaw and used it to brush away loose particles and mop up grease. Reclining then on his mackinaw, he covered himself with the raw skin and dozed, his fingers locked in the thick fur upon his chest.

Mistrustful on awakening, even in the perfect darkness of the underground cavity, he tried to be still before he stripped to the waist and knelt, undersleeves hanging down the seat of his trousers. He despised the feel of his bare ribs against the insides of his arms as he nervously cut into the heavy circle of pelt. Halfway through it he stopped, and mantled himself in its cold, wet skin.

By cinching the fur about his throat, he fashioned a snug cone. Careful slashes were made for his arms, and when the whole was tautly wrapped about his shoulders and chest, the one skin was flush to the other. He tucked the bottom margin of fur into his underpants and trousers, and forced the crimson undershirts to stretch over his new and shaggy black torso. Only then did he begin creeping to the surface.

Slow-flapping ravens lifted themselves to the trees and the red fox looked over his shimmering brush to see what was issuing from the mouth of the opening. The horde of gray jays, however, continued to gorge upon and stipple the bright carcass with droppings. The jays scattered in a dither when the fox trotted back to the carcass after the intruder's flight.

Fear drove him due north, schooling his tense eye to pick out the smallest incongruity in a monotonous field; he had always to look *between* rather than *at* the landscapes of his chaotic rambles beyond the striped maple and birch forests, seeking that secluded and empty land of ledge-hard slopes where ice winds crippled even the design of balsam and spruce, and the human face would never gaze upon him.

Rest multiplied his fear swifter than hunger and fatigue; makeshift shelters were abandoned as soon as built; and if the craving to join the life of other men took hold of him, he ventured higher into the north country.

By the heart of winter it was less a man than a state of lookout and loneliness that ranged the territory, checking cubbies and snares, sampling the freshness of every mound of black pellets, and the spoor that crossed his path; ignoring the larger prospect of ridge and hill-line for the single bough shuddering on a windless day or in a snowy thicket, the bronze iris of a snowshoe hare.

From the outset when he had stumbled upon the bear's den, an uncanny luck seemed to watch over him. No snare set in a funnel of withes failed to yield a strangled rabbit, marten or fox; and the first deadfall he contrived fell squarely upon the skull of a wolverine.

Months went by, months lived in such brutal estrangement from humankind that he came to believe something powerful was bent on keeping him alive. Survival became his assumption, and his pride. Not infrequently, while trying to sleep in some cache of pelt bales, he wondered if he would ever die.

And with the completion of his outfit, it scarcely appeared a mortal or earthly being that weaved among the prostrate spruce at the timberline. Long, black-tasseled lynx ears pronged his brow. Gray ruff of lynx bearded his chin. His chest was bearskin, his girdle yellow-striped wolverine, and he wore a mosaic of skins for breeches. And no matter now where he turned or what he heard, there, pressing ever closer to an eternal reckoning, was Mordecai Rime—albeit this Rime grew with each vigilant day and listening night; and grew, finally to overshadow the last grand pines, his footfalls shelling hoar from pine needles, until grown to the extent of Sarsen's brain, he was north winter itself.

# The Price of Pine

Pine, the rising price of pine, gave Jeshimon Plantation its life. The Record tells how logs stacked each winter were trundled down ravines into the freshet-swollen Starks River and driven to the sawmill in Starks, named in honor of the legendary Amos Starks, sole proprietor of the Starks Purchase, who, in order to promote speculation, donated forty free lots to veterans of the Revolution. Caribou fled north. Settlers, intrepid prolific figures, bought up cheap, cut-over land, pulled stumps, planted orchards, dragged boulders, drank cider, piled stones into walls and organized into the Jeshimon Plantation. When the pine near the river was depleted, roads were cut deeper in, to the stands at the base of the mountains. The prospering founders of the plantation—the Drivers, Looks, Peeveys, Grieves and Nileses—incorporated themselves into the town of Jeshimon. According to the Record, once the big pine was used up, spruce drives began in the wild reaches of timberland to the north and west, a vast region that to this day has escaped incorporation so the Company (which acquired the bulk of Starks Purchase after Amos Starks passed into legend by way of death in debtor's prison) might enjoy the gentler tax laws of unorganized territory and thereby pass unmolested from

Timberlord to Pulp/paperlord to the future Lords of the Four-Season Kingdom of Recreation. As for Jeshimon, however, the Record tells of a long waning time that commenced with the dwindling of the spruce: of farms worked in poverty and sour exhaustion, of many farms abandoned, pasture and orchards yielding to poplar, birch, ash—cover for deer migrating from the south, shelter for a legion of varmints. Then came a landscape painter who depicted the sublime pine on a crag above boiling falls in storm light, the exclusive Wassus Angling Association, admirers of autumn foliage and latterly, from the cities, a heterogeneous army seeking asylum, restoration, silence, tax shelter, alternative. Weathered pine and hemlock barns are dismantled for interior decoration. Retired businessmen return to the melancholy prospect of looted farms after the spring mud, replace shattered picture windows and depart as the deer season opens. Bands of young people appear, weave and make pottery, garden in an intense bookish fashion, then disperse. Descendants of the founders of Jeshimon continue to call the outlying farms by their old names, the Bean place, the Driver Pond House. These natives of Jeshimon scoff, gossip about the price paid for a ramshackle farmhouse and bitterly despise the invaders who have locked them out of their places without a shot as yet fired.

One can still decipher the extent of once-cleared land by rusted blades in a thicket, barbwire issuing rootlike from a remote maple. One can follow stone walls into alders to a strangled orchard, fix the site of some farm by a shallow interlapped stone well or granite slab foundation enclosing a mature beech on a ridge. Land to landed estate to real estate.

Although the story of this second invasion will have no end, the original invasion which ended two centuries ago fills the first fabulous chapter of the Record and is commemorated by the small granite obelisk on the bluff overlooking the village. And in the brochures available at the wooden prison—reshingled and painted barn red with TOURIST IN-

FORMATION hung above JAIL 1788—at the entrance of Jeshimon, is written:

> Come to our plush woodlands and sparkling rivers. Vacation by our lakes and see our bountiful game. Hike picturesque mountain trails through country unchanged since the time of the fierce Bagog Indians and visit the historic monument of Daguet, their fighting priest.

## 2

They survived because Senuchus (the "Mary" and "Mary Mussoc" of Urian Driver's *Journal of My Life with the Aborigines*), so close to the end of her first pregnancy, persuaded Wassus George, her husband, to forego vespers and stroll with her along the sandy banks of the Bagog River. No sooner had they left the stockade than Captain Sylvester Hedge, concealed in the forest above their village, heard the voices of the assembled Bagog tribe swell into hymn and fired the shot which triggered an avalanche of one hundred and eighty-seven Englishmen upon the log chapel in the midst of the settlement, a footrace whose laurels were the coveted and hoary scalp of the zealous Anglophobe and Jesuit missionary Father Odilon Daguet—"by means of insidious accounts of Our Savior's death, he inflames and proceeds to dispatch packs of Bagog Indians to roam the wilderness like wolves intent upon murder and dismemberment of the English," Governor Wharf had charged when the warrant and bounty were posted.

Wassus George and Senuchus also heard the signal shot and the succeeding screams amid the din of musketry. Senuchus could not wrestle Wassus George from the bank where he knelt, closed his eyes, and prayed for the life of his teacher, Father Daguet. At last Senuchus pounded her husband's shoulder and pointed to the red flames which waved in the crackling air above the pinetips and shone like a sun rising out of the black waters of the Bagog. Wassus stumbled beside impassive Senuchus to the edge of the forest. He wept and resumed such an interminable litany for the soul of his priest and the souls of his tribe that were it not for the thunderous conflagration, their hiding place would certainly have been found out.

Despite Senuchus's curses, the next morning Wassus George crept to the blasting coals of the village, gathered what he believed to be bits of Daguet's corpse, and carried them in his bearskin smock to a bluff overlooking the Bagog River. There he buried the smock and, notching two sticks of cedar, planted a crucifix. Tradition has it that before Wassus descended from the bluff, he stood over the rude grave and vowed to forgive the sins of all his enemies and to live a life of peace.

Wassus George approached Senuchus, who was eating a picnic of smoked moosemeat, raspberries, and maize pudding. He described to her all he had seen and what he had done. Stunned, Wassus George regarded his pregnant wife as she completed her meal and sparked a fire to smoke on the bark of the red willow. Appalled by her silence, Wassus had begun to repeat the description when he noticed a large bark basket behind her. It was filled with provisions: smoked meat and fish, herbs, additional tobacco, maize, and kernels of scamgar, a wheat to plant the following spring.

Wassus questioned Senuchus. Unmoved, she told him that she must eat, that she despised Daguet, and to the horror of Wassus George, she proudly explained how she had informed the English of the missionary's whereabouts and daily schedule, along with a sketch of the village, in return for knowledge of the time of the raid so she might prepare her departure and escape. Daguet assassinated, she was content. Like a rabbit wounded in the flank, Wassus George squealed and contorted before her in a paroxysm of despair and pain until numbed into a sleep.

Senuchus was gone when he woke. She had traveled hastily, taking no trouble to cover her way. Wassus trailed her northward along the narrowing Bagog, perplexed as to how a woman so near to childbirth and further burdened with a heavy basket of supplies could traverse such a vast and ever-rockier terrain with such speed. He discovered her prints by the rut of a canoe's breastbone leading into the river and for two days pursued Senuchus upstream. At nightfall he reached the confluence of a dozen small streams which spilled down ravines in the mountains before him. Wassus detected the small canoe under a mound of fresh-cut spruce behind a groove of broken and bent reeds. Here, by the origin of the Bagog River, Wassus made camp and rested.

Morning light was sliding over the mountains when Wassus set out and followed the trail of Senuchus into marshes, through a dark basin of cedar into hemlock and sloping yellow hackmatack, climbing steep rocky hills to the hogback which formed a barrier between the country where he had lived his life and the northern land he had never seen.

Wassus shinnied a pine to a high perch in its first branches and in the noon sun traced the white Bagog twining in and out of the familiar timber basin far below. Northward, he scanned the landscape of forest and meadow, saw a distant round pond, a silvery gash in a violet ring of pines, and layer after layer of mountains beyond. Wassus had momentarily forgotten his pursuit when he saw a gray spiral above the ring of pines vanish, and rise again.

It was dark when Wassus George reached Senuchus by the margin of the round pond. She was propped against a scaly trunk beside a small campfire, with blood on her lips and the infant Ona Mussoc (for so Driver called the beautiful girl), gnawed belly cord tied with vine, alive, couched in warm placenta between Senuchus's drawn-up legs. Wassus cleaned the infant in the pond and washed his dazed wife's thighs, hands and face. He wrapped the baby in Senuchus's blanket and examined her by the firelight. Senuchus revived and with a fearful scream begged Wassus George not to cast her child into the fire. Bewildered, Wassus declared that their daughter was a miracle he would never harm, and that furthermore he would work to forgive Senuchus.

A long while they lived in isolation beside the round pond. Ona was a sickly child. Senuchus ignored Wassus George whenever he beseeched her to journey to Canada in order that Ona Mussoc be baptized. She railed while Wassus prayed before the altar lit with candles made of bayberry and the tallow of venison. Senuchus never ceased in her efforts to turn the blood of Ona Mussoc with herbs and barks, saps, roots and strange-shaped leaves. She tramped the pondside forest and the meadows to collect spleenwort, the black berries of sarsaparilla, skunk cabbage, horehound and gold thread. But regardless of the soups and potions Senuchus contrived, Ona remained beyond cure, a vague languid child who kept indoors once the winter and her cough returned. Wassus George loved the thin gray-eyed girl and dreamed of the day Senuchus would understand the nature of her sickness and consent to the baptism.

Ona was a long-limbed young woman the spring when angry Senuchus, pregnant a second time, clubbed to death the tame dog which had strayed to the pondside. Senuchus considered this dog a harbinger and burned it where it lay. From that moment she lived in watchfulness and terror. She ordered her husband to construct a palisade around their dwelling and warily she roved the surrounding high country, accompanied by Ona, surveying, and infusing her placid daughter with hatred of French and English alike.

Whether weakened by the child she carried or the vigilance she had sustained so long, Senuchus became unnaturally complacent toward the start of winter. She moved less, often sitting quietly combing and binding Ona's coiling hair with

beads and shells. Senuchus stopped chiding Wassus George
when she sleepily watched him use a similar bead chaplet for
his prayers. Wassus observed the change, the mellow resig-
nation which deepened with the snow and the advance of
pregnancy. Once more he entreated Senuchus to permit the
conversion and blessing of Ona Mussoc, but was told only
that Ona needed fresh meat. Wassus molded caribou-hide
socks, fashioned thongs for his snowshoes, and one morning
departed in the dead cold air to hunt the marshland.

At the onset of a blizzard not two days later, Senuchus
gazed across the frozen pond and sighted Wassus George
dragging a travois on the crust. Neither moose nor caribou,
but the wasted frostbitten body of Urian Driver, one of the
English founders of Jeshimon Plantation, was lashed on the
travois.

Wassus cut open the mittens and boots of the brown-
bearded Driver and saw the bloating dark flesh. Ona Mussoc,
who had never before seen another man, drew back and
stared with consternation. Wassus stripped the gaunt body
and covered it with furs and blankets. All night Wassus forced
porringers of hot water, broth and tea between the burned
lips. Wassus was happily astonished when Senuchus moved
forward and soaked the discolored feet and hands with warm
peat and wrapped them in strips of blanket. At first he had
feared his wife might kill the white man.

In the years since the massacre of his beloved Daguet and
the brothers of his tribe, Wassus had struggled to forgive the
treachery of Senuchus, to revive a trust which had exploded
in sparks above his ravaged village, to swarm like bats in the
heated night sky. His eyes and the quizzical eyes of Ona
watched the fist of Senuchus swab the smoldering brow. Wassus was overcome with joy and a peculiar reverence for the
stranger who unknowing had rekindled his love for Senuchus,
and aloud he chanted for the life of the bearded Englishman.
Ona Mussoc lay on a rush mat and could not comprehend
why her mother attended the long shocking body. She fell

asleep wondering and was soon awakened by her fever and stuttering cough. Senuchus broke her nightlong silence and commanded Wassus to return to his hunt.

He set out for the marshland immediately. Were it not for the renewal of trust he felt in his pregnant wife, Wassus George would have been tormented by the thought he had so easily dismissed as he stalked a young caribou caught in the cedar swamp, his knife latched to the end of a long pole—that Senuchus, never a convert, had fed sickly Ona the roasted liver of the stranger.

Urian Driver recorded this account of his return to consciousness, reception, and ensuing recuperation:

I started from my delirium and my ears heard a most doleful sound, the sound of a mighty tempest in the sea. I parted my eyes a crack and thought, like Jonah, I had been swallowed by a great fish, for above me arched a backbone from which curved many ribs, the entire cavity being encircled by coruscant crimson flesh. Fervidly I beseeched the Lord to deliver me from this sorrowful estate in a fishes belly. I felt a terrible fire in my hands and feet whereupon I twisted my head and beheld such a sight as to believe myself *already* dead and, furthermore, thrust into the steaming maw of Hell itself. Veiled in minted vapors but two arms' lengths from where I lay, sat a half-naked maiden unlike any my eyes had seen. A profusion of hair was parted atop her skull and swirled over each bare shoulder to the flushed circlets on her bosom. The pungent grease which coated her face and slender frame lent her a waxen doll-like mien, an aspect not at all dispelled by her clouded insensate gaze. Behind her appeared a corpulent bundled Indian matron with a rounded countenance the color and texture of baked apple. This formidable woman was in the act of smearing a balsamic salve on the throat and chest of the maiden and to my disquietude, she grinned at me as she reined back the stolid beauty's mane and garnished the latter's distending breasts with a multitude of colored beads. Presently, distress in my blazing extremities increased to consume even the scant perception which had allowed me to witness the aforesaid.

Whatever the duration before I once more regained awareness, I found myself in the midst of a most hideous domestic ceremony. The hovel reeked of incense and slaughter. Long strips of meat dangled from the ribs of the hut and the roly matron was bent over a side of some fresh-killed beast, butchering in a sullen methodical way. By the fire in the center of the hovel, the comely maiden, fully appareled in coarse-woven blanket, skived the pelt of the selfsame creature. An incomprehensible, sing-songing and lugubrious wail, interspersed I thought with a French phrase or two, erupted behind my head and I rolled to consider a grown Indian man stretched prostrate before a whittled Crucifix hanging above a hewn candlelit altar upon which lay a gray male infant, immobile as if painstakingly carved of stone.

For what seemed days on end I observed the reverent Savage smoke the darkening infant's corpse like a ham over a chimney of green peltry in the center of the hovel. This gruesome process apparently completed, the distracted Indian wound the infant in softened skins, filled a rucksack with supplies and the tiny mummy, and without a word to either the matron or maiden, with not a glance for myself, he vanished.

The very evening of his departure, beneath the dripping slabs of venison, the woman kneaded and greased the lean torso of the maiden, sometimes with balsam, sometimes a viscous mentholated lard, but always with a queerly provocative smile in my direction. The exercise reoccurred each evening following supper, after which the maiden slept and the Indian woman squatted by the fire and smoked some sort of cheroot.

During the man's long absence, I at first convalesced quickly despite this alien environment. As if her own redemption hung in balance, the stout woman, "Mary" I called her, nursed me with a succession of bitter mashes, puddings, thick soups, and aromatic broths, gradually enlarging my menu to include breads cooked directly upon the fire, hazelnuts, and acorns, a variety of tubers, some of which tasted like our potatoes, others like turnips and finally, fruity blocks of fat and meat, fish, and I believe fresh caribou.

Generally, Mary fattened my stomach while the enchanting maiden, Ona, pampered my limbs, for in truth they had been so badly damaged that chunks seemed to drop off as the regenerate skin tenderly took its place. Ona saw to my personal needs with a baffling indifference and the infrequency of our discourse, together with the massage I could not help but witness each evening, began to torment me mightily.

Then one evening after Ona, coyly ornamented, had retired beneath a knoll of bearskins, I resolved to put my progress to the test: employing a staff, I stood briefly before Mary's stare. Unacquainted with the customs of these exasperating people, I did not know if Mary's sharp imperative celebrated, mocked, or was altogether unrelated to my effort. It was *not* in a dream, however, that rising suddenly from the bearskins, Ona drifted to my bedside, raised the blanket which hung from her waist, and *hooped* it over my raised head! Presently I heard a second muffled command, the humid cowl lifted, and like a marionette, glazed Ona withdrew to curl beneath her bedding. Many hours I wriggled in Hellfire.

The first time since my rescue, I prayed for strength, guidance, and sanity, for release from the uncanny witch who smoked a cheroot in the russet fire glow.

Disconsolate following his trek over the icy mountains to Canada, Wassus George returned before the spring freshet. Nowhere had he found a priest to bless his stillborn son and the preserved remains were again placed on the altar for the day the frost would rise out of the ground. Little by little, beginning with the few French words they commonly understood, Wassus and the Englishman learned to converse. Each time he acquired a new word, Driver proffered it like a gemstone to Ona who sat weaving and dying baskets in the thawing afternoon sun. Emerging from a blind like a hunter to reset a decoy, Senuchus thwarted each initiative of the distracted suitor, deriding his agitation when her husband was gone, stonily occupied if he was present. The nocturnal ritual in which Driver had lately participated had abruptly ceased with Wassus George's arrival.

When the ice had melted from all but the center of the lake, Driver would limp beside Wassus, punch his crutch into the muddy shore, and watch him net trout from the turbid mountain streams. Driver related how he had left Starks, the settlement sprung from the ruin of the Bagog settlement, and explored some fifty miles upstream with seven other men, four women, and two children, with designs to homestead at the mouth of what he called the Starks River; how his party had been unprepared for the early winter; how he had become lost hunting in marshland, the deep wet snow of a vast cedar swamp, the freezing night that brought forgetfulness. Wassus George recognized that his friend was not yet restored, for as night came Driver grew restless and often sat upright in a sound sleep and screamed.

After the rains, wind swept over the drenched earth, and soon Wassus and Urian Driver ascended the rocky meadow slanting to the round pond and buried the tiny corpse. The burial united the two men. Together, it was decided, they would journey over the hogback to search out the homesteaders. Prior to their departure, Driver asked Wassus for the hand of Ona Mussoc. Anxiously Driver observed the gesticulations and charged gabble conducted over the sleeping maiden. Wassus's serene approving countenance was answered by an outburst of mirth and Driver swelled with hope and confidence. Suddenly, Senuchus chattered heatedly, indicated Ona, decisively thumped her own chest, and the majestic composure drained from Wassus George's face. He nodded to Driver and, severely humiliated, stooped out of doors.

Wassus ascribed Driver's relapse to his rejected proposal, their ensuing journey to the site of the makeshift settlement, and foremost, to the grisly scene that awaited them there. Of the thirteen pioneers Driver had left behind, only two skeletal women and a man remained alive in a shanty two hundred feet back from the river. Tall stumps of trees, chopped after the snow had drifted high, stood eerie sentinel around the moldering hut and great stubbled swaths stretched far down the riverbanks. The stack of corpses behind the hut (the survivors had been too weak to bury the dead) had started to liquefy and attract swarms of insects and scavengers. Before the sun had set Wassus dismantled the shanty and constructed a wooden wigwam around the carrion. Frogs belched, owls and wolves hollered and moaned that evening as Wassus ignited the crematorium and, with it, shrill memory of the night Father Odilon Daguet was murdered.

"The paradigm of Samaritans" . . . "the cures he wrought" . . . "with the zeal of a missionary"—if not recorded in Driver's *Journal* and the diaries of the Widow Hubbard and Benjamin Peevey, the heroic labors Wassus George performed in the weeks and months that followed would seem the concoctions of an inspirational taleteller. Singlehanded he nursed the emaciated survivors back to flesh, mixed potent nervines for Driver, erected shelters, burned stumps to make clearing, cultivated, planted maize and scamgar, fished, hunted game, and taught a thousand ways to cull riches from the wilderness. Settlers from Starks, adventurers, speculators, a surveyor, trappers, and lumbermen invaded with the summer, and Wassus George, become indispensable, began to long for Senuchus and Ona Mussoc.

At last he sent Urian Driver to summon them to the hamlet he had created. The newcomers had heard menacing stories about savages and in the beginning they were skeptical of Wassus. But when they remarked his pious industry, benign knowledge, and generosity, when they were informed of how he had rescued Driver and the first settlers, Wassus George was treated with a curious deference and dignity. The Widow Hubbard rewarded him with fitted trousers. The men who offered their camaraderie, cider and beer were covertly amused by his abstinence from all liquor and merriment, and privately many regarded him a holy fool.

One week, two weeks more passed by, and neither Senuchus, Ona, nor Driver appeared at the Jeshimon Plantation. Driver had told the people of weird Mary and the strangely beautiful Ona, and all awaited their arrival with much speculation and interest.

Ugly thoughts began to worry the mind of Wassus George however, thoughts verified the morning Grieve returned from cruising the northern woodlands with a string of colored beads taken, he maintained, from the wrist of an Indian's fresh corpse. Old fears revived in the people as the cruiser described the burly body, how her head twisted the wrong way and her fingers were lacerated and broken.

A bold group led by Benjamin Peevey tried to accompany Wassus George as he bolted from Jeshimon for the last time, but they could not keep pace. Alone, Wassus had moved swiftly through the cedar, ascended the narrow ridge, and while the string of beads was still being fingered by a circle of nervous villagers beside the Starks River, Wassus reached the edge of the round pond.

No cooking fire rose from his dwelling. Inside, by the entrance, Driver napped. Curled beside the central beam, stripped and bedraggled, Ona Mussoc seemed blandly to contemplate Wassus rather than greet him. Hide thongs lashed her ankles to the base of the timber. Wassus hurriedly freed Ona and questioned her. She continued to sit as before, stupefied. With much effort Wassus shook torpid Driver to his senses. It looked as if Driver had been attacked by a wolf. The flesh on his forehead, cheeks, and whole clusters of beard were gouged out and the wounds barely scabbed. Driver's infected eyes cleared, his mouth went horror-slack, and he jumped from the bed and shrank beneath the altar, unfolding a narrative with such tremulous rapidity that mystified Wassus understood nothing.

At nightfall Benjamin Peevey and several fatigued companions straggled down the meadow to a spiked palisade under large pines by the round pond. Inside the earth, wood and hide dwelling, beneath a rough wax-veneered altar, peered the terrified gored face of Urian Driver.

The next morning Peevey and another man briefly searched the high meadow, ridge, pondside, and nearby woods, but found neither Wassus, nor Indian maiden, nor trace of a body. Later that week the cruiser Grieve guided another party to the spot where he had come upon the corpse and there indicated only a rumpled, darkening cluster of fireweed.

Despite the ritualistic markings which disfigured his face and prompted a cold inquisition from the settlers of Jeshimon Plantation, Urian Driver denied any knowledge of Mary Mussoc's murder. He was shunned. People considered him unlucky and for twenty years he was not seen in the territory. Conjectures as to the fate of Wassus George and Ona Mussoc abounded, facts were weeded out, and the conjectures grew

into tales and legends. Whenever a hailstorm shredded crops
before harvest time, a house burned down, a child vanished
into swampland, or a falling dead branch impaled a logger,
suspicious elders talked of Poison Mary's retribution and
Driver's betrayal of her saintly husband.

Perhaps these rumors would have faded or been ridiculed
if explorers who ventured into the granite mountains beyond
the round pond had not reported an abandoned hut above a
flume. More than once, a faraway human figure was sighted
darting into the forest edge. A trapper's discovery of the small
crucifix bizarrely fashioned from rock maple was widely regarded as a hoax. Hoax or not, the presence of Wassus
George had so imbued the landscape and history of these
settlers that on the first maps the hogback between the Jeshimon Plantation and the round pond was designated Dead
Mary's Ridge; the pond, Indian Eye or, popularly, Evil Eye
Pond.

3

Jeshimon Plantation was a quiet lumber and farming village
and supply post when a robust, well-dressed, middle-aged
gentleman with an extravagant beard and hair brushed so all
but his nose and pale eyes were concealed, arrived with a
fragile wife and rumored wealth. He was identified as Urian
Driver and a stir attended his movements. In vain, eyes
searched his bushy head for guilt and a brand.

He had made his fortune by the pen, Driver declared, and
was a rather celebrated reporter in the large Eastern cities.
Not long after this admission, a copy of the scandalous *Journal
of My Life with the Aborigines* was obtained through a peddler
in Starks and was scrutinized by a gathering of men before
old Peevey's hearth. Peevey began to read aloud and the
audience listened with astonishment:

". . . and as the wintry days passed, my infernal lust for
the haunting Ona mounted, subtly fanned by Mary Mussoc . . . again and again the malignant hag obstructed the
sole remedy for the very disease she had insinuated into
my bloodstream . . . under the nose of her good and
guileless husband, the fiend baited the trap with the most
sublime meat while I, starving and nerve-worn, could
but sniff, ogle, and circle . . ."

Finally the rapt tenacity of the Peevey circle and that of
the *Journal*'s author was tersely rewarded:

". . . so I took the musky and mechanical doll at the
zenith of that summer ceremony orchestrated by stamping ululant Mary herself . . ."

Though the *Journal* made no mention of the murder of Mary
Mussoc, its subsequent furtive circulation renewed indignation toward Driver.

Shock coursed through Jeshimon when Driver purchased
a large tract of land encompassing Evil Eye Pond, Dead Mary's
Ridge, and adjoining woodlands. Many thought Driver
shameless, others wondered why a man would buy his own
doom. Most people awaited only word of his catastrophe.

Unaccountably, calamity hung fire. Driver's frail wife bore
him seven sons and three daughters, all sound stock, and the
dire expectations gradually died with the deaths of the people
who had waited and wished. On the cant of the meadow,
where long before the smoked infant's corpse had been buried, Driver's house was built, frequently enlarged, and surrounded by large apple orchards.

The great pines on the pond margin were felled and hauled
by oxen to become masts and spars. Driver's own sons cleared
more woodland and outlined the spreading pastures with
fieldstones; hemlock barns went up; the daughters were

sought and married; and at his end, patriarch and centenarian Urian Driver had outlived every other man who remembered Wassus George in the flesh and, furthermore, was supposed the richest man in Jeshimon Plantation, then steadily bustling if not booming from the rising price of pine.

# How the
# Oval Hill Wajosis
# Became Starkmont

"**T**he Way be not easy," counseled expiring Eleazar Keep, prodigious, slate-blue, with eyes that yet justified the sobriquet *Terrible Index Finger* earned thirty years before during the Ramasacook Troubles. One of the original undertakers of the Corporation, Eleazar spoke with the authority of one who had borne the most remarkable afflictions since the landing of the advance guard, yet proved himself ever ready to execute the holy codes as defined by the magistrates and justified by the clergy despite the death of his first wife out of whom he had six children, a loss necessitating his swift remarriage to the widow of a fur merchant whose arthritis required him to purchase the young black girl Talitha who had stayed on after this second wife was carried off by a hectic fever in order to aid the third wife, a buxom girl of small means and twenty years who was claimed the following year by the pox which had infected every room of the Keep residence and swept away every child save the eldest, Prosper, who was nursed by Talitha until the night Eleazar Keep had discovered her daubing filth into two incisions made in Prosper's thigh, grabbed her throat and when pustules burst out on his son's brow several days later, watched her hang from the gallows not a week before his son's distemper broke, the scabs scaled off and Prosper Keep recovered, many years later to receive the call to the ministry and his father's deathbed advice, "The Way be not easy, my son, so prepareth ye to drench in sweat, yea, and to bleed."

One wretched springtime years after the *Terrible Index Finger* had died his placid, much eulogized death in the port capitol of the Colony, Prosper Keep led a regiment of his parishioners to plant Starkmont upon an oval hill some forty-five miles to the northeast. Eighteen families had petitioned the General Court to grant them this remote tract and Prosper Keep, not yet become apostle to the Indians of the Colony, convinced the magistrates that his congregation adhered to the very design of the founding Corporation; that the prospective township was readily obtained from one Glossian, sannup of a small band of Olamecs that fished the Rivers Pogamug and Guagus in fall and spring and camped winters beneath the oval hill Wajosis, hunting and trapping the surrounding forests until spring planting and the coming black-flies harassed them to summer on the seacoast. The General Court reluctantly allowed the grant and the summer preceding the actual occupation of the township, the tract was explored and measured. Two woodsmen assisted the surveyor in stringing chains through poplar thickets and lugging the theodolite into sloughs and over beaver canals, blazing the largest trees along the fifteen-mile square as it was vaguely traced in both Glossian's title and the sharply drawn patent of the General Court. An initial plat of the terrain was exhibited to the grantees in the house of the merchant Richard Thorndike the winter preceding their departure. On clear days, the surveyor explained, the entire township could be viewed from a deserted shanty atop the hill Wajosis: a stand of hickory, maple, oak and some chestnut dominated the expanse to the west; Pogamug, a wide gravel-bottomed stream, flowed along the northern line and then wriggled southeasterly across rich meadowlands, there to be met by the marshy Guagus before swelling in the poplar and alder to form a beaver pond inside the southeastern corner of the parcel. Town officers were selected during those winter sessions and the ticklish job of meting out the township according to the size of one's contribution, family and calling commenced. It was agreed first off, that the name of the oval hill be changed from Wajosis to Starkmont; that upon the site of the abandoned shanty the meetinghouse be raised. Although subject to debate and alteration once they actually occupied the site, tentative allotments were made: adjacent the meetinghouse, the parsonage of Master Keep and family; nearby, Isaac Vining's schoolhouse; a stout garrison house; constable Brinstall's gaol; a cemetery. House lots were appointed, the merchant Richard Thorndike and Deacon Simon Door receiving the largest, choicest portions because of the former's wealth, the latter's family of twelve; the goodmen drew lots. It was decided that a causeway be built atop the stout beaver dam to provide access to the cedar swamp for whatever shingling and clapboards the builders should require; to the northeast, a second bridge was to cross into meadowlands which were portioned into long strips for tillage until harvest, after which they were to be utilized for a common pasturage. The remainder, an enormous undesignated zone encircling the consolidated nucleus of the diagram, was to be held jointly by the townsmen and exploited for timber, game, maple sap, forage for swine, and, in future time, to accommodate the systematic growth of the plantation. And so, even as springtime came to the port capital, this organization which was successfully to cultivate, enclose and fortify a landscape which nearly all their number had never seen, completed a detailed abstract upon which a discrete, compacted community was in fact modeled.

Their departure date arrived and, despite the raw drizzle

of that May morning of a remarkably tardy spring, the exodus commenced as scheduled. No matter they had chosen a season of mud, they planned to sow at the start of June, were a resolute and united lot and fully anticipated trials and sorrows along their way. They were not to be disappointed.

The better part of the journey cold rain fell. The centuries-old trail used by the Olamecs to and from their winter hunting ground had washed out, was lost in fog, seemed to lead into the heart of swamp. On through the mire and ravenous swarms of blackflies the caravans dragged behind the ox-drawn wagon of their pastor, his pregnant wife Submit Keep and Joshua, their two-year-old son. Ranks of ducks and geese swept noisily overhead, unseen in gloomy skies that flung down such rain the gullies thundered with dun freshets and mire stalled the company's advance until Josiah Wing could lay another of the many trestles needed along the obscured route. Spring peepers, owls and wolves oppressed their nightly encampments. Morning count was made, of children, flocks and herds, and at first light they prayed and pushed on until somebody's cartwheel lodged to the hub in mud or a spoke gave and everyone had to wait until the wheelwright Sedgely whittled out and set a new one.

Nonetheless, if the damp mildewed Bibles and primers and the gaudy woolens which the five merchants among them hoped to barter with Olamecs passing through the township with their winter harvest of peltries, nothing dampened the zeal of that mission to carve order out of unregenerate lands, the place where they would multiply and merchandise. Whatever troubles beset them, their minister Prosper Keep searched out the significances of them, providing an ongoing commentary to the unfolding narrative of their enterprise. Indeed, once, when the congregation rested by the edge of a pond, Prosper Keep had spied his son Joshua leave a cluster of children to waddle into and part cattail spears, gabbling for the yellow lily blossomed on an emerald-green pad. Straightway, Prosper Keep rushed to the margin of the pond and ordered his son to the bank. Turning to his gathering pastorate, Keep firmly chastened his son with a cautionary parable concerning the desert wiles of the old Deluder and the beauty of the water lily which had seduced many a child into deeper water where one sinewy root could entwine a thigh and many tendrils more coil about thrashing limbs to draw him, crushed flower in fist, down into a nether dark without end. That same night Nim's flock strayed in a thicket and, as if to illustrate the Pastor's admonition, eleven were lost to the roving packs of wolves before they could be collected after sunrise. Indeed, before that expedition—three weeks to traverse forty-five miles—reached its goal, it was illustrated again and again: all Thorndike's poultry began to wheeze and slaver and, shuddering, died of pneumonia on the eve of the day Deacon Simon Door's wife slipped on a greasy boulder while fording a stream, broke her leg and nearly drowned in the rips below the crossing; Blodgett's toothache flared to the blasphemous point he threatened to end his life within the hour; Obil, the stalwart young black acquired by Richard Thorndike on business in the Zoraydores, was bitten by a snake and screamed louder than Brinstall's daughter when the gnats returned to her swollen eyes. Nonetheless, Prosper Keep mustered them and they inched their tortuous way through the erupting ferns and skunk cabbage of that singularly miserable May until they stood, weary and bedraggled, their cold red feet in the marshy flats from whence at last they sighted the foggy oval hill of their destination. There, amidst the reedy flowage of the beaver dam, Prosper Keep offered up thanksgiving. "Exalt the Lord God he bid them, For he hath delivered us from perils along the way and He hath given to His chosen ones these idle lands of the heathen, praise ye the Lord." Seventy-odd voices rose in immediate concert of praise. "Let us rise now. Let us climb. Let us worship at His holy hill for the Lord God is holy."

It was grown dusk as they willed themselves and hauled

their belongings the final mile of ascent of the misting hillside. As they drew nearer the crest of Starkmont, there came wafting through the drizzle the musky reek of cooking. Not far off dogs howled. Soon, crouching, snarling dog packs clacked teeth at Prosper Keep's fists and mud-cased boots. One truculent dog tore his sleeve as he continued on his brisk way through gaunt puppies tumbling under a bitch's jigging teats. Outside the shanty entrance from which hung a thick, ink-blue rug the minister stopped, astonished to find none other than Glossian, the corpulent sannup who had sold them the township. Three of Glossian's retainers slouched around him, eyes narrowed on two bone dice clattering in the wooden bowl he tilted. All four men sported new steel knives on hide necklaces. Keep regarded the rifles leaned in a dry area against the decaying wall of the shanty, the rum-filled calabash passed around the small circle after each toss of hubbub. Two middle-aged squaws, long black hair matted and trailing lumpily down rain-darkened leather smocks, tended a potage frothing in the kettle suspended over a cook fire. One busily hacked brown eels drooped over a split log, the other dumped chunks into stew. None of the Olamec band so much as acknowledged the dim spectators huddling at the edge of the firelight. When Prosper Keep tried to distract Glossian from the dice game a half dozen Olamec children left off whipping a crimson top in the shelter beneath the shanty's overhang to watch this stout and dauntless man with pointy grizzled beard and angry eyes begin to shake Glossian's arm and shout. Squinting unhappily, closing his eyes entirely and rolling onto his belly, Glossian resisted the dogged minister's labor to rouse him. Glossian answered with a long croon and an intricate sequence of baffled and harassed noises. Then he fell silent, sulking. In a fury the minister leashed the green stone suspended from Glossian's nose and tugged.

Of a sudden, the ink-blue flap was drawn from the shanty entrance. In the midst of this scuffle and din there emerged a tall bearish man with flaring chestnut whiskers, his woolly brown hair drawn into a bead-wrapped queue that stuck out like the docked tail of a horse. His large dark and red eyes wheeled lazily over that forlorn assembly before landing hard upon the irate countenance of Prosper Keep. Suddenly the insolence of his soot features took on a bemused aspect. Like a warning he bestrode the shanty entrance. His raw bright orange lips broke into a positive grin and clanging out a laugh, he withdrew behind the rug.

Patience used up, Prosper Keep fell upon Glossian with such spirited menace bone dice spilled from the bowl and Glossian, cackling softly, grabbed hold of Keep's wrinkled boot to pull himself into a squat. His tormentor scolded him for his deceit, recounted their contract of the year past, endeavored to learn why his band still occupied sold land and if they had acquired the guns and liquor and knives from the man within the shanty. Glossian agreed to each point in its turn; then, as soon as Prosper Keep hesitated, Glossian launched into his lament: "Glossian give you Wajosis," he declared with a slap on wet ground and describing a circle above his head added, "Give Pogamug and Guagus true . . . winter bad hunt . . . winter fur runs, hides . . . bad winter . . . laughs at snare of Glossian . . . bad winter, bad luck . . . Glossian two wife die . . . all sick eat dog." He contracted his features gesticulating toward the shanty, "Man come back Wajosis . . . ," fervidly smacking the dirt, whispered, ". . . Glossian give man Wajosis . . . give Man Pogamug . . . give Guagus true . . . Man give Glossian good luck . . . Glossian give man wife Kweeteet give wife Nonanis . . . Glossian share all true." Sweeping a great circle above him then jabbing an index finger toward the seething kettle, Glossian went on in expansive lordly fashion, "All eel Pogamug cut one / two / three . . . ," emphasizing the fairness of it with even chops of his hand. "Man we cut one / two Glossian cut . . ." Years later Glossian, alias Jonah Glossian preacher of

Hareth, described this very moment on that covenanting day when he stirred the crowd of worthies with a catalogue of his abominations before the light had irradiated his way. On that drizzling evening atop the oval hill, however, it was by jerking kicks and jolts that Prosper Keep freed his thigh from Glossian's burly embrace and stormed to the shanty entrance. He boldly demanded that the man show himself at once. After much unanswered hollering, Prosper Keep announced that he intended to enter. After several minutes, he lifted the rug flap and ducked inside.

Stacks of otterskin, rundlets and bundles of beaver and wolf and wildcat skins lined the walls. Scattered on the earthen floor were boxes of knives, bells, mirrors and pistols that surrounded a small fire, a prone, shirtless man and two Olamec women who knelt over him kneading and pounding sheets of muscle along his spine. Three times Prosper Keep insisted that the man identify himself and civilly explain his presence. Both women sucked pipes as they worked. Pale orange coals tinged the smoke and sharpened the stench of sour grease, fur, hot flesh. Under a rain of palm and knuckle the man groaned and Prosper Keep turned his head and tried to ward off the ugly quickening in his chest. It was then he saw the wizened, balding woman in the corner probing the damp orange curls of the small child in her lap. Four or five years old, the child wore a breechclout and skin leggings, its taut naked chest and scrawny arms smeared with grease. Suddenly the crone hooted, her quick fingertips having got hold of something which she popped into her mouth and cracked between her gums. "Your name and business, sir?" screamed Prosper Keep.

"Nonanis, Kweeteet, leave off," exhaled the man. Scowling he twisted onto his gleaming back and sat. "Rising, the name is Nicholas Rising. Fur is my business and all hereabouts belong to me." Rifling through the crate beside him, Rising found a satchel and from it withdrew a chamois scroll. Glumly Prosper Keep perused the document, a deed similar to that held by the Starkmont grantees, with Glossian's self-same mark of the toad at the bottom.

"And what of that boy?" asked Prosper Keep, inclining his head to the corner.

"Boy?" grinned the fur trader. "My daughter, Amy Rising."

"I pity thee, Nicholas Rising, too long a time hast thou sojourned in this wilderness. But more do I pity that child, who must needs suffer the results of it."

"There's truth," said the fur trader, "and once you have gone I'll look to the matter. So rest this night on my hill. But heed me, on the morrow be gone!"

The first town meeting on the soil of the Starkmont township was convened around a bonfire on the hillside and by midnight a course of action was, by the consent of the generality, agreed upon. Early the next morning four goodmen headed by Constable Brinstall struck out for the port capital with a well-bound Nicholas Rising in custody, along with a missive for the General Court which gave brief account of their emergency proceedings:

As the enterprise of establishing a plantation at the place called Starkmont hath proceed by encouragement, next under God, of the letters of patent granted by the General Court according to the land-title gotten by just and honest purchase of lands belonging to the Olamec petty-sachem, Glossian by name, whose signature hath sealed the transaction; and as we whose names be hereunder subscribed hath journeyed with our families and sundry properties and by the providence of God surmounted many difficulties in order to attain this remote place whereupon our community hath been designed and shall be raised: We, the inhabitants of this infant township having no speedy redress to the wise deliberations of the General Court, have therefore appointed RICHARD THORNDIKE to execute the office of magistrate within this our lawful jurisdiction until such time as further intelligence hath been received from the General Court.

Humbly Subscribed,

| | |
|---|---|
| Deacon Simon Door | Benj. Hollingsworth, |
| Isaac Vining, *1st selectman* | *2nd selectman* |
| Samuel Haggle | John Brinstall, *constable* |
| | Richard Nim, *3rd selectman* |

So it was that an hour before daybreak Wing, Brinstall, Haggle, Blodgett and Obil had fallen upon the shanty. Glossian and his cohorts, being in profound stupor, were taken and tied without resistance. Barking dogs and screeching Olamec children scattered in the gray light, alerting Nicholas Rising. Brinstall had led the charge into the shanty which cost him the tip of the little finger on his left hand. Exactly what happened inside remained unclear but after a skirmish of five minutes Rising was subdued as he lunged, slashing open the seat of Josiah Wing's breeches with a crooked knife. The only other casualty was inflicted in the aftermath of the fray. Thorndike tried to comfort the stony daughter of the fur trader, receiving an inch-long gash before the child's sharp, tenacious incisors were prised from his wrist. All the munitions were seized, the rum kegs, trinkets and furs confiscated pending the decision of the General Court, and by sunrise, the shanty was burning. "And so it hath been determined," Acting Magistrate Brinstall wrote in hasty summation,

that the savages he hath deceived and made drunken shall be satisfied for the outward injuries they hath sustained and the girl-child he rears in filth to no warrantable calling and who is possessed of a wierd and bellicose nature, shall be placed in an orderly and sober Christian household, there to be instructed in civil ways and good housewifery. We entreat the Court to receive this troubler Nicholas Rising in such wise as he shall nevermore abuse the poor savages into an inebriate and slothful condition and nevermore foment amongst them promiscuous disorders and other mischiefs with illicit vendables that do threaten our families and misshape our purpose.

That was how Amy Rising came to reside in Starkmont, there to develop into the minister's signal creation and aide, until taken into captivity at the onset of the Black Cat Uprising. As for Nicholas Rising, the General Court sat at the close of that summer to sustain the emergency action of Magistrate Thorndike and void the spurious land title gotten by Nicholas Rising since the transfer had never been endorsed by the court; furthermore, warning was issued that any future insolence, subversion of the general welfare, or other manifestation of erroneous, contrary-minded ways, would warrant the severest censure.

At the close of August Nicholas Rising was freed from the stone gaol in the port capital and early one morning the second week of September, a clean-shaven, cropped-haired tinker strolled the causeway above the stagnant pools where the beaver pond had been and climbed the dusty cartway up the hill of Starkmont. Squat, thatched frame dwellings lined his route, great piles of cordwood stacked along their unpainted clapboard walls. Beanpods twined hanging ears of corn in the dooryards. Gourds, squash, the men and boys toiling in the mown stretch of meadow where the tinker surveyed the massive haycocks and tawny green pumpkins—tillage readied for winter crops and, in a large enclosure on the stubbled banks of the Pogamug, grazing livestock—everywhere the imposter gazed he was confronted by the inexorable industry of the Starkmont planters. At the substantial dwelling of Simon Door, he was acquainted with Starkmont's brief and amazing progress by the loquacious Goodwife Door who still hobbled on a cane and wore the splint Prosper Keep had fashioned for her broken leg. Although given no utensils to patch or scissors to sharpen, the tinker did learn of the small girl at the parsonage whose improvements seemed the very emblem of their special blessings. The tinker took his leave, soon rapped upon the parsonage door and encountered a gravely depleted woman with a narrow head and massive, pregnant belly. Submit Keep wearily declined the services he offered and was shutting the door when the tinker's shoulder rammed it open and sent her sprawling onto the parlor floor. Jumping over her, he searched the house, found his daughter clutching a corncob doll away from Joshua Keep on the hearth and, clamping her rigid body under his arm, he jostled past Submit Keep, rushed from the parsonage, stole the minister's gentle mare and, frantically driving in his heels, bolted north toward the ponds and chain of lakes from which the Pogamug rose.

Minutes later, Submit Keep managed to stagger into the meetinghouse next door and toll the small bell hanging from the rafters. The men in the fields below quit at once and taking up the arms which they carried to the fields, to sermons on the sabbath and nighttimes propped by their bedsteads, converged on the meetinghouse. Bawling Joshua Keep had toddled into the meetinghouse by the time they arrived and held the long skirt of his mother as she held fast to the bell rope and continued to toll alarm. Prosper Keep had forcibly to wrest the fingers of his wife from the bell rope and carry her to their bed.

None of the townspeople, and many had known Prosper Keep since his childhood, had seen such fury take hold of him. His pale eyes glazed over and jaw closed so hard his temple and cheeks quivered. Constable Brinstall, who as a youngster served in the militia under the *Terrible Index Finger* Eleazar Keep, later asserted that if the son lacked the father's massive frame and martial carriage, he had seen that precise mixture of aloofness and rage seize hold of the old warrior whenever one of his armored company, drilled in close-knit bodies and taught to fire as from behind the walls of a movable fortress, broke rank tearing a breach in the fortress wall. On the day of Amy Rising's abduction, Prosper Keep left his wife's bedside and it was he and not Constable Brinstall who mustered the mounted party and led them clattering over the bridge and along the banks of the Pogamug. By the time they reached the northern boundary of the township where Glossian and his remnant band had set a weir and watched their squaws dry fish and harvest beans and maize, no one in pursuit of Nicholas Rising had any notion of where to follow him. The footsore mare belonging to Prosper Keep was tied to a clump of willows kicking at flies clouded about her frothy hulk. Glossian not only volunteered that the man and child had hurried by an hour before, but he guided the minister's party so skillfully through the brush and darkening forest that crowded in on the Pogamug as it neared its watershed, the ponds marking the entrance to Macwahoc territories, that both fur trader and child were caught, after dark, at the gray boulder where Nicholas Rising awaited a rendezvous with the two Macwahocs whose bark canoe had come sliding downstream toward the signal fire moments after the capture.

How Glossian piloted his father up the Pogamug to catch the outlaw that day was the first story Joshua Keep remembered. If he crushed it out of mind for so many years afterward because it hazily called forth the agony of his mother who commenced labor that evening and had shrieked until her voice gave out twenty hours later, he was to remember the story during the worst days of the Black Cat Uprising when, considering Prosper Keep's impromptu use of an Indian pilot, perceiving the genius of it, he would begin to forge, refine and methodize the mode of holy violence that was his calling. That day's venture was to occasion much besides: Prosper Keep later termed the cooperation of Glossian the first clue of Jonah Glossian's coming reversal and the grisly origin of his own apostolic works. He had heard his wife's shrieks a mile from the parsonage the following noon as he returned, Amy Rising asleep in his arms, her sullen father once again heavily bound and tripping between two men on horseback. When he reached the parsonage Submit Keep was shrieking rotely, oblivious of his approach and the bustling frenzy of the half-dozen goodwives who had tried everything from rum to pressing on her stomach, stuffing cloths in her mouth to make her bear down, and in the end, tugging the infant's blue leg that hung limp between her thighs. She bled to death an hour after Prosper Keep attempted to cut through the wall of her abdomen and removed their dead infant girl. The following day the site designated for the Starkmont cemetery on the surveyor's plat received its first occupants and not a fortnight after the single syenite slate was lodged at the head of the double grave, Nicholas Rising, nostrils slit and seared and a hole bored with a hot awl through his tongue, was warned out of the Colony under threat of immediate execution should ever he return.

# The Strike Hound

Strike cages were bolted to the front of the pickup truck. A small bowlegged Walker hound stood on the cage platform jutting from the bumper. This was chief strike hound, Bone. His broad, creased brow and pendulous ears and loose skin gave him a most deceptive, antic aspect. Spook, a taller Walker hound, was harnessed in the left cage. Only their averted, filmy eyes and the constant pulse of their nostrils suggested the nature of the bearhounds. Whenever the truck cruised along they stood motionless, their knobby legs apart for balance. Spook leaned out over the road in stony readiness. Bone slouched in the strike cage, head depressed, nose searching the road like a blind man's cane. Their ears jigged in the current. Otherwise they rigidly hung over the road like a carved figurehead on the prow of a ship.

During the leisurely first days of the hunt, schoolchildren waiting for Unorganized Territory buses yelled, goggling when they saw the strike dogs sweep past. Old men paused from raking leaves; farmers dressing fields nodded from their tractors. Indeed, those days of traveling back roads to untended orchards, cornfields, sheep pastures, open dumps and ruined apiaries, the thud of shotguns, the long whistle of the turning mill when shifts changed, the incessant squeal of

chainsaws, the sight of hogs and cattle off to butchers, cordwood stacked at every roadside, banked houses, bedded gardens and pumpkins—everyday preparations for winter calmly
proceeding as October ended—those days appeared so sensible and pleasant to the sport and had such a sedative effect
upon him that the hunt was all but forgotten.

"Hear 'bout the guy who wanted his wife dead?" began
the bearhunter to take up such slack times, and the sport
braced for that peculiar world of pink and blue nighties,
honeymoon trauma . . . "Frenchman, he sniffs from the tips
of his fingers clear to his armpits, rolls back his eyeballs and
says 'Suzette!' " The truck swerved from the bearhunter's
laughter after he hit the punchline. "Hear it before?" asked
the bearhunter, regarding the sober features of the sport.
"Don't get't, huh?" ended with the challenge, "Don't like my
jokes, that it?" So the bearhunter would grow sullen and
concoct some jest like stamping his fist in the soil along the
edge of a fodder cornfield to make facsimile bear pawprints
for the duped sport to discover. On the fourth day the bearhunter released the strike dogs. They worked a cold trail
until a bear was roused from its bed. The bear had slipped
the pack in a brown ash swamp, reappearing, they learned
the next day, atop a stone wall beneath an apple tree where
it was viewed by a delighted busload of schoolchildren.

Early on the fifth morning the truck entered the high country beyond the village. Daybreak set the ragged outline of
hills and mountains against a drab, furrowed sky. The truck
drove quickly, frost sparkling in the headlight beams. Fallen
leaves parted and spilled over the broken tar road. The strike
cages were empty. Tethered to the floor of the camper the
bearhounds dozed, curled tight in the straw. While the truck
skirted the ridge, neither man spoke. In the distance ahead,
the ridge road split upward onto county roads which, extended by logging roads, opened into the barren flats where
timber had been yarded and, higher up, a maze of skid roads.
If a chase led beyond the skid roads that scored the black

softwood ruffs of the mountains, the bearhunter knew there was no way to drive up after his hounds, no roads for forty miles.

The bearhunter seldom hunted the high country so late in the year. Wind made listening difficult. And the deer season opened the following week. A stray hound, if spotted then, was a target.

The sport rested his head on the shotgun and rifle hooked across the back window of the cab. Sitting in front of the heater, his legs sweating inside woolen trousers, the sport watched the chain harnesses dangle from the bar of the empty strike cages. At the junction, the bearhunter turned onto the lowest of the dirt county roads and stopped. Scrabbling the metal floor the bearhounds rose—four Walkers, two Plotts, a blue-tick and a black-and-tan—at once shaking the camper with yelps and moans.

"Hear?" said the bearhunter with a sly, proud look. "Sound ready?"

The sport nodded and smiled. He had engaged a guaranteed hunt. If he did not get his bear, the bearhunter received nothing for the five days.

"Bet your ass they're ready," mumbled the bearhunter. Then he kicked open the cab door and shouting down the bearhounds, stomped to the rear of the truck. As he jerked up the camper window, the hounds fell silent. He unleashed Bone, took a fistful of skin on the dog's back, held the collar and hoisted him over the tailgate. The Walker hung limp while the bearhunter carried him to the strike platform. The harness was snapped on.

The bearhunter placed Spook in the left side of the strike cage. Deeper-voiced, colder-nosed than Bone, Spook was a zealot, apt to backtrack or strike on the scent of something besides bear. The bearhunter admired and mistrusted him. Spook lifted his muzzle and glanced back at the windshield until the ignition turned. The truck lurched into gear and Spook pressed forward into the harness.

Splintering ice webbed across potholes and ruts, the truck jolted along. The strike hounds began to read the air. The bearhunter cased the stands of beech, poplar and birch on the tawny cant of the ridge.

An early snow had kept on the highest outcroppings of ledge and the peaks flashed orange in the rising sun. Mist winding along the river in the valley below flushed, spreading to seal the village and valley. The bearhunter shut off the headlights.

"Scarce a nut on the beech this fall," he complained, "an' damn few acorns an' mountain ash berries."

The sport crouched forward and peered into the dim treetops.

"Nuts'd've dropped by now," snickered the bearhunter. "Problem is, they wasn't there to start with."

"Posted!" the sport announced, catching the flash of the red tin signs—NO HUNTING · NO TRESPASSING · WITHOUT OWNER'S PERMISSION—nailed at intervals to the roadside trees.

" 'Course it's posted," jeered the bearhunter, " 'course it is, an' no cocksuck'll be 'round t' ask permission of." He set his jaw and snorted. "Posted land, some whore says he'll shoot my dogs, gangs o' women 'at ain't never seen a bear scream at me, an' not a Christly nut on the beech.

" 'Spose you think bear read friggin' signs, too. Hounds run bear a dozen miles 'fore they tree. That's a lot o' ground, some posted, some not. Look at 'm," he said of his restless strike dogs, "an' don't you forget it. Those are one-thought hounds, mister, an' I'm a one-thought man."

Through the mellow corridor of hardwoods the road twisted, mounted and plunged before a steep grade peaked and a desolate landscape came into view. A crosshatch of alders hid the disheveled stone walls that bordered an orchard. Gray sheds leaned in gaps of the broken arch of maples and assorted outbuildings lay heaped around two intact chimneys and a gutted barn. The bearhunter parked near the leafless thicket of sumac that had taken over the farmhouse dooryard. Spook bellowed with desire and then all the cooped bearhounds hooted and whimpered.

"Got a bear in behind this orchard coupl'a weeks ago."

"A good bear?" asked the sport.

"Dressed maybe two fifty, sixty," squinted the bearhunter.

The sport slapped his knees. He pictured the bear they had glimpsed and lost on the third day, a shining blue-bristled ball that sped over the valley road and into a swamp of cedar and brown ash a half-minute ahead of the pack. The sport reached back for his rifle and joined the bearhunter behind the truck. The bearhunter had already freed his check dog, a stout, gray-muzzled old Plott hound named Chomp. Whenever a strike dog caught a scent and hollered, the bearhunter released Chomp to confirm the strike before he would empty the camper of hounds. And if as now, the bearhunter chose to scout an area on foot, the check dog accompanied him.

Crackling through the brittle ferns Chomp circled the remaining charred timbers of the barn. Close behind the two men followed, raising chestnut-colored dust from the trampled ferns. The check dog weaved his sedate, purposeful way around blackberry brambles. He stopped to urinate on the crimped purple leaves before snuffling over the bleached juniper meadow, gone now to burdock, milkweed, goldenrod, and bright-berried, spurred hawthorne. At the orchard entrance Chomp quickened his trot, as though something underneath the leached-out soil had him hooked by the snout. The bearhunter watched the check dog rove and scanned the orchard. Weathered deer stands perched in every large tree on the margin of the orchard. Poplar saplings, small fir and spruce crowded the apple trees and the apple limbs bristled with sucker branches. Woodpeckers had ravaged the bark and like a hornet's nest against the gray sky, a porcupine hugged a topmost limb. Many trees still yielded stunted, pocked, tasty apples and windfall apples rotting in the orchard grass scented the air with their cider.

Throughout the plundered orchard were signs of bear. While Chomp crisscrossed the far end of the orchard, oblivious of grouse erupting from the overgrown aisles, the men also searched: here and there limbs, hinged by twisted orange fibers of applewood, slanted to the ground; climbing bear had chipped the scaly bark, their claws leaving deep yellow gashes.

Beneath one tree the bearhunter paused and grumbled, "Oldie," nudging a pile of shrunken bear droppings with the toe of his boot. "Two, three days back," he concluded, scowling at the black pile studded with dozens of white chokecherry pits.

The sport discovered a loose mound of apple chunks nearby and called, "*Real* fresh turds over here."

The bearhunter hesitantly walked over and smeared the pile in the pale grass. "Ain't so fresh."

"Looks fresh," countered the sport.

"Ain't."

"Fresh enough to smoke," grinned the sport.

"You all talk that kinda bullshit," said the bearhunter. "Turds was steamin' on the ground, turds was smokin' in the snow," he mocked gleefully.

"I've seen it happen," maintained the sport.

"Colder day 'an this I *seen* deer shittin' and I walked straight where the shit was an' it wasn't smokin' a bit."

"All right," laughed the sport, holding up his arms to concede the point.

"Shit right here mister an' let's see how long it smokes," suggested the unsmiling bearhunter.

"Okay, I believe you."

"Damn right," he declared. "Shit don't smoke." Shaking his head at the sport, the bearhunter jogged away shouting for his check dog. Suddenly he boomed, "Turds was smokin' in the fields," and continued after Chomp.

The sport watched the bearhunter hurry toward the corner of the orchard and into the maples on the rise. The morning had turned colder and the sport buttoned his quilted vest.

He set out after the bearhunter, stopping to inspect stacks of rusted pails and a saphouse tumbled beside a ravine that drained a long untended sugar bush upon the slope. The sport eased himself down into the ravine and started up the slope.

The ravine, during freshet a thunderous spillway, was now a trough of maple leaves and granite boulders that trapped icy pools of water. Upon one of these boulders higher up the ravine sat the bearhunter. "What you think o' this?" he asked, tilting his head at the leaves below.

The check dog shuffled around a nearby maple, rooting in the thick mold. The sport reached the bearhunter's boulder and the dark mass, half-concealed by twisted leaves, that sprawled at its base. "What is it?" asked the sport. He brushed away the leaves and gazed, trying to make sense of the shape. "Jesus!" he gaped at last, realizing it was without a head and hindquarters.

"Woulda went two sixty anyways," said the bearhunter. "Treed'm over by Chomp, in that maple."

The sport touched a rib and tapped the hard black meat between ribs. He fingered the white balls of cartilage on the mittenlike front paws. "Where are the claws?" he asked, getting to his feet.

"Claws go with the skin."

An afternoon cloud cover blocked off the sky and the land took on a darkened blue radiance before they stopped for water. The bearhunter slid down the gravel embankment and dipped the pail in the stream below the shiny corrugated edge of a culvert. The road had been recently built up for a logging operation. The sport heard the squadron of chainsaws at work higher up the mountain. Eating a stick of dried sausage, he strolled along the seedy stalks of evening primrose while the bearhunter watered the strike dogs, refilled the pail and opened the camper.

The sport returned to the truck and watched the pack dogs strain to wedge their muzzles into the pail. "What does a bear do after it's treed?" The beheaded, haunchless carcass in the ravine had stayed with him.

"Gets shot."

"I mean, how does it behave?"

"Best lay off them hot sticks, they'll burn every hair off your asshole."

The sport tore the wrapper off another stick of sausage. "Want some?"

" 'Tain't very likely. Burn down the outhouse."

The sport grimaced. "How does it act, tell me?"

"Might piss an' shake. Some yawn, some slap on the tree to worry the hounds, or might sit there doin' nothin'. 'Pends."

As the truck started up the logging road a sunbeam lanced the thickening clouds and lit a russet splash on the slope ahead. "Lotta oak," pointed the bearhunter. Then considering the murky crests of the mountains the bearhunter snapped, "Noplace," and his lower lip grew into a severe pout.

They were crossing a plank bridge at the base of the oak slope when Spook let out a quick string of wails. Bone drooped beside him, rolled his head quizzically and kept silent.

"Ain't right," said the bearhunter. He pulled off the road, jumped from the cab and glowered at Spook. "Better be right, whorelips."

The young strike dog continued his bellowing and the bearhunter fetched the check dog. Without conviction now Spook's hollering went on and he twisted anxiously in his harness to see what was happening behind. Chomp nosed about the sallow cattails in the gulley, urinated, and ambled indifferently to the rear of the truck. The bearhunter lifted Chomp and fastened him inside the camper. Angrily, he paced back toward the plank bridge, scrutinizing the road. He no sooner noticed the fresh moose tracks splayed wide in the hard mud than he wheeled about and stormed to the strike cages.

Spook quailed in the cage, *ki-yi*ing even before the bearhunter grabbed hold of both his ears. "Moose! Moose! Moose!" yelled the bearhunter each time he knocked the hound's skull on the side of the cage or wrung his ears. The strike dog kept his tail curled flush to his belly until the truck was again underway.

"Think whorelips'll strike on moose again?" asked the winded bearhunter. "Too much fire in that hound."

The logging road became steeper, passing a boarded-up farm and several prefabricated hunting camps tucked in the ledge. Bone hunched in the strike cage. Punishment forgotten, Spook leaned into his harness with a frozen alertness.

"Cold, Christly cold enough for 'em to den," grumbled the bearhunter. The tires began to churn and he shifted into four-wheel drive.

"How high do they climb?"

The bearhunter morosely eyed the sport. "Why you askin' all these frig-off questions, anyways?"

"Curious."

"Curious, bullshit! 'Cause you quit."

"There's a storm on those mountains."

"Day ain't over."

A crew was working on a plateau of woodchips, stumps, roots and deep, hardened ruts. The limbs and tops of spruce and fir made thick walls of slash around the yard. Two men loaded a pulp truck and a mammoth-wheeled skidder was twitching spruce logs down the mountain and into the clearing. None of the men acknowledged the bearhunter's truck as it circled the yard.

He idled alongside one jobber stacking cordwood. Rolling down the window, the bearhunter nodded. "Bitter up here."

"None too pleasant," answered the jobber. He planted his birchhook into a butt and looked over the strike dogs.

"Good chance?" inquired the bearhunter.

"Bearhounds, huh?"

"Yeah, seen anything 'round?"

"Dogs rile deer," murmured the jobber.

"Not my dogs."

"All dogs," said the jobber, yanking out the hook and returning to his work. "Prices now, we need deer."

" 'Preciate the help," sneered the bearhunter closing his window. The truck jolted slowly out of the yard. "Runt poaches more deer'n fifty dogs lay eyes on," he fumed. They descended the rough logging road in silence.

The sport was relieved to see the first flakes of snow, like flecks of mica, touch the windshield and dissolve. Before the truck reached the plank bridge, a flurry of snow dimmed the countryside and the frustrated bearhunter slouched behind the steering wheel.

At almost the same spot as before Spook jerked up his muzzle and bellowed with all the volume of his lungs. The sport expected another beating. This time, however, Bone trumpeted alongside Spook.

"Hot trail!" whooped the bearhunter rocking to a halt with his leg half out the cab door. One bugling volley lapped another and the camper trembled from the furious commotion inside. The blaring strike dogs repeatedly lunged into the harnesses, twitching like dowsing rods.

The sport hustled out and saw the check dog Chomp spill headlong over the bearhunter's stooped back to the road. Straightway, Chomp opened up. He leaped the ditch, was upended by a deadfall and, unruffled, charged into the oak grove emitting wild spasms of noise.

The bearhunter hurriedly forced Spook back into the strike cage in order to slacken the harness enough to unsnap it. Spook plunged from the strike platform in full cry. Seconds later Bone dove off the cage, and soon Meg the freckled Walker bitch, the blue-tick Strop, Droop the black-and-tan, two newly acquired hold dogs and, lastly, Horn, a cymbal-throated Plott hound, hammered up the slope and out of view.

The clatter of paws through the leathery oak leaves faded but the voices clanged on. The men remained at the foot of the hill, listening. The bearhunter cocked his head to figure the pack's direction, the distance they had covered, the data relayed by eight separate voices giving tongue at once. The sport also tried to interpret but in his ear, all the voices dashing through the oak forest fused into a single insane moan that jarred the slope and carried off the hills.

"What's going . . . ," blurted the sport before the bearhunter's hiss cut him short. There was no belligerence in the demand. Until the bear treed, the sport was simply a witness.

Although the sport heard nothing besides oak leaves chafing in the slight wind, the bearhunter kept on listening, hands in his pockets, uplifted eyes vacant. "C'mon!" he yelled suddenly, rushing for the truck.

The truck careened down the logging road, jounced over the culvert where they had hauled water. "An' you was set to give it up, 'member?" chuckled the bearhunter. "Mother ain't got five minutes on'm. Weather holds you'll have't, decent female, small male the looks o' the track."

The truck swung right and advanced to a spot overlooking a marsh and dark pond. Here the bearhunter pulled over and, holding the cab roof, concentratedly listened.

At once he sat back, threw the shift into reverse, turned, and spun toward the junction to cut off the hounds. The pack sounded closer at the next stop, somewhere on the hardwood ridge they had cased earlier in the day.

A quarter mile in on the county road the bearhunter stopped, tilted his head and smiled as the sport had not seen him smile the week long. "Spook's right on his ass," explained the bearhunter, "an' Bone ain't far back . . . Chomp's outa shape . . . five litters an' can that bitch tongue?" he said fondly. "Don't hear Strop, where in hell's Droop? . . . That's Strop talkin' now. Hear that Horn? Ever hear such a voice?" whispered the transfigured bearhunter.

Every two or three minutes the bearhunter stopped along the hardwood ridge, left the truck, held his breath and cocked his ear. With each stop, however, his ebullience diminished.

The strengthening wind drove the hazy snow and racketed through the thinning hardwoods. The bustling leaves and the tap and scratch of limbs drowned all other noises on the ridge.

On the knoll before the orchard the sport's straining ear picked up a hollow tromboning and he pointed hopefully in the direction of the village.

"Three-o'clock siren," the bearhunter glumly replied.

"This rate be dark in an hour."

They had lost track of the bearhounds.


The truck hurtled down the incline, past the orchard, but their luck was no better in the sheltered place where the farmhouse had stood. The bearhunter wheeled about and, checking every half mile, sped toward the junction at the tarred ridge road.

Whenever the bearhunter scurried out the cab, the sport leaned quietly out the door and listened. Up and down the network of disused county roads the men searched, stopping, listening, the bearhunter angling frantically for a trace of his hounds. On the logging road where the strike had been made they came upon a trucker down from the mountain, tightening chains on a pulp load.

"Seen hounds?"

"Ain't seen a thing."

"Hear any?"

" 'Round chainsaws, you don't hear nothin'!"

The bearhunter nodded blankly. "Wish this suckin' wind'ld . . . Ssst!" he blew through his teeth, although he was the one talking.

The blurred, distant gong of the Plott hound sounded at the rear of the pack.

"Horn earns his meat, a'right!" exclaimed the bearhunter. "No legs on 'im, but the lungs of 'nelephant. What's on the far side o' them oaks?"

"Swamp to the bottom of Sluice Hill," said the trucker.

"Pond, too, ain't there?"

"Railroad bed used ta cut 'cross't. Don't know if't does still."

"Find that out fast," waved the bearhunter. Speeding backward, the truck almost capsized into the gulley before it jumped forward. The bearhunter flicked on the headlights and the luminous flakes streaming into the beams appeared to thicken.

They swerved sharply right at the junction of the ridge road and slurred upward. On the spine of the dirt road, a gray skim had collected. Sitting in the hot cab, baffled by the manner in which the pursuit unfolded, had put the sport at an ugly pitch.

The bearhunter swiped the wet film off the inside windshield. "Runnin' circles," he said, speeding by the overlook. "Must be the railroad bed there." They nosed into a branch road scarcely wider than the truck and stopped.

The entire marsh wailed.

"It sounds like it's coming straight down from the sky."

" 'Cause they're talkin' straight up a tree," roared the bearhunter. He indicated the sinuous tops of hackmatack rising into the smudged air of the marsh ahead. " 'Bout half mile in."

Thin birch and striped maple pressing in upon the right-of-way raked against the truck sides. The rail had been scrapped long ago, but the bed was still intact and the truck jostled along, nodding between the rotten, moss-covered ties and remnant ballast. The bearhunter refused to slow or stop for a moldering blowdown. The empty strike cages rammed it, plowing it aside as the truck barged on, willows lashing the windshield and flicking by.

"Frig," gnashed the bearhunter, wavering to a halt. "Trestle's gone."

The earthwork bed dropped off suddenly, into a black channel twenty feet across. "Move't, bear's liable to slide down an' have it out all over."

Grabbing his rifle, the sport bolted from the cab. He hesitated on the rim of the channel. The hoarse raving of the bearhounds split the thickening sky.

"Quick," shouted the bearhunter, "fifteen minutes an' we won't see shit."

The sport trailed the bearhunter down into the channel. Sinking to their knees in the glazed muck they waded to the opposite bank and climbed the granite foundation of the trestle.

The bearhunter broke into a run as soon as he reached the continuation of the railroad bed. The right-of-way steepened toward a thicket of spruce looming jagged and black in the gray air.

The bearhunter traveled with surprising speed, his thick arms pumping beside his great paunch. Running awkwardly with the rifle, the sport watched the slope-shouldered bearhunter roll through the drizzling snow and tried to keep pace.

"Don't shoot till I say," huffed the bearhunter without altering stride. "Hear?"

"Okay."

"Want the skull?"

"What?"

"Skull. You want it?"

"No."

"Then 'f you got a good head shot, take it." They entered the cluster of spruce. Bare, dead branches spiked out from the spruce trunks and a sharper dampness rose from the ground.

"Listen good. Once it drops, no shootin'. Hounds'll be all over it. Long as it's treed, shoot all you like. Drops down, shootin's done," he repeated gravely. "Got it?"

"Right."

"Drops, I take over."

The noise of the bearhounds was deafening now, like violent retching amplified. When the sport caught up with the bearhunter he saw them, less a pack of hounds than a cult in the snowless circle beneath a canopy of spruce. All seemed

afflicted with a mighty grief which they worked to rid themselves of in rote and strident lamentations: hounds dashed
themselves high off the trunk, pruning brittle limbs at the
peak of their jump; gnawing hounds girdled the base, pausing
only to cough up swallowed chunks of bark; more hung back
several feet, braying as fast as their lungs swelled with air.

The sport drew near to the edge of the circle and peered
up the spruce. For a moment he saw nothing out of the
ordinary and it unnerved him. Then he spotted it, like a large
black burl above the first black-needled boughs. It clutched
fast to the bole and, despite the tumult twenty-five feet below,
did not stir. The bearhunter stormed into the berserk jumble
of hounds and struggled to gather the most valuable of them.
He grabbed Chomp. Gums torn and red froth splashing from
his lips Chomp kept biting at the tree. The bearhunter managed to collar Bone, Horn and then Spook who launched up
the tree with such thrust the socket of the bearhunter's shoulder groaned. Only a blue ligament held Spook's right ear to
his wide head. The four hounds were magnetized to the tree
and it took all the bearhunter's strength to budge them.

The sport edged back and, gazing upward, skirted the tree
to locate that opening in the dense branches where the bear's
shape might come clear.

Twice he heard the hard clack of its jaws and a string of
eerie sizzling pants.

The bearhunter finished hauling the bearhounds to the
perimeter of the circle beneath the spruce. He clenched his
grip on the four collars, jerked them back, and glanced into
the spruce. "Now," he signaled. "Hit the top o' the middle."

"No, it's not clear."

"No," said the bearhunter evenly. "No?"

"I'll get the other dogs."

"What?" Dumbfounded, the bearhunter had lost the power
of his voice.

"The hounds, I'll . . ."

"What?" shrilled the bearhunter. "You shoot *now*."

The sport emptily stared into the tree and fidgeted.

"This is a guaranteed hunt, weasel. That's your treed bear. Shoot it."

"I'll pay."

"Shove your money, weasel dick, that's your bear."

"I'll pay."

"Piss off," commanded the bearhunter. He loosed the four hounds and they charged the spruce. With fresh zeal the rasping pack assaulted the trunk.

"Piss off," he screeched, approaching the sport. Confusion, not rage, inflamed his features.

The sport tensely jacked his bullets, and slowly walked beneath the umbrella of spruce, down toward the railroad bed.

He had not emerged from the spruce when the first blast of the .44 erupted. Then a second. Both shots and their echoes were swallowed at once by the bearhounds' din.

The sport quickened his stride as a third, final report waved over him. Soon the undulating howls of the hounds broke into barks, yelps, snarls and then all sounds died off. Light wanly suffused the dimming marsh. For an instant the snowfall appeared suspended like rose-yellow dust.

In the grainy nightfall under the sheltering spruce the bearhunter skinned out the black bear. The bear was a small male. The hounds circled about and rested. Licking their pads, elbows, and groins, they kept sidelong watch of the bearhunter's progress.

The bearhunter worked on his knees. He used a bone-handled jackknife to separate the skin from the carcass. He could not see well enough for the delicate task of skinning out the head, so when he reached the base of the skull he wiped the small blade clean, closed the knife and returned it to his back pocket.

In darkness now, he unsheathed the larger knife at his hip. The bearhounds started to whine. The bearhunter rubbed his slick palms on his trousers and cut through the bear's thick neck. He rolled the unskinned head into the hide and secured the heavy, tight bundle with webbing.

Then he began to cut slippery lumps of bearmeat from the quarters and along the backbone. The hounds snapped the pitched meat out of the air. The bearhunter went around the circle again and again, opening the bear finally to divide the liver and heart. His hands misted from grease and hardening blood. Composing himself, this night he let them gorge.

# The Austringer

A taut woman, Edith Leon was of necessity a methodical woman. She could not abide the world to float about her as it chose. Mysteries, ambiguities, tormented her. So she retaliated. She marshaled the world into patterns. She embraced a System. First-born was Theory, but soon after came Idea, and lastly, Perception. The world ceased to float. The world became fixed, coherent, sensible as a bucket brigade from a cistern.

Gestures, words, pictures, art—all became clues, surrogates, flares lit by the troubled in their darkness for those who could translate . . . so concluded Edith Leon, formerly college student of psychology, now translator of events, wife of Walter Leon, a clothier, and mother of Warren, a clever and disturbing young doodler.

Once, she had gathered together Warren's abandoned high-school texts, margins littered with grinning birds about to kill, killing, or having killed grinning fish. In a small black booklet concealed in a dresser beneath Warren's socks and underwear she later unearthed a sequence resembling the hieroglyphs of an ancient ceremonial tomb. Page after page was populated by a breed of men whose foreheads sloped without indentation to acutely angular nosetips. Most of the faces were drawn in profile. Lips were singularly thin with downward turns at mouthcorners. Eyes were ovoid and large, encasing circular uncolored pupils. The eyes lacked brows and lashes. But the most shocking particular was their martial helmets—falcons with dark lizard eyes peered over human heads until headpiece fused to head and falcons nested in human brains.

A mutation resulted toward the end of Warren's booklet. The fine skull structures of the men broadened; their noses coarsened and hooked down, eclipsing their thin lips. Their rounding eyes blackened and at the last shone from either side of a strongly cleft curling beak. The headdress had become the head and it sat on a thick-ribbed human trunk.

Bristling with evidence, Edith Leon brought the drawings to her husband. The fact that Warren drew pictures pleased Walter Leon from the start. He owned a garment shop for ladies and alone fashioned its window displays. The den, a square wooden caboose coupled to their brick house, was of his design. To his specifications the rich wood had been tongue-and-grooved, he had chatted supervisions to a plodding carpenter over his own blueprints, and afterward spent early evenings reclined in his creation, scanning garment bulletins beneath a sunken ceiling beam. That Warren drew pictures was natural.

Edith insisted they were *abnormal* pictures. Her hazel eyes flagging urgency and a paucity of iodine, she unraveled what she deemed her son's "fanatical hatred of fish and fowl." As proof of and perhaps antidote to his malady, they would purchase animals, install animals in their house and observe Warren's responses. She had decided to purchase two goldfish and one parakeet.

Edith watched, but Warren took little notice of the racket issuing from the wire-bell birdcage or the goldfish bowl set on the television beside the miniature cactus. She did her best to give the fishbowl appeal. Besides the two fish Edith

anchored a gray ceramic castle and deep-sea diver in an inch
of smooth chartreuse, purple and blue pebbles.

Nonetheless, Warren declined to feed the fish. So daily
the fish rose to the tiny flakes Edith salted on the surface of
the water. Warren refused to watch the fish. And so each day
Edith sat for a time before the bowl while the fish hung in
the water waving their tails, their mouths opening and closing.
The bowl became gray, and meandering strings of white excrement trailed the fish. In an effort to clean the murky bowl,
Edith dumped the water down her kitchen sink. The fish
hopped from the poured water, eluded her net and were lost
flipping and slapping in the well of her grinding garbage
disposal.

The parakeet fared better. Edith named the turquoise and
yellow bird Cuckoo and elaborately outfitted his cage with
diversions and obstacles: bells of seed, ringing bells, wooden
and plastic perches, oblong beak sharpeners, mirrors, a lad-
der, a removable sandpaper floor for droppings, a snowman
with spring legs for butting and an embroidered gauze blanket
to ease the darkness—Cuckoo wanted nothing. Edith spent
hours talking to the bird as he bobbed before a mirror and
picked his perch. Gradually his random chirps, yells and
squawks abated and a limited but intelligible jabber emerged.
Cuckoo bid Edith good morning and evening and all the day
said "prettypretty" in a high voice.

Late evenings there was silence intermittently splintered
by the shrill fixed voice of the parakeet. Edith slept in
the den, pale in the spotlight of the ceiling beam. Cuckoo
perched on her collarbone, his head cocked to the side, quizzically. Edith's lids masked her eyes into coyness. There they
slept, Edith's eyes ajar slightly, Cuckoo's purple lids perfectly
sealed.

Had Edith Leon been a sibyl as well as a translator of events
and seen Warren hunched over an attic desk in the cricket-
ridden country night of future years, had she seen his desk

piled with books entitled *Birds of Prey, The Misunderstood Raptors, The Noble Art, Hawking for You,* and *The Complete Falconer,* and known that he had a doeskin gauntlet, a rawhide-wrapped metal perch, and lacked nothing but a hawk, she would have celebrated the confirmation of her System, her Theories, her Ideas, and her Perceptions.

And had she known her son's rapture as he perused his maroon drawing book (particularly the entries he imagined to resemble a sequined lady releasing herself from the trapeze, somersaulting in the air and at the last moment clutching the steel forearms of a gent in caramel-colored tights), how jubilant her own celebration would have been: a speck hangs high on the top of Warren's page; below a dun partridge flushes from a green copse. The speck enlarges, a falcon banks, surveying, and dives, its wings pulled tight, unclear for its speed, like a comet. In a brown circle of detached quills the smaller predator penetrates the partridge with hooked hands clenched, binds to, and drops the stunned bird, watching its graceless tumbling descent. On the ground the blackheaded falcon rests on the brown body, dips its toothed beak, and with an abrupt twist, unlinks two neck vertebrae. The sharp wings of the falcon encircle the partridge breast, mantling. Again the black head dips, depluming the short tan chest feathers. Cleaned, the breast meat is white and prickled. The final picture shows the falcon straddling the vermilion bird, a thick neck, crop packed with the whiteness of breast meat—had Edith Leon but an inkling such acrobatics were to be performed in her son's brain she should have leapt from the sofa tousling her short gray hair and fixed her turbid eyes on the mantic black eyes of her parakeet. Understanding, the bird would have fattened his brindled gorge and chanted, "morbidWarrenmorbidWarrenmorbidWarren," with the toxic roteness of a conscience.

2

Warren courted Gretel throughout the snowstorms, sleet, hail, sun and warm downpour of March, wooing her with sketches of her naked torso. She posed on a stool between the silver-painted radiator and the gas stove, her toes curled around the dowel supporting the stool legs. Sometimes she wrapped a fuchsia-and-gray-banded blanket around her waist and goosefleshed thighs. She fanned her arms and undulated her body, embellishing the description of her day: the expedition to the toilets where little girls flapped their arms and were angels, the little boys sidewinding beside in a separate line, miming snakes. How Denise may or may not have stolen Randy's milk dime. Crystal's right eye swollen shut.

Gretel's wavy brown hair filled the deep V scoops between her collarbone and neck, hanging down her pale back in uneven lengths. Her breasts seemed larger for the fineness of her rib cage. Balanced on a dark but sparse line of down, her navel protruded slightly and the tips of her jutting pelvis deepened the grooves that outlined her pubic crest.

She liked the way Warren concentrated, whisking a charcoal stick over his large tablet or pausing to rub the stick on sandpaper and blow away black powder; his irritation in rolling a caramel block of eraser on an errant line until gray twists cluttered the floor.

Art school was teaching Warren an architectured human body—how the skull was a dome capping clavicles and scapulae which provided awning for the rotunda of ribbery; how the pelvis (secondary supports) snugly socketed balled pillars, the whole resting upon the arches of the feet. With the mind of his studies Warren erected queer and gabled human buildings. He rubbed his lines into what he called "shadow studies," blurred to the degree his pages appeared spat upon and licked. Once charcoaled in his sketch pad, Gretel's ruddy nipples became dead as cigar ashes; her torso the same that hung from wire and stocked shelves and tables of his studio classroom—plaster of Paris trunks of classical statuary.

Dissatisfied, Warren avoided his lectures. He skipped studio instruction. His pictures only changed—and changed abruptly—the first of April when Gretel blandly said, as if describing the daffodil sachet her principal, Mrs. Winkeller, stashed in the right side of her bosom, that she was not having her periods.

The human building of his studies began to quake. Like a child who in play has so earnestly erected a castle of wooden blocks, Warren with one sweeping blow toppled the spires and turrets, cleaved the pyramidal base of the classroom thumb from the balled middle, cleaved the balled middle from the pear-shaped tip, and like a child, found more mirth in collapse than construction. Secretly he purchased a box of crayons and with bright primary colors roped by fat black lines, started Gretel's pregnancy.

For five days he made pictures of the changes he supposed her childbearing would manifest. As the red embryo enlarged, her stomach skin stretched taut and blued. At the last Warren drew the bulge as something discrete; sometimes a fantastic saffron balloon or a transparent globe veined with waterways, whitish land masses, oceanic; sometimes buffed, a mirrored sphere reflecting the sky, the silver bars of the radiator. The fifth day, delivery was imminent. The navel had popped out long and straight like the stem of a great hard blue fruit.

At night Warren's fingertips tested her unchanging nipples, his palm alert for wetness. His ear, cradled between her hips, listened to the snaps and squeals of her digestion. He bought newspapers and analyzed the classified sections. He scanned job opportunities and realized he did not know how to do anything. He tried to imagine a distributor cap. Through green goggles he saw his hands solder together pieces of copper tubing, stitch uppers to shoe soles, adjust the floating balls in backs of toilets. One morning a week before Gretel's kindergarten classes ended he went so far as to introduce Warren Leon, window stylist, to Mr. Ransom, proprietor of the Swallow Shop.

Ransom told Warren he had done it himself once a week for fourteen years. He pressed his flattened palm on the speckled tie over his breastbone and said his heart was the reason. He led Warren through a drab green-curtained dressing room in the back of his shop, down stairs into a dim basement, a long corridor with small perpendicular recesses. The cellar walls were brick and fieldstone chinked and patched with concrete. The air was damp and water trickled between the black stones. Ransom pointed out a workbench to the right backed with shelves of odd tools and spattered paint cans. They passed the alcove of the boiler, toilet-paper and light-bulb closet.

The prop room was at the remote end of the cellar. The props were in crates and boxes marked by seasons. Ransom said his summer merchandise had arrived and that Warren should "center on brights." Together they would coordinate the summer windows and display cases. What they needed, explained Ransom, was a bouncy summer panorama—all McIntosh red, grapefruit yellow, and tangerine. "Geared" to lure people in off the wet streets for a taste of summer. He coughed into a paisley handkerchief and left Warren alone in the basement with the crates containing the seasons of the year.

Warren opened an enormous box marked AUTUMN. It was stuffed with picket fences, vines of red and yellow leaves, a blackboard announcing "Back to School Days" and a brilliant orange and green plastic pumpkin. Under the leaves Warren saw a rigid brown hook. He dislodged the hook which became the tail of a brown Airedale dog with a broken ear and a scarlet collar and leash.

Placing the dog aside, he opened SUMMER. It contained fishnets, opaque green and red glass bubbles, sand dollars, seashells, and fragile crab bodies. A second box was layered with bathing caps growing soft rubber flora, scaled bathing caps, and sandals. The brown, red, gold and black hairpieces and wigs beneath, shiny and coarse, blanketed a tangle of legs and fingers. The hands were poised to offer a harlequin scarf, a beaded handbag with a yellow flower. One of the legs was chipped and revealed a wire bone. Another had been repainted on the calf with an orange in uncomfortable contrast to the pink-fleshed original. The bald lower half of a mannequin, its right buttock impaled on the metal shaft of a stand, rose out of a red-berried holly wreath in the WINTER crate.

Warren never returned to the Swallow Shop from his first lunch hour. In a glass cubicle around the corner he phoned Walter Leon long-distance, to secure a large check for the summer. From the booth he jogged the entire way to Maple Street School. There, through the chicken-wired window of a door, befuddled Warren was watching Gretel chalk *H* and *h* above rows of tiny heads when a squat woman redolent of daffodils, eyes ever-alert for a child molester, asked aggressively, "Mister, are you looking for someone?" Warily, "Excuse me . . . mister, can I help you?"

3

From the attic space serving as his studio/study Warren surveyed his rented domain. Behind the farmhouse twenty or so acres of thistle and witchgrass tangled to a blighted elm in the ravine. He could not see beyond the firtops behind a knoll of pine seedlings planted in rows, but after her hike Gretel reported that the meanders of a stream, high from the rainy June and tawny from the pulp mill in Starks, described the far boundary of their land.

Much as he began it, Warren concluded his first week of country life—gazing across the field through the branches of the elm. This elm towered so foolishly barren amidst the lush ravine, so gloomily contrived with the plump raven squatting on the remains of a limb, that Warren devised through its branches the busyness of a Brueghel winterscape: on the knolltop he set a kerchiefed woman to collect faggots; in the left foreground weary hunters waded through drifts of snow; sharp-chested hounds poked their muzzles into snow crust near a fire; the ravine was a frozen canal where boys played hockey.

Suddenly one incongruous boy braved the chill dressed in a striped green and yellow jersey. He ambled down the knoll of seedlings, across the skating canal and vanished behind the elm trunk. His torso emerged from the ravine, arms waving away Warren's winterscape, waving up at Warren in the window.

Hurriedly Warren turned from the window. His back parallel to the slope of the hewn roof timbers, he moved to his desk by the brick chimney cutting through the attic floor.

Soon voices and the splutter of an engine lured Warren back to the window. Gretel was pacing out the size of her garden plot below in giant steps. A bald man astride a quivering rust-orange tractor concurred by nodding his corded neck. The boy in the striped green and yellow jersey leaned on a glacial boulder nearby and watched. His stiff reddish hair covered his forehead and shaded his beaked nose. Perhaps he was twelve or thirteen. Gretel completed the outline and piled her thick brown hair on her head to catch the breeze on the back of her neck. A sleeveless ruby shell molded her unbridled breasts into the gentlest curve. The boy sat cross-legged in the sun chewing a blade of grass, his back against the boulder.

The wedged blade dropped and the machine traced Gretel's steps, turning up heavy overlapping lines of black earth. The plowman was exceedingly serious and neat. He checked his progress behind. Shortly a small dark rectangle was notched in the gnarled field. The farmer stopped the noise of his engine and walked stiffly up to Gretel. He squatted, picked up some dirt, and for a quarter of an hour all Warren managed to intercept were the fragments: "sure to crop your tomato suckers," "three to a hillock," "nothin' like blood-meal," and a preening invitation to "come see my pigeon-house." The boy rose to join them, his arms folded on his chest. The farmer laughed (how pointless, causeless, laughter appears from a distance, scowled Warren from one window corner), daubed his neck with a blue sheet of a handkerchief, and remounted his machine. He aimed his tractor at Warren, idled, and shouted over his engine to Gretel, "Don't expect too much the first time. It'll be a lot better next year when all this rots. I'll be by to harrow in the mornin'," and he steered his jolting machine over the clotted field to the road.

Gretel squinted up at the attic, her hands curved along the lines of her dark eyebrows. It was too late for Warren to remove his head from behind the windowframe. "Warren, come outside." The boy smiled widely into the lowering sun. "A minute," said Warren. He slanted past the chimney toward the stairway, paused at the top of the stairs to gather himself, and descended.

"This is Anthony," Gretel said. "He wants to know if we have any odd jobs for him." Anthony sat on the pepper-speckled granite porch steps and examined Warren. Incest, decades of inbreeding finally produced such eyes, thought Warren. Wide rubberoid lids concealed half Anthony's eyes, giving the impression of an ocular drift into the forehead, a fear the boy was about to swoon or was preparing a backward somersault.

With index finger and thumb of his right hand Anthony kneaded some flesh on the left underside of his chin, his head cocked to one side. He scanned the shabby lawn and said, "Looks like you wanna have your lawn mowed. I mow lawns, you know."

"No, I didn't know," said unhappy Warren trying to lift his mouthcorners into an inquisitive yet sympathetic smile.

"I do," said Anthony flatly.

"Do you have a lawnmower?"

"Nope."

"Well, I don't have one."

Anthony eyed Warren, shrugged, hung his left hand over his right shoulder and walked down the driveway to the road, scratching his shoulder blade.

Warren sensed Gretel was now sucking her soft inner lips tight to her long incisors in her conception of a glare. The looks she gave him! He had first glimpsed her lips' enviable gift of contortion when she brought Crystal, a sullen red-haired five-year-old, into their apartment. Clamped under Gretel's arm was a stack of finger paintings by her kinder-garten children. Crystal and Gretel proceeded to thumbtack his olive kitchen into a crazy quilt. Warren had scuttled into the bedroom and closed the door. Together Gretel and Crystal looked at the pictures and talked about cows, gardens, chickadees and cats. Wearied of listening behind the door, Warren opened it a slit and beheld Gretel and Crystal spooning flesh-colored chunks from a carton of peach ice cream. Gretel had raised her eyes and of a sudden, cinched her mouth into a miraculous spasm of triumph, antagonism, repulsion, willfulness and cold ice cream.

This face in particular Warren remembered. He sat on the steps and fingering the warm granite said, "What did you want me to do?" He looked up for an answer and saw Gretel's back, arms akimbo, hands girding her waist, retreating to the garden. "He didn't even have a lawnmower," reasoned Warren.

Gretel straddled a black corrugation of earth, bent at the waist and commenced throwing stones and mats of turf outside the garden's perimeter. She tugged at an obdurate root when Warren shouted, "Do you want to abort right in the middle of the garden?" Without turning, Gretel shot her right arm erect in an obscene gesture, reclutched the root, and with a heave wrenched it from the ground.

———

She had been too busy to notice the dusk. Catching herself on her knees, feeling the garden in darkness for rocks, Gretel laughed softly through her nose. The clouded moon was nearly full circle. Except for the amber rectangle of the attic window, the farmhouse was gray against the moving black clouds. She straightened, arched, and pressed her thumb-pads into the knotted small of her back. Before her like a colossal antler, the black elm pronged the sky. She sauntered toward the farmhouse alternately kneading and drumming her back with her knuckles.

Far up the road she heard the approaching drone of a truck. A pale beam of light curved into the night. Just before the logging truck rumbled past she sighted the silhouette of a bicyclist pedaling along the opposite roadside. Momentarily, Anthony was washed in the truck's headlights, one hand on a fringed handlebar, the other hanging lax by his thigh. In the scarlet of the truck's wake both his hands gripped the streaming handlebars. He was pedaling strenuously, his buttocks pumping off the seat, his neck extended low. A fine rain sounded pleasantly to Gretel as it pricked the grass. The wind blowing from the knoll of seedlings strengthened.

Gretel went inside and paused by the shed entrance. Warren paced the attic. She slipped into the bathroom and closed the door. A shiny disc of metal nailed above the porcelain washstand (a peephole of a mirror discouraging all but the piecework of shaving and hair tweezing) reflected the reddish-brown smudges highlighting Gretel's cheekbones. Her face had been smeared by her fingertips in the garden, pushing her pesky hair away, fastening it behind her ears. Her bare feet and her hands were stained with dirt. She undressed, turned the spiky shower as hot as she could bear and stepped under it, her chin on her chest, waiting for her muscles to unstring. The doorknob turned and Warren's head popped from behind the plastic shower curtain, smiling vaguely into the humid shower stall. "How do you feel?"

"Sore," said Gretel, twisting water out of her hair. She shut her eyes, threw back her head and let the water bounce off her face and shoulders. Rivulets streaked between her breasts, hung on her belly, and dropped in a steady stream from the point of hair between her thighs.

"Like a hothouse here," offered Warren. The door reclosed and Gretel began to turn the soapbar in her hands, working a lather.

A hard rain slanting through the open attic window darkened the floor. Warren shut the window and sat idly thumbing through *Birds of Prey and Art,* a tome tracing raptorial art from the petroglyphs of Lascaux through bird-souled Egyptian relics to Tranquillo Cremona's somber canvas *Il Falconiere,* or *Love and Jealousy,* depicting a woman guardedly resting on a mustachioed picaroon's chest while his irked falcon, uneasily jessed to his raised glove, beats the dusky air around them. Disquieting rain was tinkling steadily on the window glass.

In the steamy bathroom below, Gretel bent over, her stringy wet hair hanging nearly to the linoleum floor. She wrapped a towel around the back of her head and straightened, adroitly fashioning a turban. She rubbed the clouded metal disc to see herself and opened the door. Mist rushed into the kitchen. She wiped the moisture from the bathroom window with her wet towel. Her body felt nicely spent. In the clearing window she held out her arms and gyrated them in small circles, enjoying her turbaned nakedness. Moving closer to the window, she flexed her jaws open and closed. She started. Her face's reflection did not correspond to her face. Anthony's unabashed lidded eyes peered through the streaked glass. His wet hair was matted on his forehead, his sharp nose flattened against the outside glass.

Gretel did not overtly acknowledge him. She powdered herself, unwound the turban and ruffled her hair briskly with a towel. Uneasy, she at last pulled the string overhead, shutting the light off.

Long after midnight Warren slipped into bed beside Gretel

who half-turned, murmured and covered her head with his pillow. He folded his hands over his stomach and readied for the interminable hodgepodge of episodes, unwinding installments "to be continued" after his somnambulant return from the water faucet or the bathroom still faint with Gretel's lilac-scented talc.

He experimented with methods of falling asleep: he aligned his inhalation with sleeping Gretel's; opposed her exhalation with his inhalation; ignored all her night sounds. This failing, he waited for a distant engine noise to mount, braced himself during its brutal climax (its light show skimming across the ceiling and down the wall), and relaxed as it diminished to the sough of Gretel's lungs and unperturbed open mouth.

Finally he dreamed, of a hilltop, of making love on a shaggy female creature. They trundled over and over, laughing down the slope, hugging through goldenrod and lupine, rolling into the river that appeared below. Together they splashed and whipped the water into excitement. They ran up the hill, hands clasped. Asthmatic Warren paused powerfully to sneeze into a gaudy tiger lily.

Gretel imperiously strode over the hillcrest, heavy with laundry. My children, she said, I will teach you to wash clothes in the old way, pounding dirt away on the stones of the river. Warren scampered himself and his increasingly hirsute lover into the suddenly available and vacant abode of a subterranean animal.

Gretel spotted movement on the hillside. Resplendent in scarlet jacket, golden buttons and white silk stock shirt, she raised a brass horn to her pursed lips and brayed a metallic *ta-ta-ta-ta*. Hordes of unkempt dog-faced children, their frothy tongues elongated, charged up the hill. Master of hunt Gretel led the hallooing phalanx while on either side whippers-in Crystal and Anthony flailed the grass.

Sconced deep in their den, the furry succubus massaged Warren's jangled spine to calm him. Gretel glowered one hundred jeering eyes of fifty indignant heads over the hole's edge. Warren turned to his conspiratress. She was gone! Warren was alone. A final rallying flourish of Gretel's horn plangently abridged Warren's private cinema.

Outside a horn honked and bleated. The front door slammed. It was noon. The bedroom was dark except for a blue strip of sky between the incompletely drawn green canvas shade and the windowsill. The room was damp from the night of rain. Warren resolved to vacate the rumpled bed, extricate himself from his gluey pajama bottoms, dress and welcome the day.

He pulled on green flannel trousers he had bought especially for the country and his green billiard-cloth shirt. He scratched his stubbled cheeks and walked to the bathroom where in the circular shiny metal, gruesome histrionics accompanied his pistonlike toothbrush movement.

No sooner had Warren dropped the flannels to his ankles, lifted his shirt tongues and become warmly situated on the horseshoe of the toilet than a queer-voiced "Hello? Hello?" sounded in the kitchen. Grumpily, Warren hitched his trousers. He opened the door to his own piqued head twinned in the mirrorlike sunglasses that sealed the trespasser's eyes.

"She wants you," said ubiquitous Anthony. "Down to the garden." Wetness darkened his dungarees up to his crotch and his fists were wadded in his pockets.

"Tell her I'll be right down," grumbled Warren. The taciturn intermediary did not budge. "Tell her now," Warren ordered and he slammed himself in the bathroom and doused his face with cold water.

Three curled wisps of cloud, the only marks in the bright sky, raced high above the rotting elm. Gretel was standing beside Anthony, the reddish tip of his cowlick level to the lobe of her ear. They watched the farmer harrow the garden. Rows of tiny wheels masticated the caked ground behind the machine. The wind that blew from the firs over the pine knoll and soaked fields was sharp and cold. Warren swished through the tall wet grass to Gretel's back. Her hair was plaited against her bleached denim jacket, an image of severity to Warren. He nodded to the farmer.

The farmer, no longer civil as from the attic window, wore a red-and-black-checked hunting cap and coat. He jounced sourly in his seat, featureless save hispid ears and nostrils.

Warren hauled Gretel by the elbow to a flat glacial boulder at the side of the garden. He began (with despondent intensity) from text: "Inbreeding. The son of his father and his older sister, herself the daughter of her father's first cousin— only such a combination could spawn . . ."

"Dougal's got a bird," interjected Gretel.

"Only an impoverished gene pool could result . . ."

"A goshawk."

"Who the hell is Dougal?" asked Warren, his query draining all impetus from his projected tirade.

Gretel pointed to the farmer, who had shut off his clanking engine and was inspecting the steaming nose of his tractor.

Warren loped across the muddy garden and obliquely, accosted Dougal. "My wife tells me you keep hawks?"

"Nope."

Warren ebbed. Old MacDonald, he thought, was of the same impervious and mutant stock as Anthony. Perhaps an uncle. "You don't have a hawk then?"

"Yep, I do."

Warren sufficiently restrained the impulse to cudgel confused or contrary MacDougal to inquire, "How much will you take for him?"

"Her. And she ain't for sale just yet," said morose and inscrutable Donald, fiddling under the orange hood of his machine.

"I don't understand," confessed Warren.

"Look buddy, that damn gossuck has gone and killed my best show pigeon this mornin'. Got caught up in chicken wire. Day or two, you can have what's left of her."

"I'll give you twenty-five dollars now."

"Nope."

"At least could I take a look at her?"

"Suit yourself," said Dougal. "I'll be home after I harrow Poulin's late this afternoon."

Formerly, in his preparations to become a falconer, Warren had wandered far, wrapped in sable, cantering a coily Arabian stallion over endless dunes, a hooded peregrine balanced on his sure fist. His perusals of falcon lore had resulted in his creation of a gyral sickle-winged enchanter performing thousands of feet above his head. In the labyrinthine castle Gioja del Colle he had discussed avian pecularities with Frederick II of Hohenstaufen, the weather best to fly at herons. But now Warren was fixed in his peregrinations, assigned by the *Boke of St. Albans* not to be a King with his Gerfalcon, a Knight with a fierce Saker, not even to be a Squire with his Lanner or the Lady sporting her magical Merlin. No, feudal hierarchy cast Warren down, down, halting him a rung below the insipid Young Man with his Tree Falcon. Truly Warren could no longer be termed a falconer at all. He was but a Yeoman, his bird a short-winged hawk.

*The Noble Art,* a morocco-bound volume by Colonel Humphrey Melmoth, further elucidated: "We usually call a hawker, he who keeps a Goshawk, an *austringer* [from the Fr. *autour,* Lat. *astor, austor*]—certainly not a true Falconer." Warren salvaged grim comfort from the frontispiece photograph of the dapper uniformed author (a petite goateed man holding a snowy gerfalcon as large as his chest, shoulders and head).

Such salient data did Warren the Yeoman cull from his books after his gloomy return from Dougal's farm. That night he subdued his anxiety gleaning goshawk facts in his attic lair. Stratagems teemed in his head as to how he might burgle barbaric Dougal's farmhouse, how he might rescue his captive Gos.

The visit to see his hawk had been infelicitous from the start. Vengeful Dougal's beagle, a rotund arthritic dog with a violent temper and underbite, had hobbled up to Warren and quite without warning shredded the left leg of his new flannel trousers. Warren had sought refuge through a paunchy screen door. A wizened woman in a long gingham dress was flattening dough into a circle on the kitchen table. Audaciously, without looking at Warren, she said, "Don't you worry, Poker don't bite."

"Where could I find Mr. Dougal, ma'am?" asked assiduous Warren in his most gracious tones.

"In the barn," said the woman. The flesh on her arms rolled loosely with her motion.

Warren had located Dougal pitching hay before the serried pink noses of spotted cows. He glanced at Warren and forked on while the big-eyed cows lowed impatiently, intermittently plapping pies of dung into the concrete grooves behind them.

Warren waited for ten minutes. His eyes puffed and watered from the hay and he began to sneeze. Finally Dougal walked up to him and said, "Hay fever? What can I do for you, mister?"

Warren gazed through his tears at distorted Dougal and wheezed incredulously, "About the bird!"

"Oh, you're the gossuck fella," and he walked past Warren toward his house. The portly dog snarled. Warren hastened after its master into a kitchen where the woman was filling the browned piecrust with a viscous yellow substance. Dougal opened a door in the hall and led Warren down a flight of stairs into darkness.

He pulled a string and a light bulb illuminated the moldy stone-walled cellar with its earthen floor. A giant gray wood furnace radiated a tangle of smokestacks, the tentacles of a galvanized octopus. Dougal ducked his head under an angular stack, walked on a plank around the furnace and pulled another light cord.

"In here, root cellar," said the farmer, pointing to a wooden door. He opened the door and stood outside. His burly frame filled the jamb. On tiptoe, peeping over Dougal's shoulder,

Warren saw the glint of translucent orange eyes. In a silvery flash the bird lunged at unflinching Dougal from an oak chopping block. The hawk came to the end of its nylon tether and jerked to the ground at Dougal's boots. She convulsed. With a din of slapping wings she flounced over and over, seizured. The bird's brown-brindled ivory chest heaved. One of her wings was awkwardly extended, the other tucked tight.

Just as suddenly as she had bated and convulsed, her spasms subsided. The hawk's torrid eyes grew torpid, filmed by membrane. Warren noticed her dome feathers were either frayed or missing. In their place rose a raw chestnut tonsure. Dougal slid the bird into the cellar with a soft kick and shut the door.

"What have you done to her head?" asked Warren to Dougal's calves as he trailed him up the stairs.

"Nothin'."

"Don't tell me you found her that way."

"I found her buttin' her damn empty skull on chicken wire tryin' to get out."

"Why didn't you kill her then?"

"Seems she's doin' that just fine by herself," said Dougal. He hung his cap and hunting coat on points of an antler in the hallway and began to scrub his hands in the kitchen sink. "Well buddy, you seen her."

"This morning you said I could have her. Can I take her now?"

"Come by this time tomorrow," Dougal said, sitting with finality at the wooden table, the morning's newspaper at his elbow.

"Piece of hot pie, mister?" said the kind lady. She held out the finished product. "Custard."

"No, thank you, Missus Dougal. I really should . . ."

"Not Missus," spat Dougal, "Charlotte Dougal, my sister."

Charlotte bowed slightly.

Edging and nodding, Warren backed toward the screen door and sidled coolly by the crippled beagle into the dusk.

---

Many hours passed before he ceased thumping one wicked bastinado after another on the soles of incestuous Dougal's feet and regained the composure requisite to reading of his goshawk. Twice he walked downstairs to use the bathroom and twice he was rebuffed by Gretel's prolonged occupancy. Persistent pressure this second time led him behind the house, where his strained mind heard phantom footsteps running through the grass; far away a farm dog barked, stopped, and barked again at the echo of its bark.

Through the night Warren drowsily compiled the list of equipment he would have to purchase the next day in Starks:

> binoculars
> gun
> fishing rod
> swivel
> clothesline
> soft leather strips
> bells

He scribbled diagrams detailing the conversion of the shed into a draft-free hawkhouse, complete with screen perch and vertically doweled windows. A yawn squeezed tears into the corners of his eyes. The torpor settling over his body seemed to extend to the tip of his pencil. Warren's head swayed. Frizzles of iridescence floated across his drooping lids, his chin flush to his sternum.

His obstinate head jerked erect and Warren was awake, startled by the attic window. Like a Peeping Tom, like his mother's perspicacious eye, a full pocked moon hung centered by the cruciform sash. Warren shuffled to the window. Moonlight blanched hoarfrost, a spring snowfall over the landscape. He uncoiled the shade.

He was administered immediate and potent sedation by Frederick Landseer's treatise, *The Complete Falconer.* Across the yawn of centuries Landseer wagged his soporific index finger and opined:

Launch not beyond your depth, unfledged Falconer. The education of a raptore necessitates a labour and a love. I stress, select a bird commensurate with your Learning, your Locale, the Leisure available to you, and not least, your own Fitness. Verbum Sap.

Warren's head rocked above the bulky and salubrious volume in his lap. He felt the pricking of sleep benumb his thighs.

To have superior birds, birds that will win honour and pre-eminence in the chase, the Falconer must realize the essentials of an ancient and noble art.
What qualities must need the aspiring Falconer possess?
He should be of average size. If too tall he will be quickly spent and want dexterity. If too short he will be sudden in his motions.
He ought to be moderately well-fleshed: emaciation is a liability as he will be unable to withstand cold and prolonged toil; neither should he be corpulent for he then will be short of breath and plagued by the sun.
He must be sagacious, with a retentive memory, acute hearing, and keen eyesight.
He must have daring and tenacity to bear the rigours of climbing hill and cliff-side, swimming unfordable waters, pressing through thorny bracken.
He must know how to write the language and keep a diary of his progress.
He must possess a stentorian voice to call over the winds.
He must not sleep heavily for he must check his bird several times nightly and rouse at the slightest irregularity of jingling bells.
Training, correcting, consulting his bird shall be his main

pleasure. A Falcon under the management of such a Man will exhibit the greatest mettle and address in chasing prey and do honour to the skill . . .

Warren's head was careened on his right shoulder, *The Complete Falconer* asprawl at his feet, when Gretel snapped up the shade to the overcast morning. Her hair was drawn back with a blue headband. The sun had burned the bridge of her nose fire pink. On the metal tray she held was a glass of orange juice and a cup of coffee. Warren contracted his face into a wince.

"Why didn't you come down? Warren, are you mad at me?"

"I have a stiff neck," he said, looking from the gray room into the gray layers of sky. "What a miserable day."

Gretel placed the tray on the floor. "How are you coming with Dougal?"

"He's a butcher."

"He was awfully nice about the garden. He wouldn't take a penny." She walked to the head of the stairs. "Oh, I'm going to hire Anthony to help me plant and weed the garden, things the way they are," she smiled quickly.

"How can you bear those eyes of his, my god, a basilisk . . ."

"Ssssh," sounded Gretel. She pointed down the stairwell.

"I'm going into Starks this morning. Make a list if you want anything." Warren stood and stretched.

"Is that it, basilisks and butchers?" she whispered and skipped down the stairs. Warren fumbled for something apt but already her dark head had disappeared through the floor.

At the kitchen table, while Gretel listed various seed packets, bulk seed, plant sets, and tools, Warren asked Anthony what grade he was in. Anthony took a swallow of milk, aimed his ravaging nonplus at Warren and erased his fuzzy white mustache with a curling swipe of his tongue. "Seventh."

"You're about to enter the eighth?"

"Seventh," said Anthony. He took another swallow of milk.

"Milk and eggs," rescued Gretel and she penciled them beneath "six tomato plants."

The sun burned behind a dense cloud covering, flecking the ash sky with blue, silver and red. Warren drove into the malodorous village of Starks, crossing the concrete bridge over the Starks River. Under the ledge of sky the river appeared motionless, like livid sheets of rock. Starks was ruled by the wee triumvirate toothpicks, popsicle sticks, and tongue depressors. Suitably, three monolithic stacks were each diademed with columns of royal-blue smoke.

At Jink's Hardware an old man with a crew cut of white spikes sold Warren a cheap green plastic fishing rod and reel, a .22 rifle and ammunition, field glasses, a swivel, a clothesline, packets of seed, tomato and onion sets, a hoe, and a rake.

"Varmints botherin'?" he asked Warren, who could make neither head nor tail of his intention. "Chucks? Coons?" he yelled as Warren barged out the door.

A smiling matron who spoke no English sold him some supple maroon leather and saddle soap at Mike's Shoe Repair. On the counter a pair of off-white baby shoes had aluminum bells through their laces. Warren pointed to the bells and asked if he could purchase them; if perhaps she had another she might sell. From behind the counter the woman produced a pair of bell-less chocolate-colored boy's shoes. Warren wagged his head from side to side and shook the bells on the off-white infant's shoes. The jovial woman studied a tag on the shoes and said, "Mart-in, Mar-tin."

Warren entered the five-and-ten-cent store. They stocked cowbells, catbells, deskbells, parakeet bells and bells for the bedsides of the invalid. "The kind on a baby's laces," Warren explained to the neckless teen behind the glass candy counter.

Warren was on his way out when he spied amidst a heap of orange dolls, astronauts and black bears, a tiny rubber man with a green silk shirt and a ruby coxcomb. Threaded to the peak of the coxcomb were three round aluminum bells and the reasonable price: seventy-nine cents.

In the yellow circle of Dougal's flashlight beam the lackluster hawk hunched in the root-cellar corner. The lined wooden crate Warren had constructed to transport his goshawk was hardly necessary. Her round bulging eyes had sunken and become oval. A discharge issued from her nostrils and her wings shuddered.

"Instead of friggin' with this bird I'd help out my wife with that garden if I was you," said Dougal.

"You're certainly not me, however," said Warren.

"Suit yourself, buddy." Dougal cut the nylon cord around the bird's leg with his pocketknife. Warren, pinioning both her wings, set the hawk into the crate. She did not struggle.

Warren inspected the hawk closely when he had returned to his shed. Her feathers showed hunger traces and were soiled a pasty white around the vent. Her right leg was swollen and discolored where the nylon had eaten into it.

Warren took the attic stairs three steps to a bound. He rummaged through his books for some antidote but they were incomprehensible, archaic. Over his crucible, Landseer intoned:

Take a piece of gumdragon; the oil of earthworms and roe, with eels cut in pieces and dipped in warm sheep's blood: mix with incense and mummy . . .

Warren clapped the book shut and downstairs rifled through the medicine cabinet. He decided to paint eucalyptus oil on his hawk's nares with the cotton nub of an ear cleaner and lacquer iodine on her misshapen leg.

Gretel was alone eating at the table when he rushed in for food. He brought the hawk two strips of raw steak on a dish and set it by her side. "Here, Gos," coaxed Warren, dangling the meat before her beak. She looked askance. Warren plopped the meat back on the dish and with assuring measured movements, left the room.

Gretel was rinsing her dinner plate in the sink. "Well, what's the diagnosis?"

"I don't know. She looks terrible."

"She?" said Gretel. She magnified the arch of her brows. "I'm going in to see her, okay?"

"No," said Warren, "I want to see if she eats. Besides, I read that some hawks get riled in a woman's presence."

"Bullshit."

"You can read it for yourself."

Gretel put Warren's supper on the table without comment. She leaned against the stove. "We planted the squash, the carrots, and the beets."

"Ah, that's what seems so odd, madame," simpered Warren. "Where is your catamite?"

"Don't always jeer," said Gretel. "This afternoon while you were in Starks I screwed Anthony. He has no navel. Would you believe it?"

The hillock of mashed potatoes. The peas in a green hump. Seared meat halfway to his mouth, Warren looked up at her bright watchful and mischievous eyes until he had contained himself. He clinked his fork to the plate and said squeakily, "Fine sport for an expectant mother."

Gretel was furious. "That, thank God, I'm not!" she shouted. Her flushed cheeks pulsing, she twirled and dashed from the room.

Warren stayed at the table. He squeezed the mashed potatoes through his fork tines into intricate crinkles around the lip of the plate. He sat at the table until his plate became unfocused. Gos was his single alternative: he rose and walked to the shed.

Gos was huddled over the empty meat dish. She flapped and started to hop across the plank floor. Warren waited firmly. The hawk calmed and slowly Warren approached her. From his pocket he took a soft jess and tied it around her left leg. Once more he pinioned her wings and placed her on a perch, a young poplar trunk nailed to the shed corners. He fastened the jess to a leash in turn fastened to the poplar. The hawk nestled her clenched right foot into her body.

Warren sat, his back to the wall, and watched his bird, roosted now atop the swivel of her leash. A faint tapping at the door distracted him.

"Warren . . . Warren," said Gretel hoarsely. She had been crying. "Warren, I lied. I didn't sleep with Anthony."

Warren did not answer.

"I swear I didn't . . . I lied. I just felt sorry for him."

"How did you know that detail about his navel?" asked skeptical Warren.

"He took off his shirt in the garden. Warren, don't be silly. I lied. Christ, he's only *twelve* years old."

"Are you still pregnant?"

"You know I am, Warren."

"Do I?"

"You should."

Warren tiptoed past the august eyes of the hawk to the door. He opened it a crack to Gretel's red-puffed face. "Come to bed now, Warren."

"Why did you say those things to begin with?"

Gretel shrugged benignly and sniffled.

"Well?"

"I don't know."

"I have to stay with the hawk," said Warren.

"All night?"

"She's sick and frightened."

"So am I."

Warren opened the door wide, craned out his head, and kissed Gretel lightly on her forehead. Gretel smiled at him. Her lips contorted thinly and she said, "'Night, you condescending prick." Warren recoiled his head barely in time to avoid being boxed in the slamming door.

He smarted under a welter of vexation, and relief at the

narrowness of his escape. She had utterly misread him. That much was clear. It was a kiss of tenderness, of compassion, mused Warren, his nose inches from the pine door. It was a kiss of forgiveness.

The hawk raised her rounded tailshaft and sliced a loose splat of grayness into the corner. Warren rolled his shoulders and sighed. At the least he would accustom his hawk to his presence, the odor of his flesh and hair, his green billiard-cloth shirt and mutilated green flannel trousers.

In order to tame her Warren intended to keep watch and prevent the bird from sleeping. Simultaneously the hawk observed the man. Her black pupils swiftly contracted and expanded as if some arcane code were being transmitted.

The vigil of the hawk continued through the night. She scrutinized the shadowy creature doubled up below her, its head on its knees, a garland of cobwebs festooned to the wall above its head.

Sunrise slanted incarnadine light through the doweled window and Warren's eyelids. He blinked and looked at the cinder-and-salmon-colored striations across the plank floor. Instantly, to establish his bearings, he replayed Gretel's ruse, the jarring door-slam, his ailing hawk. The hawk! She was not on her perch.

In the dark opposite corner of the shed the hawk floundered on her belly, entangled in the leash. Her eyes were fastened on Warren. He pushed himself to his feet and replaced the mute goshawk on her perch. She tilted, gained her equilibrium, and clutched the poplar with both her feet. Her breastbone bulged from under her brindled ivory breast.

Warren left the hawkhouse and with resolution strode up to the attic. He filled his trouser pockets with ammunition, looped the leather strap of his field glasses around his neck, and grabbed his rifle.

He met alluringly disheveled Gretel downstairs. She wrapped her quilted yellow bathrobe close about her and froze. Warren swept gingerly past her apprehensive face, the barrel of his .22 depressed.

From the granite doorstep he scanned the fields behind his house, first with his naked eye, next through his field glasses. He unbolted his rifle and fed it one lead and copper cartridge. He prowled around the garden in the dewy grass. Again he raised the glasses to his eyes. Adjusting the dial, he transformed a nebulous kaleidoscope of colored mist into the knoll of pine saplings. He focused on a flock of starlings strolling through the grass like violet-green mechanical toys. He raised the cold stock to his cheek in rehearsal. He shuddered and stealthily crossed to the ravine.

Warren had never shot a gun. He had killed a bird once, a goldfinch, in the chrome grill of his car. The wind had meshed its pale feathers into the studding and he was forced some days later to extract the rigid bird parts piecemeal.

He paused behind the dead elm. From his lowly vantage the starlings were not visible. He crept slowly up the knoll-side. The unwitting colony of starlings came into view. Warren aped the prone posture he had seen the sniper assume on Technicolor mesa tops. He isolated one bird and aligned its breast with the sight of the barrel. The starling dunked under a pine bough.

Warren pressed the trigger gradually and gradually squinted his eyes shut. His mind heard the explosion it expected and he leapt to his feet to locate his quarry. The air filled with a flurry of fleeing black triangles. He scoured the ground beneath the sapling but found no trace of violence. He unbolted his rifle. The cartridge popped into the air. Warren clenched his teeth: he had overlooked the safety.

From that point on, birds uncannily disappeared at Warren's approach. Stalking fowl in suffocating spring growth was a tedious affair. The sun glared. His field glasses became a millstone. He unbuttoned his billiard-cloth shirt and circled back toward the road. Warren remembered he had not eaten supper the night before. He shifted his rifle from hand to hand and trudged along the ridge above the roadside.

A pulp truck labored up a short incline. Warren waved to the driver. The obtuse trucker in turn beeped his horn twice and shot Warren with the improvised gun of his index finger and thumb. Chagrined, Warren plopped down under a wild apple tree. Brown wisps of petals were strewn around its trunk. He mopped his nape and brow and stretched out, his fingers locked behind his head.

A foolhardy twitter commenced above his head.

Oh, unlucky descendant of the moronic Bird that capered upon the menacing snout of the Serpent—a sparrow had lit on a branch above Warren's head. Cunningly, smoothly, Warren groped for his .22 and pulled it to him.

The sparrow scolded.

Warren fired.

The bird dropped by Warren's ear and scooted unevenly into thick grass. Warren crawled in pursuit. He parted the grass and clubbed the wounded sparrow to death with the stock of his gun. He inserted the hot limp-necked bird into his shirt pocket. Swallowing his quickening secretion of saliva, he traipsed down the embankment to the road, the rifle resting in the crook of his arm.

The bird was grotesquely small.

Warren estimated his expedition had covered two or three miles. He trekked along the pebbled shoulder of the road, then, to gain better prospect of his location, tugged a jutting root, and hoisted himself up the incline. Less than one hundred and fifty yards away sat his clapboard farmhouse. Through his field glasses Warren discerned Gretel, squat on her haunches, shaping mounds of earth around the corn kernels that sprinkled from shirtless Anthony's palm. Above the waist of his dungarees a long pink scar smiled from his tanned flesh.

To frighten them, Warren approached quietly, his rifle

raised. Gretel spotted him first. She screamed warning. Crouched low, Anthony tunneled through the shaking grass to the ravine.

Warren walked up to the garden, shaking his head in amazement. "And what was that all about? You didn't actually think . . ." He grinned.

"I have no idea what's in your head, so—"

"So you sounded alarm." Warren laughed gleefully and by the tailfeathers plucked the battered sparrow from his pocket. "This hunter is after bigger prey." Mockingly he jiggled the birdlet before her nose.

"Is this your idea of a game?" Gretel said scornfully.

"Certainly," said Warren. "You see to your Kestrel, me to my Gos."

His hawk was sitting alertly where he had left her. Warren slipped on his doeskin gauntlet and shook the sparrow a step below the perch. The hawk examined the tiny meal and bobbed reluctantly; then she pounced down on his fist, lowered her head and began to tear.

## 4

First page center of a garnet-colored vinyl notebook, Warren block-printed HAWKING DIARY on a sky-blue line. The twenty-third of June he penned his initial entry:

I have nursed Gos diligently. I have roved hilltops, foraged the ravines, tramped thicket and field to provide her three small daily meals.

To date, her diet consists chiefly of sparrow, chickadee, and starling. She convalesces rapidly. Pleasant mornings I weather her for an hour in the yard on a metal perch. Still, small reminders of her captivity persist: a black scab on the top of her head and a brown ring around her right arm (much like a burn).

When I enter the hawkhouse, she flaps excitedly. There is more to manning a hawk than the calculated equipoise of food and the lack of it!

### JUNE 24—

Despite the scorching day I wore my customary outfit so as not to unsettle Gos. At noon I shot the raven in the elm. This was overdue. For too long it had harassed me with its Halloween poses. The gardeners, I think, were taken aback at my marksmanship. Good. I put them on edge.

I fed Gos half a cropful of the raven's greasy breast meat. She is slicing with increasing vigor.

Late this afternoon I promenaded her around the fields for a full hour or more. She adjusted to the rhythm of my gait at once. She was enjoying this stroll when a road grader scraped by. She became flustered. Promptly, I headed her home. I was unprepared for the pinpricking sensation a glance at the ground elicited: my shadow stretched in the grass before me, the cruel profile of Gos on my fist.

Later this evening I will dismember a wing of the raven and attach its nub to the clothesline for a lure. It occurs to me as the days pass that this household has become severely polarized into two ancient camps: Farmers and Hunters.

### JUNE 26—

Gos jumped the entire length of her leash for the head of the chickadee garnishing my glove thumb.

Constant arduous work is toughening my body. I begin to comprehend why the true hunter has long observed rules of abstinence. Without a spartan continence is this rate of advancement, this one-mindedness, possible?

## JUNE 29—

I jessed Gos's right leg yesterday. This morning I fastened a bell above each of her jesses. The bells seemed to annoy her. She pecked at them and ate little.

Once daily I feed her a moderately full crop. A hard rain cooled the air this morning but the afternoon was muggy. I kept her inside.

I extended the length of her leash and she will readily (at the trill of the police whistle or the call of her name) leap the distance across the hawkhouse to my fist. Sometimes I reward her with a strand of meat. The hand of my gauntlet is crusted with gore.

Under my attic window now the ping-ping of the shuttlecock is most distracting. Gretel is teaching the basilisk the game of badminton. This is yet another exhibition on her part—she will do anything to convince me she is happy. I know better. She contrives an ebullient girlishness. She wears beige shorts.

Still, I am insufficiently neutralized.

## JULY 5—

Today a clouded milestone! Tonight an auspicious crescent moon; yet it is painful to write.

I tied a fifty-foot length of clothesline to the leash and launched Gos to the lowest branch of the elm. She hunched there and gazed about. Like a scarecrow, I extended my gloved arm, called her name, and blew my whistle. She darted obediently to my outstretched arm. The single negative aspect of this episode was that she miscalculated upon landing and punctured my unsheathed upper arm.

I put Gos back in the hawkhouse and rewarded her with a titbit. Gretel interrupted her bucket brigade to the garden to attend my lacerations.

My green shirt, emblazoned with eight rents, forms an admirable ensemble now with my slashed trousers.
Slyly, to taunt me, the pinging recommences beneath my window. I will repeat Landseer's dictum—*Training, correcting, consulting his bird shall be his* MAIN *pleasure.*
Damn them. If one of them overshoots, if that shuttle-cock is stroked through this window, so help me I will fall upon it and yank out every feather.

### JULY 11—

For the fifth day running the weather is unbearably hot. I cannot raise my right arm above my head. Today, after swinging (left-handed) the meat-jeweled raven's wing (lariat-style) above my head, I let it drop in the grass. Leashed Gos swooped low from the branch and fell at mark on the wing.
Now she has been tested and proven to whistle, to lure, to voice.
A robin I shot from the telephone wire was greedily and beautifully devoured. Gos pecked away the skullcap of this robin, dipped her horned curve into its brainstuff, leaving a red wick of spinal column; this she tugged with such ferocity the headless robin turned inside-out—bursting into a crimson tulip.
Afterward she stropped her beak merrily on my thumb. The test is not far off.

### JULY 13—

This kind of commitment, of discipline, is doing its work. I am hardly tempted now when I spy them from the window. Gretel and protégé resemble lotus-eaters. They pull weeds, they water their minuscule plot; then, pretending the harvest is over, they wallow in the grass and bask—legs wedged open, codpiece awry, slumbrous, besotted. The roast pig will never present to them the knife to slice its own succulent flesh as in that drugged land of Cockaigne.

They are pretenders! They are miserable.

JULY 17—

In the ravine I shot a rabbit that was paralyzed on a stump, sure I would pass by. Later I tied fishing line to its hind leg and Gretel (hidden behind a clump of briars) reeled it across the field. This failed. Either Gos did not see the rabbit dragged through the tall grass or else she balked at Gretel's presence.

Whichever, I know Gos is in trim; that she is properly trained, manned, and prepared for the great test—free flight.

If the day is clear, tomorrow.

On my way back to the house the young crocodile (hot to capitalize on my disabled member) challenged me to a game of badminton. I ignored him. I ignore them both. Had Gretel not tried to compete with me she might have been happy. As it is, her artificial happiness sickens me. At heart she is miserable. And now, it is too late. I am beyond pity now. When winter comes, when Gos brings home grouse and woodcock—then the grasshoppers will come knocking and obsequiously kneel.

And I shall say GO DANCE.

5

Halcyon afternoon. Warren weathered his hawk in the shade of the house. Under the baking sun Gretel sprayed the garden (leafy and pointed shoots already sprouting between stakes) with extensions of newly purchased hose. Atop the glacial boulder, Anthony catnapped on his stomach, his cheek resting on the backs of his hands.

At two o'clock Warren returned Gos to the inside perch. To ensure a reciprocal keenness, neither austringer nor hawk had yet eaten. Warren's cumbersome right arm was swollen from shoulder to wrist. Dully, leadenly, it hung by his side as he rechecked his apparatus.

He employed Gretel's cast-off leather pocketbook for his hawking pouch. Into it he stuffed the compactly wound raven-wing lure, an extra set of jesses, and his official police whistle—brilliant metal encasing a hardwood ball.

Gos shifted and began to rearrange plumage on her back. With his curled index finger Warren stroked her rolling dark-capped head. "Cobra," smiled Warren, "cobra de capello." Her flashing orange irides sent waves of nervous anticipation over him.

He slung his field glasses over his neck and carried his rifle into the bright field. The garden was abandoned. A rake lay in an aisle, teeth up. Warren unbuttoned his billiard-cloth shirt and tied it around his waist. He crossed the field, rested against the leafless elm and listened: the static of mosquitoes.

He scaled the hill of saplings and collapsed grunting in a heap. A cold unnatural drop of sweat hung from his nosetip; droplets glided down his sides to the beltline of his tattered flannel trousers. He cowled his head from the sun with his shirt and lurched downhill to a dense stand of firs. A chipmunk chided him curtly and vanished into the thick-laced underbranches of a fir. Warren strayed through the stand. A branch swatted his nose and he tumbled down a steep embankment to the river.

The water was badly polluted. A citron-yellow head of foam had collected before a half-submerged decaying trunk. Warren dunked his head and slapped water on his neck and chest. His eyes burned. A jay rowdily flitted overhead before he could swing his .22.

He chose each step along the bank, noiselessly. Cedar and

poplar lined the banks and shaded Warren as he made his
way to a sharp bend in the river. He sat on a warm stone
outside the elbow of the meander and scanned downstream
through his field glasses. Trunks dammed the river below,
forming a moss-rimmed pool under a birch tree. Warren let
his glasses fall to his chest and twisted his knuckles in his
stinging sockets.

A crackling, a splash, and through the haze red-eyed Warren beheld a spectral dryad wading in the pool. He was hal-
lucinating, he thought, his arm had gone septic. She floated
on her back as white light glinted through the birch leaves
and dappled her breasts, naked belly and loins. A faunlet
rudely appeared and gamboled on the mossy bank.

Warren's field glasses dispersed the sylvan sham, focusing
lucidly and cruelly on Anthony's navel slash; depressing to
his furless contracted and uncircumcised spout. Anthony can-
nonballed into the pool with a great splash and Gretel frolicked to the bank. Sunny waterdrops stippled her body. She
laughed as Anthony stood on his hands in the pool and wiggled his toes.

Crablike the intruder backed into the brush. When he was
thirty feet from the water he rose and scrambled feverishly
up the incline. He crumpled on the burnt-umber floor of the
fir needles. "Slut," he muttered, "pathetic slut."

The sun was lowering when Warren's .22 yapped like a cap
gun and a redheaded woodpecker plummeted to the foot of
the fir tree riddled by its gimlet beak.

In the hawkhouse he secured the woodpecker's breast to
the raven-wing lure. He slid the strap of the hawking pouch
over his shoulder. Awkwardly, he fitted the gauntlet upside-
down on his left hand. He unhooked the leash and wound
the jesses around his fingers. Hungry, sharp-set, Gos straddled his ungainly glove and clenched.

Outside she revolved her head, puzzling at the distant moan
of a farm dog. Warren halted at the far end of the field, one

hundred feet short of the elm. With a thrust of his arm he cast Gos off. She beat her wings swiftly (he heard the whoosh of her fingers pressing down the air) and sailed to the lowest dead limb of the elm. There she humped. Her head cocked from side to side.

Warren fidgeted, his eyes fixed on the hawk, as long as he was able. He extended his good arm and gave a blast of his police whistle. The hawk flapped her wings and pruned them close. Her bells jingled lightly. She settled on the limb.

Warren followed with two shrill blasts.

Gos did not move.

Warren sat in the grass and waited. Patience. He counted to three thousand. Presently he took the raven-wing lure from his pouch and swung it around his head, shouting "Gos-GosGos" with each revolution. The weighted lure dropped in the grass.

Gos sulked on the limb. In the lavender twilight her silhouette resembled a turkey vulture's.

Warren blew brief strident blasts on the whistle until he felt dizzy. He tramped to the foot of the elm and called up to her. He drummed his palm on the rotting trunk.

With a tinkling and a rustle of wings the shadow of the hawk left the elm and skimmed over the knoll toward the firs, her jesses trailing behind.

Warren snatched the lure and stumbled up the pine knoll. He sickened at the appearance of the enormous saffron balloon bouncing on the horizon. Perceptibly it rose, diminished, and diluted to an ocher moon.

Warren bleated his whistle with all his breath.

He whipped the lure over his head.

He called the name of his hawk at the top of his voice.

Impulsively he discarded the lure and moon-eyed drifted into the firs, his ears pricked to catch the tinkling of bells above the hissing trees.

# The Toad

After rain the bees huddle upon discs of sunflowers so full of seed the tall stalks bow. At roadsides, chokecherries dangle and the mountain-ash berries flare. Winter pears are dull, hard, and the book says that if cared for by a skilled physician the seven-month fetus, her first, has a fair chance to survive if born this moment.

Beets drying on the counter, she takes up a batch of string beans in her purple-stained fingers and blanches them. A squirm and flutter sweep one side of her hardening belly. Again she opens the book and examines a cross section of pregnancy's seventh month: a woman's pink outline, billowed from its crimson insert. She closes the book, diagrams too ugly to be of use.

She puts up a kettle of water for corn, takes the wicker basket and goes outside. Plucking a raspberry and some blueberries along the beaten cold grass, she returns to the garden. The snort and shriek of the chainsaw rises from the ravine. Twisting maroon ears of corn into her basket she works down the narrow rows. There, beneath one stalk sits the toad. The bent leaves fling raindrops upon the toad as she crunches off a ripened ear of corn. The toad does not budge. She admires its serene frowning presence, black egg-shaped pupil in a bronze rim. Ponderous yet so quick of tongue, this patient hunter has been her daily companion since planting time when she rested her palm on what appeared a clump of sod. It had let out a squeak. She bends, stroking the crinkled satin throat of the toad. It makes one jounce, toward the dark, veined beet greens, and halts, propped formally upon its short arms.

Beside the compost she shucks the corn, tossing silks and husks into the tangle of creepers and gourds, melons and potatoes that teem there. The chainsaw has stopped. She quickens her pace. She pulls a crippled bunch of the carrots she forgot to thin and probes the tomato plants for a splash of orange. She kneels then, alongside the outcroppings of beet greens. Poking around the beets to size them and find the small, tender ones she clutches a shock of purple stems, shakes dirt from the beets and lays them on the carrots, tomatoes and cucumbers in her basket. Parting the livid beet tops, her glance once again meets the egg-shaped pupil of the toad gazing serenely out of the crumpled leaves.

The toad squeaks, shuffles its arms queerly and edges backward. It squeaks again and again until the woman spies, clamped halfway up the toad's spine, the black round pupil, copper iris of a snake.

At once she moves to break the snake's hold but her hand lets be. Again tugged backward, the toad juggles its crooked arms to keep balance and chirrups. The squared-off nose and enameled snake lips do not move and the toad falls silent, seemingly at ease except for the pulse in its crinkled throat. Although the toad's hind legs are swallowed, a knot behind the snake's head, the face of the toad looks no different than it has looked the summer long. And what of this snake with its squared-off nostril and enameled lip and precise copper iris? A round eye behind an oval eye, lips within a mouth, the slow ceremonial of bindweed coiling up orchard grass. As she watches their peculiar decorum, she suddenly wants it speeded up, done with. And slowly the enameled lips do rise, to latch higher up the toad's neck. Where the mouth had been fastened is exposed a raw patch of toad flesh. When she can no longer tell if the toad is alive, a limb of the fetus lashes the woman's diaphragm with force enough to cause her to shift footing. Chill from the black dirt shoots through her bare soles and goosefleshes her legs and arms.

It is not the slow dying of her companion the toad; it is the snake mouth. It appears the mouth can never stretch wide enough. Then the gluey pink roof of its mouth lifts and slanting, extends its grip over one stolid eye of the toad. Any more and the unhinged, discolored head of the snake looks to split. She sees the nosetip of the toad vanish at last, takes a full breath, lets it out. Now only the stout arms of the toad stick out the corners of the snake's lips. Muscular waves speed up and down the snake's length, flushing the toad deeper inside. At last the toad's arms, hands and delicate small fingers are gone.

Impossibly swollen now, the snake rests, misshapen as a gourd under the greens; then, backward, slides into the wine-colored stems. The woman touches the lump in its streaked back. The snake contracts, flattens, whips, to wriggle free. She is not yet ready for it to go. She presses it firmly to the ground.

At the far end of the garden a man sets down the chainsaw and stops. He watches his wife kneel intently at the row of beet greens.

Blankly she is fingering the toad the snake has disgorged. Its hind legs already are indistinct and liquid, wet dead arms outstretched as they had been forced, to fit inside the snake's mouth. Slack-jawed, the snake slips through the witchgrass on the fringe of the garden.

# Dog in the Manger

*I*

All nine greyhounds whimpered as their trainer approached the runs. They danced on their hind legs and clawed at the chain-link fence. Long necks craned to the ground, haunches thrust up, they lashed their tails and stretched away the afternoon nap.

The trainer raised a pin from the door of one compartment. A sleek black greyhound hurtled out of the pen, his coat purple in the November sun. The dog bounded ten yards, swerved, and twirled around his master. The trainer clapped his hands; the dog depressed his wedge-shaped head and crouched through the grass, entire body waggling, up to the man's high boots. Indignant at being so quickly curtailed, the dog flicked his hot tongue on the hand fastening a slip leash to his collar and snarled at the pickerel-like brindle bitch who lunged past her opened door. The trainer clicked his tongue, leashed the bitch quickly and jogged down the dirt road that wound to a stop at his farm.

The seven hounds left behind chorused their frustration.

The trainer jumped the shriveled ferns in the roadside gully and headed on toward the orchard and high meadow. Both greyhounds paused by the rows of bleached cornstalks scraping in the remnant garden.

A succession of frosts had withered the landscape. From a ledge above the orchard the surrounding maroon and blue hills appeared close, sullenly compact.

Both leashes jerked taut in his fists and the trainer was lurched forward.

Halfway up the meadow a fat woodchuck began to burr. The woodchuck sat on its haunches unperturbed, its black forepaws lax. The greyhounds snorted from the pressure of the collars against their throats. Their front legs pedaled the air.

The trainer slipped the leashes and away the greyhounds sprinted over the meadow.

The woodchuck hesitated and rolled nonchalantly toward the mouth of its burrow. It was too sluggish, dazed with fat for hibernation, and the trainer felt a dread mingle with his excitement. He began to run after his hounds.

The bitch was upon the woodchuck first, clamping its tail as it dove into the burrow and flinging it into the air. The dog seized the neck, the bitch its spine, and they began to shake it. Yoked by the screeching woodchuck, they cantered in circles on the meadow.

The trainer ordered the greyhounds to stop. He cupped his ears to muffle the woodchuck's long shriek. Greedily, the hounds paraded their catch. The woodchuck's chestnut belly had come unseamed and a loop of intestine popped through the masses of stored fat.

The greyhounds did not eat the carcass, but neither would they abandon it. They sprinted after one another, taking turns dragging and tossing it, playing tug o' war.

The woodchuck had lost its shape and the sky was darkening before the dogs' blood cooled. They dropped the pulp in the grass and frisked happily around the trainer in reunion.

The trainer absently slicked back the whiskers on their greased hot muzzles. It was a shock to see how a chase transformed them and to share something of it. A raccoon, a rabbit, a nerve-frozen doe triggered the blood of a greyhound's eye

and discharged tension that unstrung with the crack of the
rabbit's neck, the collapse of the doe, her lungs exploded in
a cedar swamp. Afterward, smeared and spent, they would
slouch back to him, feral creatures reduced again to hounds,
comprehensible. He knelt to the level of the two slender
heads. Ears tucked back, eyes protuberant, their dry tongues
scraped his nose and mouth.

The two hounds led him through the dim meadow to the
ledge. Mist rolled off their shoulders: there would be another
frost that evening. The light turned on below over the farmhouse porch. Shafts of light from the kitchen, dining room,
and upstairs bedrooms sloped to the ground. Despite his
distance from the farm, he saw the yellow windows of the
kitchen and dining room glint, blotted by his wife setting the
table, and the glint stirred his appetite.

He wrapped a leash around each fist and trotted down into
the orchard. Abruptly, both greyhounds stiffened. An apple
thumped in the dry grass and the branch above it wavered.
The trainer stumbled ahead and yanked them to go on, but
they balked and gazed across the orchard, ears cocked in the
direction opposite the farmhouse. He slapped the leashes on
their flanks but they did not move. They howled a prolonged,
piercing alarm.

The trainer squinted through the black apple branches. He
could see nothing but the long row of stakes on which the
snowfences were to be hung. The hair finned along his
hounds' spines. They wrenched angrily to the ends of their
leashes. He worked to restrain them. Baying and coughing,
the two hounds tugged toward the far corner of the orchard.
He wrestled them up toward the house. Hauling and hauled,
the three staggered directly between the two points, to the
road.

A bulky form, an outline darker than the air, hunched one
hundred yards down the dirt road.

The trainer whipped the hounds to quiet them. "Hello?"
he shouted. His eyes engraved a bear into the outline. The

bear was injured, he thought, perhaps drunk from bushels of apples fermenting in its gut.

The hounds shrank lower to the ground. From the farm in the distance behind he heard his wife call. The bear slouched forward.

At fifty yards, a man stooped in its place.

"Are you okay?" shouted the trainer. There was no reply.

People seldom walked the dead-end road to his farm and never at night. His hounds lagged shoulder to shoulder as he approached the stranger, halting ten feet from the lowered head.

"Hey, you all right? I didn't know what you were. In fact, I thought . . ." The stranger sidled a step closer, raised his head, comically waved his palm beside his ear, and said, "Hi, Jack."

As if fingers cinched the trainer's larynx, his voice was stifled.

The trainer stared into the face before him, a caricature of a face he once had known well. No skull seemed to frame the head or anchor the features. Indolent eyes appeared to float like buoys no longer moored in the brain. Nothing looked symmetrical, nothing solid to the touch. The hounds' jaws clacked as they absorbed the tension which flowed through the leashes and they moodily encircled the trainer's boots.

Again he heard his wife, her voice become strained and insistent above the belligerent cacophony of the kenneled hounds. "I'm speechless," he said, shifting leashes to his left hand and extending his right hand in greeting.

The hunched man lowered his head, glanced at the dogs, and limped around them to the other side of the road. "What's wrong with them?"

"They are very high-strung. Jesus, I thought you were a bear," said the trainer to fill the space between them. Dumbly, as if motion required all his concentration, the stooped man swayed ahead.

"We have a son. Did you know? He's almost three now."

The man turned into the driveway. His tortoise indifference, his laborious rocking motion, ate away the trainer's disbelief.

"You know, we actually heard last spring that you went out a window."

"Really?" The man dragged his fingers the length of the jeep.

"Yes; would you believe that last spring we heard you had committed suicide?"

He stopped and twisted back his head. After a moment he murmured, "I didn't come to see *you*." The trainer rapidly walked ahead.

A woman stormed onto the porch and seeing the green glow of the hounds' eyes, stopped short. "Didn't you hear me?" Television voices followed her outside through the ajar door.

"I'll lock up the dogs, I'll be right in." The trainer pulled the hounds around the corner of the house.

The crippled man entered the globe cast by the light and stood on the lowest step. He smiled up at the woman, porch light whitening the part in her coarse black hair. "Who are you?" she said.

The man made a pained noise, scowled, and looked away. His jaw hung and he turned back to her and gawked at her dark wide-set eyes.

"Mark, remember me, I'm Mark Craeger," and his mouth stretched into a long grin. Craeger crouched up the steps and moved around her as if she were not alive but a marvelous inanimate thing he had happened upon and wished to inspect. He touched her hand. He rubbed the fabric of her loose khaki trousers between his fingers.

"These are not your pants," he said.

"We both wear them."

Craeger grimaced theatrically as the trainer opened the door behind her. His stoop intensified. His shoulder brushed the woman's hip as he lumbered past her husband and into the house.

Straightaway Craeger scrutinized the face of the child. He stroked a twine of black hair from the boy's fleshy bright cheek and it sprang back. Transfixed in the highchair by a giraffe dunking its neck between splayed forelegs to reach water, the boy chewed a porkchop bone and continued to ogle the television. The woman watched Craeger hover near her son and quickly brought another plate and silverware to the table. Craeger sat next to the child. His acrid smell saturated the room.

"Joel," said the trainer, "this is Mark."

A herd of wildebeest smoked across the savanna, an elephant fanned its ears, a parrot squealed, and from nowhere a lion straddled the gouged remains of a zebra.

"Zebra horse," burst Joel, pointing with his chop. Joel's upper lip protruded and he rested his wet chin on the brass buttons of his overalls. Sideways, he regarded Craeger, who was bent close to the plate, noisily swallowing the porkchops, beets and salad placed before him.

"Mark eat porkchops," Joel observed aloud. "Mark eat cucumbers." Craeger contorted his face, stuck out his beet-mauve tongue and wiggled it at Joel. Joel banged his head against the back of the highchair and let out a long ticklish laugh. The vein in his temple distended and his small mouth showed sharp, spaced teeth. "Mark funny man," he announced.

Craeger took the last chop and stuffed it into the side pocket of his navy suit jacket. "Do you like him?" he mumbled. Joel climbed down from his highchair, toddled to the latched door leading to the playroom, and twisted the knob with both hands. Unsuccessful, he slapped his palm against the door.

"Does who like who?" the woman said to the bristled peak of Craeger's head.

"No, Joel," his father said. Joel flushed, fell on his rump and gaveled on the door.

"*You* the *boy*," said Craeger.

She snorted smilingly and did not reply.

"This is some place, Fran, you must love it here," said Craeger.

"We do," said the trainer.

"Must put a lot of pressure on one another, so far from people. Not to get bored, I mean."

"There's a lot to do," said the trainer.

"Gee, and those are some animals you have," said Craeger. "How many do you have anyway?"

"Ten."

"Ten dogs! That must cost a pretty penny. Why so many?"

"I raise them for the track."

"Gives you something to do, I suppose." Craeger bent forward with a warm smile. "Why do you answer all the questions, Jack; is Fran forbidden to talk?" The trainer laughed and as his laughter died, Craeger added, "Is something *wrong* here?"

The trainer slumped back and benignly enlarged his eyes. "What can I say? Fran, have I cut your tongue out?"

Joel's rhythmic hammering ceased the moment his father rose to unhook the door. Joel pulled himself up by his father's leg and turned the knob. Listening behind the door, a greyhound scuttled to its feet, its claws clattering on the bare hardwood as Joel darted into the playroom.

"This is inane," said Frances. She snapped off the television and began to clear the table. Joel returned from his toybox with a miniature dump truck and fire engine and placed them on the table beside Craeger's elbow. Craeger ignored them.

A white bitch stared from the open door. "This is Milka. We're about to breed her. See what happens, Mark, when they're in heat," said the trainer. He pressed his knuckles along her sinuous back. When he reached the base of her spine, the tail switched mechanically to the side.

"This pump truck," said Joel, steering the red fire engine on the edge of the table. "Hydraulic dumper." Craeger pursed his lips, his eye fastened on the bitch.

Twice the white greyhound warily stalked around the table, stirred by Craeger's new scent. Her serpentine body crouched at last, sphinxlike, behind Joel. "Wow, she's something," said Craeger and started to growl louder than the siren sounds that Joel made to accompany his fire engine.

"Don't make that noise," ordered the trainer.

Craeger persisted. Suddenly Craeger batted the fire engine and dump truck at the hound. Milka started before they hit the floor. Her black lips twitched back to unsheath her fangs. Craeger hissed and taunted. The trainer clutched Milka's collar, dragged her to the playroom, and held the door closed.

Joel gathered his vehicles and rushed to clasp his mother's legs. She hoisted him to her breast. Belatedly his face puckered and he wept. Craeger remained seated. He withdrew the porkchop from his pocket and, in a droll manner, commenced to chew at it.

The trainer felt his hands and feet go cold. "Take Joel upstairs. Latch this door behind you."

Craeger deposited the cleaned bone on the table and, as if he would nap, sank into himself.

"There are rules, Mark, human decencies. I don't know what has happened to you and I don't hold myself or Frances responsible for it. Do you understand that? This is our house and if you stay here you'll act like a human being. You won't provoke the dogs, you will not . . . do you understand? Are you listening to me?"

Craeger's compliant posture had deflected all his words. For emphasis, that some contact be made, he seized Craeger's wrist. Craeger's parted lips dropped to kiss the back of the trainer's hand. His hand retracted. Craeger raised his varnished sulphur-colored eyes and scrolled his upper lip beneath his nosetip.

"What do you want here?" said the trainer. He fixed upon Craeger's white skin, hairs separate on the boneless cheek. He had no more words. Craeger's exorbitant expressions failed to signify any state of being which he recognized. "Human decencies, human decencies"—uncanny, drained of sense—resounded like a heckler's voice and heat compressed around his eyes.

"He's a great little boy," said Craeger. He wrinkled his nose and averted his head.

The trainer turned wearily and paced through the kitchen to the dark corridor of the shed. The cold burned his wet face. In the kennel below, the ears of the nine hounds crooked to follow his footsteps. The hounds scurried from their stalls down ramps to the runs outside. They fidgeted hungrily, barking, anxious to be let out.

He switched on the floodlights and descended to the kennel. Hardened by the wind, the ground was already crisp beneath his boots. He let out two males. The larger sauntered over the moonlit field and waited for the smaller fawn greyhound to challenge. Nose to the ground, the fawn dog carefully meandered, urinated on the smoking grass, sniffed, all the while closing the space between them.

Swiftly the challenger bolted and left the other champing in pursuit at his flanks. Their sharp-knuckled paws drummed across the field. They shrank in the distance, merged and vanished. A faint drumming continued, grew loud, and neck and neck they pelted toward the trainer, humped, lashed out, humped like giant ferrets. The fawn greyhound rippled past him, a muzzle ahead. His tongue slapped on his lathered cheek, his lemur eyes emerald in the moonlight. The fawn greyhound, the trainer decided, would sire Milka's litter.

Craeger stood back from the kitchen window, sucked at the milk carton spout, and once more reeled forward to peer

into the yard. He hooted contentedly. Under floodlights outside, the greyhounds wriggled like snakes around the trainer.

Craeger jeered and tilted back the milk carton.

Frances's voice cautioned Milka. Girded by an air of preoc-
cupation, she slipped into the dining room, hooked the playroom door, and directly strolled to the kitchen. Craeger set
the milk carton on the windowsill and crossed to the sink.
Silently he hunched beside her. He watched her strong fingers scour fork tines and spoons. He confronted her quietly
with his close huddled presence until she acknowledged him.
"Joel takes to me," he said.

"He doesn't see many people," said Frances.

"I think this is a bit extra special, don't you?" Craeger
nudged her and with a grunt, stood straight.

"Why do you walk all doubled over if you can stand up?"

Craeger whistled admiration. "Fifty-four bones I broke. I
am a cripple. Fifty-four bones." To stress the point, he clown-
ishly resumed a deepened slouch.

"How are you doing? You're not as pretty as you used to
be, you know that?"

"No?"

"And I know why."

"Well, then, tell me," she said archly.

"Because Jack is a *bad* person," he declared.

"Think that," snapped Frances.

Craeger pressed against her hip. His lower lip drooped and
he stretched to kiss her blunt jawbone. Frances lightly shoved
him and he collapsed at her feet. He smirked, reached up
and patted the buckle of her belt. "You're going all rotten
in there. All rotten." He knit his limbs and folded up at her
feet like a great-headed fetus spilled from a jar of
formaldehyde.

Frances petulantly filled the sink with dishes, made a bed
of the playroom couch, and led restive Milka to the isolation
pen at the side of the house. "You can sleep in the playroom,"
she informed Craeger stiffly. He lounged at the table like a

drunkard, swished the carton and swallowed, milk drooling down his neck into his collar. "There will be towels on the bed. The bathroom is on the left," Frances concluded and headed upstairs.

"I wouldn't shit in your toilet," he exclaimed.

Craeger rolled the empty milk carton from one corner of the table to the other and waited. When he heard the heavy footsteps on the porch he listed forward on the table and closed his eyes. The trainer softly locked the front door, turned off the porch light, and stepped to the playroom door. His fingers were checked on the doorknob: "It was this time of the year five years ago we first saw Fran," said Craeger. He had not shifted position. His gray lids remained shut.

"I remember," said the trainer, uncertain whether he should go on, stand, or join Craeger at the table.

"On a red horse. She looked so fine." Craeger's words seemed to roll out by themselves. "What a beauty. I loved her, did you know that?" Craeger shivered and sat up. He chewed as if his mouth had gone dry. "What's happened to her anyway?"

"What do you mean?"

"Frances is a *bad* person now," he pronounced.

The trainer stood. "And why do you say that?"

"You know full well." Craeger's smile assumed complicity. His lids flagged. "Good night, Jack," he said with a nod of dismissal.

"Good night," the trainer repeated. That he had not refuted the charge in Craeger's smile annoyed him the instant he left the room. He climbed upstairs and paused. He listened to Joel's breathing, crossed the landing and sat on the foot of the bed to tug off his boots.

"Well?" The shade-blackened room amplified her voice.

He undressed and lay beside her. He reached out and touched the flannel over her hip. "Nightgown?"

"You shouldn't have let him come. My God, he was supposed to be dead, I thought."

"I didn't invite him."

"Make him go," she demanded, "tomorrow. I don't want him around Joel. He stinks."

"How generous."

"Isn't it true? And he's crazy, Jack."

"You have an awful short memory." She did not answer. "Besides, where can he go?"

"That's not our problem," she said. "You can't help him."

"I care about him."

"Why? He hates your guts."

"Oh?"

"He said as much. He said you were a *bad* person."

In the next room Joel thrashed a bar of the crib and squealed in his sleep. Frances tiptoed to the crib and patted his back until Joel hummed briefly and at last resumed an even sleep.

"He didn't come to see me, you know," the trainer said decisively on her return.

She was silent, thinking for a long while before she said, "Sometimes I wish I didn't even exist until we got married."

"That's stupid."

She was still awake when her husband twitched and his breathing deepened into sleep. She heard the dogs stir in the kennel and moan dismally for access to Milka's swollen heat.

Past midnight the high-pitched moans changed to a fearful and aggressive summons. She shivered from a doze. She leaned over her husband and wrinkled back the shade. She shook him. "He's leaving, he's leaving," she cried.

In the white moonlight below, Craeger trundled toward the orchard. He rummaged in the frost-stiff grass at the edge of the garden. Then he lowered his trousers and for some minutes crouched on his white hams. Then, he shambled back to the farmhouse.

2

Impatient that his day get going, Joel clutched the crib bars and rocked the crib.

"Fine thing, to dread going down your own stairs," said Frances. She wrapped her trouser leg into the woolen sock and laced her boot.

"I said I'd talk to him. It doesn't have to be brutal," he said.

"It is already. Why did Joel toss all night? And the dogs? Get him out, Jack. That's more important than your sentimental manners."

"Sentimental? He was a close friend, you were in love with him. Is that sentimental?"

"Get him out," she repeated.

"All right, I said I'll tell him."

She left the room and with Joel slung on her hip reappeared at the door. "Morning, Joel," crowed the trainer. Joel happily whipped his body.

"We'll be outside today," she said and went down.

Untouched, the two towels hung on the back of the couch. The bed had not been slept in. She kneed open the door and saw Craeger's back curved over the table. Eggshells circled a stack of Joel's books, the milk carton, and the pork bone. "Look! Look here, Joel. A panda snoozing in the bamboos," said Craeger. He flagged the picture at Joel. Joel squirmed and reached to Craeger. "Get down, get down," he insisted.

"Help Mommy make the oatmeal," countered Frances. She humored him into the kitchen and while she prepared breakfast, held him on her side.

When she perched Joel on the counter, however, his lips refused to unseal for the spoon. At last she yielded and sat at the table. Craeger flattened his ear to the table and frowned like a physician discerning an irregular pulse. He proceeded meticulously to cleave the eggshells with his thumbnail. Each time a shell cracked, Joel's mouth gaped with hilarity and

Frances deposited a spoonful of oatmeal. She felt blood rise suddenly to the surface of her face; Craeger's decoy was not for Joel—he had tricked her into sharing a domestic travesty, and each time an eggshell was splintered on the table, it was as if he cracked a beetle's shard.

The trainer heard Joel's laughter before he entered the dining room. This day he had not expected to hear laughter and find everyone seated together. "Good morning, Jack," said Craeger, lifting his head. "Are you as hungry as I am?" He smirked askance at Frances, who had offered him nothing. She worked Joel's feet into the gum-rubber boots and snapped up his coat. She failed to catch her husband's eye as he ambled to the refrigerator. "There's enough oatmeal for both of you on the stove," she said, grabbed her jacket, and led Joel tripping outdoors.

He put up coffee and dished the thickened oatmeal into two bowls. He placed a bowl at Craeger's littered end of the table. "Been eating an egg?"

"Eggs," said Craeger.

The trainer ate his oatmeal. He watched Craeger's forefingers swab viscous cereal from the bowl.

"Well, what do you have planned, Mark?"

Extravagantly perplexed, Craeger tilted back his head and narrowed his eyes.

"What do you want to do, I mean?"

"Visit."

The trainer noticed the red light glowing on the percolator. "How do you have your coffee?"

"Cream and two teaspoons of honey."

"Honey?" He smiled, shrugged, filled the order and served the coffee. He swished hot coffee through his teeth and said in a tight pleased voice, "So, you really think I'm a *bad* person?"

Craeger concentrated on the trainer's soft eyes.

"I know you said it. How could Fran have known you used

the exact same words about her?" The logic braced him and he sat.

"She does know, then?" asked Craeger. "Very good."

The trainer paused a moment too long, nodded, and Craeger drank coffee and spoke nothing.

"It would be better if you left."

"But I just arrived."

"We both think it would be better."

"Better?"

"We have to breed dogs today. You antagonize the dogs. And last night Joel . . ."

"Joel likes me," interrupted Craeger, "a lot."

"Yes, but last . . ."

"I wanted to be with you and Fran. There aren't many people I want to see again. I've spent too much time alone in hospital rooms, so much that I forget how to talk. I wanted to visit you first . . ."

"It's not possible right now."

"And then maybe afterward I'll travel around, maybe go to Peru with somebody, or British Columbia."

"I'll drive you to town this afternoon."

Craeger drew in his neck and settled sulking, contracted in his chair.

"You'll be able to catch a bus." Resolve drove each word out his mouth. His eyes avoided Craeger and he walked outside to the porch. If he remained in the room, discomfort would prime more words and in the end, he would relent.

He ignored the hounds' hallooing and strolled down to the garden. Cusps of frost lingered in the shadows of the house. In the open the day was brilliant and warm. He pulled corn-stalks and flung them onto the pile of frost-lurid tomatoes, purple squash and wizened black peppers. With a stick he chiseled the hard ground and crawled down rows where tur-nips, beets and carrots had grown, his fingers rooting the cold broken earth to harvest whatever Frances had overlooked.

He stopped working and knelt back on his heels. All at once the fact that he had left Craeger alone in the house surged through his body strewing images of a room on fire, a rifle aimed at a greyhound's brisket. Anxiously he scanned the side of the house. His eyes fastened to a darkness shifting upstairs behind his bedroom window.

He sprang up and ran to the house. He charged through the empty dining room, the playroom, and up the stairs.

Gazing into the rectangular mirror which rose behind the opened drawers of the commode, Craeger gritted his teeth as he raked a brush over his stiff cropped hair.

"What are you doing here?" gasped the trainer, pounding into the room.

Craeger replaced the hairbrush on the marble top of the commode and said, "You never even showed me around your house."

Only after he had noticed Craeger's navy suit jacket pouched on the sheets of his unmade bed did he realize that his own tweed sport coat was draped around Craeger's body. "Get out of here," he screamed. He bunched Craeger's suit jacket in his fist and halted. Beneath the jacket was an album of photographs taken from a shelf in Joel's bedroom. The album was turned to a page on which Frances crouched in a meadow to forage for blueberries, opposite Frances in her gold swimsuit counting periwinkles with naked Joel on a pink granite shore by the ocean.

"Do you need this jacket?" Craeger asked, holding out the wide tweed lapels.

"Get out of here," the trainer said. "Here." He tossed the blue suit jacket to Craeger. The jacket hit his shoulder and fell to the floor. Craeger disregarded it and lurched slowly downstairs. The trainer picked up the jacket and followed. Craeger returned to his end of the table and sat.

"Let's go, Mark, you can catch the bus."

"I don't have any money."

The trainer walked to the kitchen counter and wrote a check for one hundred dollars. He slapped it on the stack of Joel's picture books beside Craeger. Craeger officiously read the check and folded it in half. He slanted on one buttock to slide the check into his trouser pocket.

"Now let's go. I'll drive you to the station." Craeger refused to move. "Don't make me force you."

Craeger chose a book about steam shovels and leafed through its pages. The trainer wrenched him from the seat by his elbow. Craeger slackened and was dragged out to the porch. "Now get in the jeep."

Craeger squirmed loose. "No," he simpered.

"Walk, then," and he threw shut the front door. He spied the suit jacket dumped in a chair seat, rushed it to the door, and slung it onto the porch. Craeger stood where he had left him, the suit jacket coiled about his shoes. Once again the trainer closed the door. He listened a moment, locked the door, and with his open palm began to sweep the bone and eggshells over the edge of the table into the empty milk carton.

Outside, Craeger scuffled to the end of the porch and as if he had reached the prow of a dinghy, stopped short to survey the long hazardous swell of field, orchard and tapering road. Around the corner of the house he glimpsed Milka prowling the margin of her isolation pen. Craeger stretched and, crooning, squatted against the clapboard wall, his knees drawn under his chin. He took the check from his trouser pocket and from inside his tweed sport coat retrieved a small photograph: Frances's head was lowered and her cheeks facetiously bulged as she perused her pregnant belly; her fingers interlocked to measure, to substantiate its impossible girth. Expressionless, Craeger examined the photograph carefully before he inserted it in the creased check and replaced both inside his new sport coat. He felt the tremor of pacing through the downstairs. The tremor diminished, dogs began to bark, and Craeger watched the road. A truck had stopped far down the road and he saw two tiny figures begin to unroll slat fences and fasten them to the row of stakes.

Joel took him by surprise, roaming from behind the shed. He climbed the porch steps and approached, coyly drawing cider from a brown apple. "Where's Mommy?" Craeger asked.

"What Mark do?" Joel asked and quickly answered, "Mark sit on porch." Craeger giggled and pointed out the men putting up the band of snowfencing. Delighted, Joel tittered and sucked on the thawing apple. Presently Frances tramped around the shed, fronds of asparagus and empty milkweed pods bunched in her fist.

"That's a pretty bouquet," remarked Craeger.

"Isn't it lovely?" said Frances. "Is that Jack's coat?"

"No," said Craeger, "he gave it to me. Know what those fence guys are doing out there? Quarantine."

Frances smiled, pushed on the locked door, turned the knob, and rapped. "Is he home?"

"I don't think so," said Craeger.

Frances knocked again. "What?" answered the trainer fiercely.

"We're back."

Craeger chortled as the door opened and Joel heaved his apple off the porch. Frances took Joel's arm and pulled him into the dining room. The trainer slammed and locked the door.

"I forgot the watchword," bantered Frances.

He shoved her against the door. Joel scooted to the kitchen chewing his fingers. "It's no joke, he's warped."

Frances sidestepped meekly and placed the palms of asparagus and milkweed pods in an amethyst-colored jar. She centered the arrangement on the table. "What's happened?" She restrained Joel as he streaked toward the playroom and removed his coat.

"I wanted to give him every chance. Malignant is the only word, malignant."

"Did you ask him to go?"

"He made me kick him out." She saw the edge was gone from his anger.

"Aren't you going a bit overboard?" She opened the cupboard and pushed cans.

"I caught him ransacking our bedroom."

"Are you serious? What was he doing?"

"He'd been into the drawers. The photo album was out. He was using my hairbrush."

"And so you gave him your tweed jacket?"

"He already had it on. I don't want a thing he's touched. I threw the brush in the trash."

Frances locked a soup can in the can opener and ground off its lid. "Then call the county sheriff," she suggested calmly.

"Just keep the door locked. Ignore him. He'll get hungry. How long can he stay? Pretend he isn't there."

"What should I tell Joel?"

"Nothing. It would confuse him. Keep Joel away from him."

"He's gone out of his way to be friendly to Joel."

"It's a trick. Just pretend everything is the same. During Joel's nap we'll breed Milka. We'll use the shed door, that's all. Stay away from the porch."

"It's not reasonable, Jack. If he's out there we can't ignore him."

"You heard what I said."

He selected two short leashes from a peg in the shed. In pairs he exercised six of the greyhounds. The dogs tried to maneuver toward the isolation pen. The brindle bitch, who slashed jealously at the dogs, and a large surly red dog, he ran separately. When he attempted to coax the red hound back to the kennel, the dog bucked and pinwheeled but failed to slip his collar. The trainer whipped the leash twice. The red dog glared and cringed into the run.

The fawn greyhound seemed to understand he had been selected for stud. Leashed, he trotted obediently at the trainer's thigh. He brushed the hound's fine yellow coat in the shed and they entered the house.

"I'm not sure Joel's asleep yet. He was all keyed up," said Frances, turning from the sink. She walked to the landing, listened and returned. "Don't you want something to eat first?"

"No. Get a roll of gauze, I don't know how Milka will take to this."

Frances trailed them to the isolation pen. Milka greeted the fawn dog at the gate with a charge, then darted into a corner. The trainer shut himself and Frances inside the pen, released the dog, and waited.

The hounds stamped formally and frolicked. Frequently they halted and the dog nuzzled the bitch's ear or butted her shoulder and throat. She stood rigidly, switched aside her tail, and he dabbed his tongue over her unfurling heat. The dog mounted. The white bitch yelped, twisting back to gash his tensed neck. He dodged and paraded about her. His eyes bulged from his narrow head. Upright, his tail stirred the air like a sickle.

The trainer took the gauze roll from his wife. "She's too flighty. Hold him." He straddled Milka and wound the gauze around her closed snout. "Now bring him here to me; you steady Milka." He tugged the dog away and his wife held Milka's collar. His wife knelt on one knee and with the other braced the bitch's concave belly. She blinkered Milka's eyes with her elbow while her husband directed the fawn greyhound from behind.

The dog's glistening red nozzle emerged as he reared to clasp Milka's haunches. The trainer bent to guide it. Muted by the gauze muzzle, the bitch's screams persisted until the sperm jet was lodged, fully dilated, inside her.

"A tie," he said happily. He was sweating. The clonic lunges of the dog's body softened and the bitch relaxed.

Tousled black hair stuck to the bridge of Frances's wet nose. He looked at Frances and began to laugh.

"What modesty," said Frances. "Poor Milka." Frances scratched Milka's ear. "Christ, my legs and arms are all cramped."

"Why don't you go back in?" he said. "It could take another half hour."

"You can manage by yourself?"

"I think so." He switched positions with Frances. He supported limp Milka and held the dog's tawny withers to prevent him from rolling off. Frances kissed his brow and groaned to her feet.

"Bravo, bravo," shouted Craeger before she had unpinned the gate to leave the isolation pen. "Do it again. What a show." Craeger racketed from the edge of the porch. His neck was lewdly crooked around the house corner. "Encore, encore, encore."

Frances indicated her disgust and trudged stonily to the shed entrance.

3

Saddled on the arm of the playroom couch, Joel peeped noiselessly out the window. Like the white wing of a moth, the back of Craeger's left ear was suspended outside the lower corner of the window. Joel pressed nearer to the glass. The navy suit jacket turbaned the rest of Craeger's head and his body was clenched against the chill.

"Dessert, Joel," Frances called into the playroom.

Milka looped back her neck and haltingly licked her loins. She gobbled the bit of chicken breast the trainer pitched by her snout and resumed the methodical bath. "We'll breed them again tomorrow."

Frances placed three dishes of pudding on the table. "Tapioca," she hollered.

The trainer considered the white bitch sprawled by the front door. "This litter should be something special." Frances nodded and marched into the playroom. Joel hovered by the window and watched her shadow stretch over Craeger's head and fill the cube of light cast from the playroom onto the dark porch. She cupped her hand on Joel's shoulder. "Come on, honey, tapioca pudding." He jumped to the blankets covering the couch. "Mark sleeps on porch," he said.

Frances carried Joel to the dining room and inserted him in the highchair. He dug his teeth into the center of the dish and wiped tapioca on his chin and throat.

"Are you tired?" his father asked him. Joel scooped more pudding and greased the deck of his highchair. The dish was confiscated. "He's overtired, Frances."

"Mark sleeps on the porch," said Joel.

The trainer glared at Frances. "What did I say about that?"

"About what?"

"Mark sleeps on the porch, Mark sleeps on porch," Joel agitated. His incantation worked.

"Not to say a thing to . . ." He completed his meaning with a nod at Joel.

Frances reached over Milka and snapped on the porch light. "What do you think Joel is, a moron?"

"Turn off that light."

"No."

He rose and slapped down the light switch. Milka moved skittishly to the kitchen. "Because you wanted him out *today,* I put myself through living hell this morning. I did what you wanted. Don't go back on it."

Frances lifted Joel between them. "And? Is he gone?" she said pointedly. "No, but we slink in and out of the back of the fort. You think that's what I wanted? To play this asinine game?" Joel gabbled loudly. "And don't say I'm upsetting Joel," she added. "He sees him camped on the porch. He feels how unnatural all this is."

The back of his hand flashed up, faltered, and his fingers

lightly stung her temple. Redness stippled her throat and ringed her eyes. Joel went silent, vague. "You had better get hold of yourself, Jack," she said blandly. "Go outside. Feed your dogs."

He followed her into the playroom. She picked out the farm puzzle and the circus puzzle and said, "We'll be upstairs." He loitered, resting on the blanketed couch. A wrecker truck, cement mixer, Ferris wheel, two wagons, a sprung jack-in-the-box, Noah's ark and dozens of plastic barnyard and exotic animals had overflowed the plentitude of Joel's toybox and were strewn on the braided rug. Unnatural? Her adamant hostility toward Craeger, Craeger's uncanny, insolent, obsequious and idiotically sinister behavior—that was unnatural. And now, after she had prodded him to turn Craeger out, she called him asinine. He glanced out the window behind him and discerned cowled Craeger huddled serenely in the half-light, asleep.

Listlessly, he walked through the downstairs and into the shed. He clustered nine dishes and filled them with dry meal. He left the floodlights off. He watched the woolly blue clouds mass along the hills and conceal the moon.

Blocking the entrance to each run with his body, he slid the feed dishes past the doors. The greyhounds tried to squeeze outside. Milka's season dwindled their appetites.

A thin cap of ice had formed on the water pans. The trainer cracked the ice and refilled the pans. Tonight the hounds were all the same to him and it was a chore to feed them. Bitter wind seared the matted field and forced him to the shed. He decided to renew his offer to drive Craeger to town. Perhaps the chill wind had changed Craeger's mind.

Milka accompanied him to the front door. As if she were readying to break from a trap, the white bitch crouched below the doorknob. He dragged her to the playroom and hooked the door. Then he flicked on the porch light and went out.

Craeger dropped a drumstick into the tiny heap of picked chicken bones on the porch deck and snuggled the patchwork quilt about his neck. He revolved his head and raised his eyes. "Yes?" he asked.

The trainer stared at the remnant of his meal. He stooped, and one by one gathered the moist bones. "These can injure dogs," he said remotely. He turned and walked to the door.

"Very well, then," said Craeger, "dispose of them."

The trainer softly closed and locked the door. He switched off the porch light, threw the chicken bones in the waste can and for a long time cleaned his hands at the kitchen sink. His body moved heavily. A nerve mass in the base of his neck had begun to sting, and each step through the house and up the stairs made the sensation of burning grow worse.

He watched from the door of Joel's bedroom. Frances hushed him and resumed the lullaby. Her legs were tucked beneath her and one arm rubbed Joel's back through the bars of the crib.

He leaned on the doorjamb and isolated a puzzle piece by her heel, a ballerina in a handstand on a speckled draft horse. Humming the song, Frances got carefully to her feet. She checked Joel and whispered, "I thought he would never fall to sleep. We made those puzzles fifty times." She moved close to the trainer at the head of the stairs. Her broad angular features appeared to him unusually distinct, yet much farther away than he knew she was.

"Are you okay, Jack?" She did not wait for his answer. She passed him quickly and walked downstairs to wash.

"Why did you feed him?" he asked, but she did not hear or did not wish to reply.

He was leaning on the doorjamb, his back to her, when Frances returned and she was frightened. "I'm bushed. Are you coming to bed?" she asked, retreating to the bedroom. He held the banister and as if plated in mail, descended.

He sat on the couch. Hanging from brass chains of the playroom chandelier, the blue coronas of four bulbs nettled him. The rhythmic clack of Milka's tread deadened on the braided rug. When he put his face against hers, the ceiling light, her long skull, and his head were momentarily aligned, just so, and he looked through her eye. A dark-red web of vessels squirmed in amber liquid. It was there, he thought, in that web, a sight hound lived.

He turned off the four lights and in the dark massaged the base of his skull and let his neck loll over the back of the couch. Silently, Milka bounded onto the couch and nestled into a ring beside him, her sharp muzzle across his lap. Again and again his fingertips traced a line from her damp nostrils to the bone ridge between her warm, velvet ears. When he quit, she whined and nuzzled his stomach. He drooped his head forward and pushed Milka off the couch. His foot bumped the jack-in-the-box and it whistled like a bellows as he moved along the wall.

He fed Milka in the shed and whisked her by the mob of hounds to the isolation pen. On his way back through the downstairs, he put out the remaining lights. He pulled back the blanket and sheet on the couch and, fully dressed, stretched into the makeshift bed his wife had fixed for Craeger.

Like a blizzard, the baying of the confined greyhounds filtered into the house and he straggled in and out of sleep. Before the night had elapsed, Joel's murmurings, the dogs' rutting din, the rumble of the furnace in the cellar all blended together and the air seemed to jangle and scream as it circulated through the playroom. He started up in the blackness, uncertain whether his eyes were open or shut, if he imagined the chaos blaring from the kennel. He turned to the window to see if Craeger had left the porch once more to defecate but could barely determine the outline of the window.

He kicked aside the sibilant jack-in-the-box, jarred three carnival notes from the Ferris wheel and stumbled his way toward the shed. The tumult of the greyhounds had grown frenzied. He groped about the mortised timbers in the shed to locate the floodlight switch.

The abrupt effulgence of the floodlights dazed him. From

the shed steps he squinted, white-blind, to comprehend the pandemonium below.

Two enormous many-colored wings flapped spookily back and forth along the block of runs. Fanning the patchwork quilt like plumage of a mating display, Craeger strutted past the fawn and black greyhounds, stamped outside the red hound's door and shook his quilt. Purple and white jaws snapping the air, spines bristled, the greyhounds lunged at the fence. The red dog thrashed and crazily rammed the chain-link wall.

The trainer seized Craeger's back and hurled him to the ground.

Craeger drew in his head, doubled up, and sheltered himself beneath the quilt. The trainer stabbed his foot into the mute cushion and waited.

Motionless as some garish fungus under the floodlights, Craeger did not respond. "Bait my dogs," screeched the trainer, and his heel came down on the quilted mound.

Timorously the quilt began to creep, over the frozen ground. Craeger draped a quilt corner on his shoulders so he could see, and lumbered out of the spotlit ring on all fours.

The trainer kept pace, exactly beside him. Craeger turned the edge of the house and crawled before Milka to reach the raised porch. Breathing quickly, he clambered onto the porch and wound himself in the quilt.

The trainer scanned the flat black sky. Little as yet suggested the coming day. He addressed the murky shape on the porch: "It will be light in less than an hour. If you are on my property then, I'm going to call the police and have you arrested."

An amused gasp erupted from Craeger's throat. "Arrest this man, Sheriff," he gruffly imitated. "The charge?" he inquired. "Well, officer, he's my child's rightful father." Dialogue completed, Craeger forced a yawn, cocked the side of his head to his kneetops and watched the trainer's silhouette melt into the clapboards and vanish.

Milka jostled the fence of the isolation pen. He drifted by her and the row of pent hounds pranced as though the pebble floor seared their footpads. He made no attempt to pacify them.

From the shed cabinet he selected a box of cartridges and took down his rifle. He pulled the cord of the single bulb above the workbench and wiped a rag along the cold barrel.

He carried the rifle and ammunition into the house. He vaguely distinguished Joel's toys now on the playroom floor. He sidestepped them and sat on the couch. He removed the lens caps, drew back the bolt of the rifle and loaded five cartridges. He worked with precision.

He lay the rifle on the disheveled couch and, one level at a time, moved up the flight of stairs. He crossed his bedroom and furrowed back the shade next to the bed. All he could make out were the ribbons on the prim collar of her night-gown. Her deep, distanced breaths did not convince him she was sleeping, but it made no difference, so far had she and their bed receded from his eyes. He let the shade fall and slid into Joel's room. He did not stop to look into the crib. He parted the curtains of the window opening on the road, raised the shade and began his vigil.

More than an hour he watched the dark enclosure of sky. Joel chirped and smacked his lips. The first light appeared, to seep up through the bone-colored road and the hoarfrost between rows of apple trees. Still, he lingered at the window and listened for a signal.

A silver-red sunspot filled a niche in the one-dimensional hill line. Like a snake issuing from a black fissure the spot stretched silver-red along the undulating rim of hills until its limbless train encircled the horizon.

Momentarily, the alert sounded, remote, inexorable, from the kennel and he spied Craeger slouching from the porch and down the driveway. He watched the pallid form veer suddenly toward the garden. It was not the form of a person at all. It was the distorted shape of wile without spine, the lies and deception on which his life had rested.

Craeger made a dozen laggard and undecided steps and halted. He stood absolutely stiff. He turned slowly, all the way around, and he looked up at the single shining pane of glass behind which the trainer kept watch.

The trainer hastened down the stairs. He clutched the rifle and stalked through the house to the kennel where greyhounds ricocheted off the chain links.

He swung open the red greyhound's door.

The red dog vaulted from the run and vanished before the trainer was able to discharge the black dog, the fawn dog and the brindle bitch, one after the other.

He replaced the pin in each door and walked around the corner of the shed.

Beneath an apple tree, halfway between the garden and the snowfence, the hounds swarmed over the bulge of Craeger's body.

The trainer sat on the frigid turf.

The greyhounds' pointed heads converged, bobbed and wagged savagely. They flipped the body on its back and the four snouts plunged to carve. The swarm became clear, stylized, the revolving figures of a merry-go-round. He steadied the circular reticle of the scope behind a dog's shoulder blade. He was deaf to the report of the rifle as the fawn greyhound twisted into the grass.

Bewildered, the brindle bitch arched her head at gaze and somersaulted when the bullet tore into her chest.

The black hound bolted fearfully toward his trainer. Steaming muzzle, throat and forelegs were dark silver with blood. Another shot and the hound sagged and flattened, kicking on the driveway.

Frances burst screaming out the front door.

The large red greyhound cowered in confusion over Craeger's body and the trainer fired. The dog yelped and hobbled toward the woods. Frances shoved his shoulder and his last shot hit nothing. Her face was deranged. She saw the figure heaped at the edge of the orchard.

"Set, Set," called the man after the red greyhound.

"Good God, no please . . ."

"Three dogs."

"My God . . . no, no, you didn't, no."

"They jumped the run to get at him." A red slash, the greyhound disappeared into the leafless trees. "The dogs, I killed them."

A squeal broke from the upstairs bedroom. Frances crumpled on the ground. He put down the rifle. He clamped Frances's elbow and jerked her to her feet. "Call the sheriff . . . hurry . . . do you hear me, quick, he may still be alive," and he glided over the streaked frost.

# Halloween
# Window-Painting
# Contest

Once again children are painting storefront windows. The Halloween window-painting contest is under way. According to contest rules, *paintings will be judged for Originality, Neatness, Technique and Halloween or autumn theme.* All along Main Street teams of youngsters are at work before the windows assigned them. From her stepladder perch, a girl giggles at the boy shaking a jar of orange paint and points out an impeccably defended, broad-shouldered small-rumped gentleman of fifty who approaches them. Nearby, while their teammate applies a grid of tape to the window, exactly to transfer their finished design, another girl stops pondering a sheet of graph paper unfolded on the sidewalk to watch the stride of this elegant dour figure, steam rhythmically shooting out his nostrils. This is Mr. D., one of the local merchants sponsoring the contest. His overcoat is black cashmere, hat chestnut-colored with a band of pheasant feather. On his long and surprisingly high-bouncing legs he goes, now four blocks from his place of business (above the foyer a black cursive *D's*, gilt-rimmed on a black enameled field) in the heart of the former business district of the town. Passing each group of window painters he pinches the brim of his hat.

Despite the bright blue October morning Main Street is devoid of traffic. Mr. D. has supported every plan to revitalize the former business district. Parking meters were beheaded, shade maples planted around a new stainless steel fountain on a traffic isle. Geranium baskets were suspended from telephone poles and streetlamps. Unattractive buildings were razed for new banks and parking space. Main Street is, these and other beautification projects notwithstanding, empty of customers. As his employees know, Mr. D. enters his four-story brick building punctually at ten o'clock. Today, reading by the second-story window, Leona glances up, shuts *The Windswept Wilds* in her lap (where in a frosty tower Geoffery finally has trapped his daughter Marion) and spots the dimpled chestnut crest of Mr. D.'s hat bouncing along the sidewalk below.

"Mr. D., Mr. D.," and Leona's signal shoots across the second floor to an emery board which stops filing a torn nail so that Joan may pull aside the dark curtain and assume her station; down to the first floor to abridge Rhoda's explanation to a disconsolate soldier in the phone booth of a nearby military complex; deeper down, to the basement, where Peter Quimby conceals his flask in his sock and slips two white mints onto his chalky tongue; and reverberates up, up through the now-vacant third floor to the fourth and topmost floor—closed to the general public—to arrest the stroke of the brush sunk in Maria Zentana's sparking, crackling black hair.

The alarm was premature, however, for Mr. D. stands quietly outside the foyer whose glass walls contain those arrangements which he contrives with such passionate attention to detail and symmetry. He is gazing upon the lone, lean girl painting a section of his showcase. Gloomy curiosity darkens his iron-colored face. "Are you working alone, young lady?" he inquires.

She sets down her paintbrush, pulls her green socks up to the points of her diamond-shaped kneecaps and stands much taller and more gaunt than Mr. D. expected. "Oh, yes," she says.

How old are you and what is your name because other children work in groups and your hair and eyelids are salmon-orange, your flesh ghostly, your features at once striking and horrible and how thin you are so here is money, says married but childless Mr. D. to himself.

"I hope to win the prize," smiles the girl.

"That *would* be an honor," agrees Mr. D., envisioning a photograph of his storefront with its contest-winning window painting, his admiration directed at the white scalp line halving her head, his hand cupping her spearlike shoulder: the local paper's front page. "I trust you will add something of an autumn theme," suggests Mr. D., "cornstalks, a witch on a broomstick, a hobgoblin, bat or perhaps a moon?"

"A moon!" she says cheerily. "Yes, a moon."

"Have you a plan or model for your decoration, young lady?"

"Not yet."

"Ah, indeed, no," Mr. D. says and steps back, the better to appraise the black outline of a long banquet table sketched on his green window. "I will place your full moon at the very top," the girl decides aloud.

"Then by all means, yes, and good luck with it," Mr. D. says with a shudder and enters his foyer. The door opens before Mr. D. fingerprints its glass and Peter Quimby, a black *D's* on the breast of his gold livery, mumbles good morning. "Hello, Mr. D.," sings Rhoda, head bobbing, pencil nodding down an aisle of stock. Peter Quimby follows Mr. D. into the small, old-fashioned elevator and slides shut both doors.

Why are normal, happy children never selected to paint my windows? Mr. D. wonders. "Did you see the child outside, Quimby? Customers will be frightened off."

"She was out there when I opened," says Quimby eyeing the downsliding intervals, walls, and as the elevator stops at the dark third floor, adds, "Shame to cover up *your* window though." Quimby opens the doors smoothly and seals his minty lips.

"Thank you, Quimby," and silently, Mr. D. mulls: But why my building? Softly, Mr. D. murmurs "Damnation," and advances to his office at the rear of the empty floor. Quimby pushes the door closed and the elevator descends to the basement where he will remain until needed.

No sooner is Peter Quimby landed in the basement than he retrieves his flask, swallows, winces and begins to muse beside the elevator door. Quimby is exceedingly fretful because tomorrow is Sunday. He must devise some scheme to absent himself from his apartment. He cannot spend the long day with his infirm mother, his wife, their indiscriminate daughter and her three daughters: four generations of bitter Quimby women in one four-room apartment; no, he will not. He will not hear his wife read, as this morning she read, another age-old tale from her magazines . . .

Patrolman Ceazon arrived at the attractive brown ranch house of thirty-two-year-old millworker Alvin Gulin and Lorraine, Gulin's twenty-seven-year-old bride of five months at 5:43 P.M. The brawny clean-cut Gulin, who was showering when the patrolman entered, had himself called the authorities. Gulin ushered the patrolman into the kitchenette where Lorraine Gulin lay in a red pool on the brick-patterned linoleum floor. Patrolman Ceazon quickly determined that the shapely brunette was dead. Coroner Egle later determined that the body had been rent in eighty-one different places.

"Eighty-one! Good Lord!" shouted Quimby's mother. "In God's name, what need of eighty-one?"

Egle said that a wedge of lower lip had not been accounted for. Gulin, described by a neighbor as a "hot-tempered hard worker who kept to himself" readily admitted to the slaying. He had found a pair of Lorraine's panties in a pot on the stove, he said, and something "broke inside." Gulin had no previous record.

The account over, the eyes of four generations of Quimby women had come to rest in certain judgment upon Peter Quimby, as if *he* and not Gulin had lifted that kettle's lid and let murder fly out.

Small wonder he is no success when he lives to support the appetites of six women, concludes Quimby; when children are encouraged to paint store windows. Windows are smudged and Quimby must come along with a remedial rag and azure spray. Filth is tramped on Mr. D.'s floors and Quimby must come with oily dustbane and a mop. Dirt and garish monotony, discord and promiscuity: it is all of a piece. Is it surprising then, that Mr. D. is unsuccessful in business? D., who refuses to bend to fashion, customers, and women? D. alone lives a coherent, continent life. Numerous times Quimby has risen from one floor to another with Mrs. D., an aloof and thoroughly contained lady. Although Quimby is ten years older than Mr. D. (figures Quimby to himself as the elevator buzzes and he drops an answering mint onto his tongue), if Mr. D. were to live for the next decade as Quimby now lives, and if Quimby were to remain as he is on this Saturday morning, a stranger might take them for brothers.

*Buzz-zz-zzz-buzzz.*

It is unnecessary to glance at the indicator on the elevator wall. It could not be Mr. D.; his ring is an admirable impersonal *ZZZZZ*. Rhoda, engaged, makes her *Z-z*, and waits. Most often, Joan the divorcee goes *Buzzz-zzz-zz-z*. Leona the formidable widow jabs her muscular thumb on the button and keeps it there—*Buzzzzzzzzzzzzzzzzzzzzz*—until Quimby opens the doors to her intimidating scowl.

*Uzz-buz-zzz-buzzz-zuhh—*

No, the fourth floor is buzzing for him; Maria Zentana

summons. Zentana considers the elevator bell an instrument on which she can prove herself a virtuoso of hot-blooded rhythm and, simultaneously, with but a press of her purple-nailed forefinger, release enough voltage to levitate the elevator from the bottom of the building, Peter Quimby gnashing quietly inside.

How strangely intimate Quimby has become with the ways of the women who move on the floors above him; how frequently this or that one makes water in the fourth-floor bathroom, how much toilet paper is used, who properly disposes of tampons; how well he knows their intricate genius for cheating Mr. D. and belittling himself.

Abundant hip slung out, brown elbow against the wall, Maria Zentana points to her neck (half-dollar between two fingers), and hoarsely asks, "My throat is so dry, Mr. Quimby, would you run out for some tea?" Stoically he accepts the money, closes both doors, Maria Zentana taps on the glass, rasps "Lemon," smiles, and starting down now, Quimby notes the purple smear of lipstick on one of her wide white incisors.

*ZZZZZ.*

Quimby stops cleanly at the dark third floor and opens both doors for gray-lipped Mr. D., dressed for walking in his black cashmere overcoat and chestnut hat. Following his earlier interview with the odd young window painter, Mr. D. has passed the morning in his private office, shades drawn, at the rear of the vacant third floor.

"Slow today," says Quimby. "First?"

"Indeed," Mr. D. replies. As the elevator glides past the second floor there is a glimpse of Leona and Joan bustling down aisles. "Witches," mumbles Peter Quimby.

"Indeed," Mr. D. replies stepping onto the street floor. As Mr. D. uncoils a black scarf from his overcoat pocket, a crumpled paper is freed, hops to the floor and scurries into the elevator corner.

"Be sure to lock up carefully before you leave this evening."

Mr. D. hears neither Quimby's earnest "Trust me," nor Rhoda's mellifluous "Lunchtime, Sir?" Stilting through the foyer, he hovers momentarily behind the young girl who stretches to dab paint halfway up the window.

At such a moment the white scalp line of a girl's russet head can become identical to a peach's cleft. This accomplished, then the next step, of biting into soft peach-flesh, becomes at once simple, usual and desirable—even for a man of Mr. D.'s exemplary mores. On the verge of clasping between his manicured fingers an extraordinarily large peach and driving in his teeth, Mr. D. hears a request for a step-ladder or a stool.

"I can't reach high enough to paint your moon," she turns to explain. But the impetuous adult is off, galloping along the sidewalk half a block away.


Five p.m.: Quivered in a soldier's fist, long-stemmed roses enter D's, and the roses, Rhoda and the soldier march into the foyer and vanish; Leona and Joan forgo the elevator (i.e., Peter Quimby), and descend the staircase, the widow stridently recommending *The Windswept Wilds* to the divorcee; and *ZZ-buz-zzz-buzzz,* loosing her thick hair from under a dyed fox collar, Maria Zentana sinks through the darkened building with Quimby. "How will you pass your weekend?" she asks and half-smiling, springs out the glass door.

Peter Quimby stands on the street floor of an otherwise deserted D's. "Cruel dry-mouthed witch," Peter Quimby exclaims, and loiters by the entrance. He imagines Saturday night, Sunday morning, Sunday noon, afternoon and evening. Such a vast space. What to do?

All too soon, Quimby has emptied the ashtrays, buffed the floors, washed windows and even rubbed dust from the lobes of the rubber plant, gently, so they gleam silver in the shadows. Finally, the street floor wastebasket is all that is left between Quimby and the four-room inferno of Quimby women. When reluctantly he tramps across the floor to empty it, he passes three figures crooked like sickles in the three-way-mirror beside him. Before he can properly defend himself against the recognition that these objective and pitiless question marks are Quimby's stooped self in triplicate, he lets out a yelp and rushes to the elevator where he sits on the collapsible stool, head adroop. Suddenly, Quimby's eyes focus upon what looks to be a white carnation, the scrap of paper rumpled in the elevator corner. He reaches down for it, smooths it upon his knee:

> 8 Sunday night. Will be waiting upstairs—
> Alteration Room.

Embossed at the bottom of the paper are the creased lip-prints of a wide-open purple mouth.

"In the name of God," whispers Quimby, "in the name of . . ." and without further ado, his feet sing a hallelujah of themselves. Quimby is dancing on the street floor of D's. His hands clap jubilantly. Peter Quimby is doing a jig. He throws back his head and shouts, "Maria Zentana! I will be there. So blind. I have been so blind. Oh, Zentana!"

He fidgets the key into the resistant front door of D's and rattles the door to make certain it is locked. He wears a mere windbreaker in the nippy October night but his body is insulated with ebullience.

Hunched in the glow of streetlamp outside the foyer, the diligent young painter is still at work. Main Street is deserted. Astonished, Quimby stops and checks his watch. "It's late," he says. "Aren't you tired and cold?"

"Just my hands," the girl replies. She whistles steaming air onto her raw red fingers gripping the paintbrush.

"You are a dedicated window artist," says Quimby with a

flush of tenderness, and he looks up at the picture taking shape on the glass: There is a banquet table upon which sits an uncarved pumpkin. A man sits in full profile at one end of the table, a knife poised in one of his fists.

"To win the prize you *must* be dedicated," the girl explains. "If only I had a stool to stand on then I could reach more of the window." Quimby streaks into the foyer and returns carrying a chair. "Here. And use these," he says, scooping fuzzy blond work gloves from the pocket of his windbreaker.

"But then your hands will get cold."

"Tonight they won't, please," Quimby urges with delight, and with a hop to his every step, he is on his way home.

Normally, as he walks to or from D's Peter Quimby inveighs against a lurid haunch on the Bijou's marquee, an obscenity scrawled on a fence. Customarily he pauses atop the hill above his apartment in order sourly to survey the town. But this is no normal evening. Nothing whatsoever provokes Quimby on this Saturday evening.

Tonight he expends all his passion on the logistics of tomorrow's meeting with Maria Zentana. A satisfactory plan is not yet formulated when Quimby hears a familiar voice cry "Do you have the slightest idea what they cost?" and he finds himself facing the door of his apartment. Quimby pushes the door open and inspects the small porcelain bowl which his wife holds out for his perusal. "Look! This is what's left."

Quimby squints down at clusters of tangerine pits clinging to the bowl like petrified tears. His wife paces, stops short, and sets the evidence on the table before the elder Mrs. Quimby and the three Quimby granddaughters. "In five minutes he ate all six tangerines. Then he took your daughter and left. You know what she'll look like in the morning?" Quimby's wife points a significant stiff index at the moist pits in the bowl. "Was a single section offered the children?"

"Your daddy was just the same way, Peter."

"Guess what they cost," Quimby's wife demands of him.

"It doesn't matter," answers Peter Quimby, a scheme for

rendezvous with Maria Zentana crystallizing rapidly, "For starting tonight, I have taken a second job. I have become," Quimby says with a newfound lordliness, "A moonlighter."

"He's lying," Quimby's wife explains to the table. "What job?"

"There has been such a lot of vandalism and robbery in the town that Mr. D. has asked me to become his watchman."

"Watchman? What about the job you have."

"I will nap enough at night to perform during the day."

"You? He's lying through his teeth. How could *you* scare off a robber?"

"With the pistol," counters Quimby plausibly. "I must have the pistol of course."

"What will come of *us* without the pistol?" asks the wife.

"Houses are robbed too, Grandpa," quavers the eldest granddaughter.

Quimby, however, resolutely enters the bathroom and proceeds to stuff a grocery bag with his safety razor, after-shave lotion, brush and mug, toothbrush, a sample tube of toothpaste, deodorant, hairbrush and a washcloth. In the bedroom he slips the pistol from the nighttable but in haste, overlooks the clip of cartridges beside it. He wraps the pistol in the washcloth, covers the washcloth with the bold orchid shirt selected from the bottom drawer of the dresser, and, grocery bag popping with the staples of his new life, skips before the stupefied women and children, hesitates at the door long enough to blurt, "If necessary, I can be reached at D's," and is climbing the hill to the town when the elder Mrs. Quimby ends the silence: "Whatever that was, it wasn't Peter Quimby."

On entering D's foyer Quimby is halted by the chair. He recognizes his blond work gloves, arranged so they pinch a sheet of paper on the chair seat. He places the grocery bag on the ground floor and, drawing the paper to his face, reads the orange painted words:

> Thank you.
> You are a Good Man

What a day it has been, to receive two such notes as Peter Quimby has received! Merrily Quimby pockets the gloves and paper, unlocks the door and carries in the chair and grocery bag. Inside D's it is hushed and sober. Just as Quimby comes to realize he has never before been inside D's at this hour, a telephone rings rapid-fire up and down his back. He leaps across the street floor and snatches the receiver off its hook. "D's," exhales Quimby.

"Checking," informs his wife's voice, and the connection is broken. Quimby is trembling. He puts back the receiver and grinds together his teeth.

He returns to his grocery bag by the entrance, stoops and stiffens. Something is standing outside the front door. A burglar, thinks Quimby. Indigo, big as a thunderhead, there is a burglar outside the door. Light shines into Quimby's eyes. There follows a double rap on the glass but Quimby is unable to stand. Again a double . . . then a peevish double . . . then a thunderous triple knock storms upon the glass and Quimby rises as his elevator must rise to its appointed floor and twists open the lock. "Yes?"

"What are you doing on the floor?"

"I work here. I am the new watchman," answers residual guile.

"You are, huh? How'd you get in?"

"With my key," and promptly, a ring of keys is displayed. "Name?"

"Eleven years I have been with Mr. D., the owner. Call him. He will verify me."

"Name?"

"Quimby."

"Never seen a watchman here before."

"This is my first night. Before I worked days."

"What's in that bag?"

"A change of clothes. Toilet articles."

The officer slips off a soft brown leather glove, fits the key in the lock and bolts and unbolts the door a dozen times until apparently mollified, he returns the wallet and the key ring. Once again the telephone rings and Quimby streaks to silence it. "You think I'm a fool? I know you're lying," says the voice, and to the ensuing static, Quimby chuckles and loudly replies, "Yes . . . of course . . . don't worry, dear . . . certainly I'm alone . . . sweet dreams to you too."

"Keeping tabs?"

"Yes," admits Quimby sheepishly.

"They all do, Quimby, all of 'em. And for good reason, huh?" and with a salute of his gloved forefinger backs outside to continue on his rounds.

Quimby manages to lock the entrance, drag his grocery bag across the floor and into the elevator, descend to the basement. There, without switching on the light he recovers his flask, snuggles its cold neck into his lips and with small, intermittent gulps, realizes he should have passed the long stretch until Sunday night elsewhere.

To get a better grip on things, Peter Quimby snaps on the light, probes into his pocket and squints at Maria Zentana's message. The underlip-print, the fat one, has been smeared, but the odor of her lipstick—of ripe peaches—remains strong and encouraging. Anxiously, he refills his flask from a bottle kept chilled in the water chamber behind the toilet, urinates, remembers he forgot to pack a clean pair of undershorts and thoroughly despondent, flicks off the light.

Hour after hour passes while Quimby weighs the advantages of riding in the elevator up to his rendezvous in the alteration room against taking the flights of stairs on tiptoe; speculates as to how, without the key, Maria Zentana will gain admittance to D's; wonders where he will ever get the extra money for tangerines and in the end, grows fearful lest his wife and/or the policeman has awakened Mr. D. from sleep, questioned him and persuaded him to view Peter Quimby as a common criminal.

No, as the unseen day dawns it seems more and more likely he can never keep his appointment with Maria Zentana. When certain of this he drains his flask and gets to his hands and knees on the cold concrete floor of the basement to search out his grocery bag. Near the elevator he finds it and inside, wrapped in washcloth, the unloaded pistol. Seated on the floor, he cinches his dry lips around the muzzle of the pistol, presses the trigger repeatedly and blacks out.

Outside the Sunday sun has almost risen to the height where its rays first touch Main Street to warm the torpid pigeons; inside D's, the muted telephone rings vainly down through the ceiling and into the basement for a proverbial third time . . . where Peter Quimby is embarked upon a daylong sleep. Whenever Quimby had met his own death in a dream, he never jolted upright in bed as some do, eager to retrieve their lives. No, Quimby accepted his death and slept on, anxious to see what would come to pass. Until now, he has never succeeded in discovering where it is he goes upon his death to see whatever it is he does see. But down in D's dim basement this Sunday evening there is Peter Quimby stirring on the frigid concrete beside the orchid summer shirt hanging out the top of the grocery bag.

Despite the fact that Quimby now presumes his fifty-year marriage to his flesh (remarkable even these days for its savage discord) has ended in divorce, he holds but a single reservation concerning his demise: he will never press those purple lips, the print-makers. Still, it is not a discontented soul who begins its supposed afterlife by scuffling the unlit length of the basement (in the windbreaker pocket, the pistol, the windbreaker itself underneath the unbuttoned orchid shirt), intent upon reaching the alteration room to deliver gruesome news of Peter Quimby's suicide. The street floor is dark. Let Peace be made between Rhoda and her mournful soldier.

Up another flight, to the day station of Leona and Joan. He catches his wind here and again is inundated by a wave of compassion for both widow and divorcee. A Good Man broadcasts love, he thinks, elated until remindful of his grim mission.

Up the banister he hauls himself, to stand at last outside Mr. D.'s locked office. God bless D. Rest period.

Not halfway up the final stairway, he hears the long-drawn *AAaaaaaahh* of a throat whose tongue is clamped by a tongue depressor, of Zentana greedily awaiting her pleasure. He will climb no further, if only to permit her an additional moment of hope. Crouched on the stairs, he winces. The pistol muzzle digs into his hip. He removes it from the windbreaker and with it, fancied memory of the bullets that tidily entered the roof of poor Quimby's mouth only to auger out those sloppy exits from the back of his head. Grief propels him up those last steps to the portal of the alteration room.

"In the basement," he announces, "Quimby has taken his life!" and altogether depleted, thuds to his knees. Twelve feet away, Maria Zentana also kneels; and besides she is as pink and rounded brown—from the waist up—as the stiff and spindle-legged Mr. D. is ashy pale—from the waist down. Maria's face sinks into her cupped hands.

"Get out," hisses Mr. D. and with the solemnity of a flag-raising, slides briefs and trousers up his long legs. "What do you want? Put away that gun. Get out of here. Damn you. Whatever you want is yours. Damnation. You are fired."

Remote, contemptuous, Quimby peers far below, and takes farewell of his corpse, its once familiar head a reeking colander. Voice sharp and censorious, he orders the brown-shouldered woman to stand with her face in the corner; then the livid man, in the opposite corner. Newly incorporated, he reaches for a scarf, expertly droops it over his neck, slides the soft overcoat off a hanger and over his orchid shirt and taps the chestnut-colored hat onto his head.

"On the contrary," he explains, "it is *you* who are fired." With that, he strides around the corner. With elegant restraint, he descends.

Fast approaching ten o'clock of a lowery Monday morning in October, the relentless young window artist adds a splash of copper to the window, takes a backward step, another, to take it all in, and is jostled by a purposeful black overcoat topped with a chestnut-colored hat with a stylish feather band.

"Hello," she says, "and thanks again for all your help."

"Pardon, young lady," he stammers with a pinch of his hat brim and strolls through the zigzagging glass foyer. The window painter sets her brush in a can of water. She does not understand but she feels bad. And presently, an escort at each of his black cashmere elbows, her friend is whisked back through the foyer trailed by a weeping, kerchiefed woman who sits in the front seat of the dark automobile that has pulled up to the curb. "I knew he was lying," she announces as the door shuts on her and on the three men squeezed together in the backseat of the car which rolls now up Main Street of the former business district of the town, climbing to the top of the hill and out of the sight of the young window painter watching on tiptoe. She looks toward the hilltop a long while, then glances into the foyer to see the arrested heads of more women behind the glass entrance. Something is wrong she decides. He is a good and generous man. She thinks hard, but nothing comes out of it so she edges back to see her window painting. It is all done: the banquet table set with an uncarved pumpkin; a child, fully frontal, staring out from behind the table; a father in profile poised to dine at one end; a mother in profile, ready at the opposite end— and risen over all, his bright hunter's moon.

# A Land Without Fossils

Down the ridge of spruce and hardwood the night winds come clattering. Flayed bark lashes birch trunks. The beech leaves rattle and convulsed spruce whine. Down the ridge and across long snowfields wind chisels at the crust and rams our northwest wall. One winter following a massive blizzard there rose a frigid night wind. Three nights it kept up. Power lines were down. Drifts extended, hardening as they buried the ridge road deeper. The farmhouse trembled, inhaled what it could and whistled; when a brutal gust caught the wall flush, the entire house staggered and let out a scream. Of that long winter's-end blow, it is the third night I remember now.

Several hours I had been gazing at a puckered bright watercolor my five-year-old son had painted and given me at his bedtime. It was another map of his land. I had become so absorbed with it that the fire had burned down and the study grown chill. I set the lapboard and watercolor on the pile of books and papers sprawled around the armchair. The black greyhound looked up, yawned and laid his narrow chin back on the edge of the stone hearth. I turned down the kerosene lamp, stirred embers, fed three logs and with a flashlight went down into the cellar to check the wood furnace.

Chocking the furnace with hardwood stacked, from ledge floor to hewn joists, along the stone foundation, I watched the blaze rise and flutter out the mouth of the wood furnace, closed the damper and hitched shut the door as smoke slipped up and spread along the cobwebbed ceiling. Returning upstairs, I hesitated at the study entrance. The greyhound crooked up his ears and rolled his bloodshot eyes. I went up the narrow stairs to the bedrooms. I looked in on my wife; then, in the adjoining bedroom, on our son, open-mouthed and serenely asleep beside the terrarium. The black eye of a torpid green lizard inside swung like a turret in the flashlight's beam. I looked at its discolored stub of tail. My son's curious, rough love had snapped it. Of late, the terrarium had served only as a night light. Finally I returned to the study, smoothed out the watercolor and again directed my attention to it. So delightful months ago, my son's invention had ceased to enchant me and on this night started to trouble me. Immediately after the existence of the land had first been made known, at the onset of winter, he started to catalogue its various features and inhabitants. The maps he plotted had grown ever more complicated. With the solemnity of an ancient cosmographer at work on circular *mappaemundi* the five-year-old labored over them. What most vexed me, however, was that insistently he spoke of the land as the place where he had lived before he was a son. So excited that he rushed from wall to wall and his breathing governed the break of his syllables, he described his land with the preface "I remember . . ."

*It is an oval land, an island country surrounded by a sea of green ice. Like Jerusalem in the oval's center is a golden palm-print which represents a house. A purple range of mountains hangs behind this house, and a tropical jungle grows in whatever spaces are not taken up by the yellow brushy deserts*

*and the rocky red clifflands that slope down to the green ice*
*sea. A volcano never erupts on this island and there are no*
*earthquakes, floods or hurricanes, and meteors never drop out*
*of the sky and hit people on the head. Indeed, very few humans*
*inhabit the island. Not that it is a sparsely populated place.*
*On the contrary, it is distinguished chiefly by an abundance*
*of winged and scaled creatures. The sky is crammed with all*
*manner of birds. It is not unusual to spy a pteranodon or*
*rhamphorhyncus gliding in the same current as an osprey or*
*sparrow hawk. Terrible diatryma share the brushy deserts*
*with zebras, tapirs, steogsauri, bison and numberless lizards*
*and snakes. High in the tropical forests the vine snakes and*
*emerald tree boas wait; while in the swampy places far below*
*the macaws, Pondicherry vultures hunch in stunted trees.*
*Rosy boas breed in chinks of the rocky red clifflands where*
*the hoatzins cling, but almost nothing dwells in the purple*
*range of mountains and nothing at all exists beyond the green*
*ice sea.*

Whatever else, the land was a compendium of what my
son had learned of the world. And yet, stranger than the
nonhuman plenitude of these vivid biomes and the hazardless
atmospheres which presided over them was the omission of
familiar creatures: dogs, cats, field mice, moose, raccoons,
white-tailed deer and black bear, partridge, bobcats and rab-
bits of the nearby woods. And strangest of all, not a fossil
nor trace of bone was ever to be found in any region of the
land.

For a long while I tried to trace out the origin of my son's
land, of the figures crowded in the oval on a ground of green
ice. Crossing the hayfields one July at dusk, my wife and, in
a carrier on her back, our infant son had seemed a fabulous
hunchback. Through the spruce stand upon the ridge she
smacked her lips at the brown thrasher, the brown thrasher
smacked a reply, and our son laughed as he laughed after
suppers when we strolled the dirt roads in the dark answering

great horned owls. We all had watched the tree swallows glue
a nest above the front door and sweep upon the cringing
tabby cat. And the tabby had contributed an evening grosbeak
which I had started to paint (after Ryder's *Dead Bird*) while
my son napped and completed just as he awakened to the
plump and handsome grosbeak laid beside its painted twin.
One summer evening while I was rocking him in the ham-
mock, the mesh of the hound's pen twanged and we went
down to discover a saw-whet owl on the peastone of the pen
floor. So gently had he cradled the tiny owl to the porch that
I hesitated to tell him that the owl's neck had broken; but
after several minutes, the owl revolved its queer head and
weaved into the dark as if propelled by my son's laughter.
Dead things the child treated with the same respectful and
objective inquiry with which he treated things alive. Shortly
after his third birthday, his interest shifted to the exotic and
alien birds whose pictures soon lined every wall in the farmhouse. The showy lashes of the secretary bird, the magnificent
frigate bird's valentine of a mating bubble, the fuchsia warts
encircling the eyes of the spur-winged goose—these were his
favorite features in the new gallery. What an awesome thing,
the memory of a child. In no time, he was able to identify
the hundreds of birds, from Anhinga to Zone-tailed hawk,
in our aviary of posters and glossy book pages. Indeed, the
nuthatch scooting vertically on the aromatic balm o' Gilead
outside the kitchen window; the pine grosbeaks, lavender
and melodious in the apple tree tops sprinkling bits of rotten
apple like sawdust upon the snow: these no longer inspired
an equal wonder. Of all the drawings, none enthralled him
so much as the hideous wild turkey gobbler of Audubon.
The spurs, armored violet shanks, disdainful eye and, of
course, the coarse beard drooping down the breast sent him
stuttering. It seemed a stroke of fortune the spring we located
a bird farm that a man operated with his old mother on a
muddy slope behind a trailer. A huge sallow-white turkey
stalked the old woman wherever she walked in the yard, and

the woman was careful not to let the officious-looking thing get behind her. "Thinks them veins sticking off my legs is worms," she had claimed, grabbing the cock's turquoise head. All day that woman's son pressed out plastic spoons in the valley mill, returning to their solitary trailer in the evening to feed his golden pheasants, Muscovies, pumpkin heads and wild turkeys, dingy shadows of Audubon's gobbler that performed the crazed struts and lunging gobbles my son had credibly imitated for months afterward. The brindled turkey chick we purchased that spring afternoon became my son's prize once the tawny down on its head rubbed off and sky blue and red caruncles began to erupt from its dome and neck. Then the boy became the turkey's guardian, keeping watch for the greyhound and tabby cat while the young gobbler strolled down aisles of carrot tops and beet greens darting yellow slugs after a rain, gargling down water. Although its wings were clipped, the turkey managed to roost atop a cedar post of the dog pen and take short, flapping leaps. It was at the beginning of September that the greyhound sighted the turkey feeding on blueberries at the same moment my son sighted the hound. With great ostrichlike strides the turkey had rushed across the mown field before the greyhound had got to it and cracked it this way and that. My son ran after them until he saw the long blue head swinging like a pendant from the greyhound's purple lips. Then he dropped where he was and rolled in the sharp stubble of the field. He accepted no comfort. He did not want another turkey. He wanted to stab the hound into a million pieces. Suddenly he stopped wailing and went inside, but the spasms of his grief were shooting through his chest, even at bedtime. To models and picture books of prehistoric creatures his zeal had been abruptly channeled, and by the first snowfall, the gallery of birds was replaced by rainbow charts of the Carboniferous, Permian, Triassic, Jurassic—potent new worlds of words containing those beings whose outlandish claws and size and fins were surpassed by nothing but the sound of their names.

Arguments over his di-*plo*-do-cus and my diplo-*do*-cus filled
the dining room before the table was cleared to make way
for enamel paints, glue and a plastic diorama of death in the
La Brea tar pit or a windup stegosaurus with faulty legs. On
walks that winter, the quick prints and tail-slash of a field
mouse had been left by podokesaurus and the frozen droppings of moose were credited to a passing moropus. It was
that spring that he knocked on the study door and asked to
see the fossils. He ignored the distinction I tried to make
between fossils and bones, the skulls of red fox, black bear,
bobcat, porcupine, raccoon and moose. Shed snakeskins, assorted antlers and the dainty bones and teeth found in the
castings of owls provoked a storm of questions, but it was
the coiled skeleton of a snake with ribs like whiskers and in
its entirety no larger than a half-dollar that made his small
back stiffen and his eyes open wide. I had found it intact
beneath the plank where it had considered itself deep enough
for hibernation. Beneath mosses the next summer he caught
rubbery salamanders and red efts. We watched tadpoles
snatch air and dive to the silty bottom of the jar on the kitchen
table. The day of the snake hunt had been the finest day of
that summer. My wife had held up the first, a big garter angrily
spanking her forearm. He caught red-bellied snakes, green
grass snakes, garters, some so tiny they ringed his short fingers like gorgeous jewelry. As fall advanced, he decided that
winter should not begin. He made up a song,

> *Snakes are hibernating*
> *Winter is coming*
> *Put up your snowfences*
> *Snow is falling.*

And as the winter set in, he was at odds with a season as
never before. Daytimes, he was so busy arranging rubber
snakes in the chives, basil and sage of the planter that he had
to be coaxed out of doors. Scuffing past the dead bees that

littered the base of the insulated hives, he said that he hated winter. A night light became necessary, so the terrarium was moved upstairs. On the door of his bedroom closet a bolt was put up as he requested. It was then, at the start of December, that he had awakened from his dream of a land without fossils.

I got up, set the lapboard and map on the arms of the empty chair and turned off the kerosene lamp. Embers gleamed in the frosted windows of the study, in the glass doors of a bookcase. The row of bleached animal skulls was washed a warm shade of orange. The darkened study began to shrink as it does in the hours before daybreak. I slapped my thigh for the greyhound to follow and left the study, deliberately latching the door. Little heat rose from the vents in the hardwood floor, so once again I started down to the cellar. At the foot of the cellar stairs the manic tabby cat flung something upward in the flashlight's beam and dashed into the crawl space.

It was a tiny shrew, velvet warm and dead in my fingers with a snout like a pencil point. I opened the damper, the door of the wood furnace, and dropped the shrew into the red and gray coals. Then I slid in a log of rock maple and a yellow birch log whose curls exploded as the cast-iron door sealed.

I closed the damper and went upstairs. The greyhound trailed me to the kitchen and stood by while the kitchen stove was stoked. A pie tin, filled with water to soften the air, was centered on the stove's single cover. I stared at the dwindled moon in the upper pane of violet sky, got on my parka and went outside with the hound. The porch floor snapped underfoot. The incessant wind had scraped bare the frozen hay bales around the sills. The snowcrust was hard as ledge. The greyhound urinated on the corner of a bale and rapidly skittered back to the door. I went on and climbed the enormous bank at the side of the buried road, an accumulation of snow plowed aside during the winter. The mailbox had vanished. Back to the wind, I straddled the ridge of the snowbank and watched the orange flicker of a snowplow which appeared during lulls, small as a campfire on the next hillside.

After a time I stood and turned toward the house. The greyhound lifted one slender paw, then the other, off the frozen porch. I was passing the porch window when I glimpsed the figure of my wife striding in the downstairs hallway. Through the blur of frost I watched her run back with a white porcelain bedpan in her hand. "I have to pee!"; our son had awakened her with his cry. Oblivious, half-asleep, hair tossing from side to side, the image lingered in the whitened glass until I felt myself witness to a gesture within my former house, a house functioning without me, and functioning in beauty.

I turned and winced into the wind driving crystals of ice down the ridge and across the long, treeless snowfields. Then I saw the black hump of ridge against the wintry sky, scanned the black apple trees in the ash-blue orchard, the shafts of birch on the rim of the slope above the cedar cuttings. Property. Boundaries and their fierce meaning. If a land without fossils was built of fear by will, my son and I shared the same occupation. Mountains, a purple range of mountains, grew behind my golden house; my orchards were a brushy desert, and a tropical jungle of alders and willows sloped down to cedar cuttings and the eroded defile of rocky red clifflands— an inviolate island country encircled by a green ice sea where nothing at all existed.

"I remember when I was there," my son had insisted. "Before I lived here. Before I was a son. I remember."

The memory of a child, what an awful thing. For the first time in my adult life, for the first time since the death of my father, I began to pray. I dropped to my knees on the snow and prayed that my son was right; that it was so; that I might believe the child remembered.